An UNEXPECTED GRACE

An UNEXPECTED GRACE

TRACIE PETERSON
KIMBERLEY WOODHOUSE

BETHANYHOUSE

a division of Baker Publishing Group
Minneapolis, Minnesota

Published by Bethany House Publishers
Minneapolis, Minnesota
BethanyHouse.com

Bethany House Publishers is a division of
Baker Publishing Group, Grand Rapids, Michigan

Printed in the United States of America

Library of Congress Cataloging-in-Publication Data
Names: Peterson, Tracie, author. | Woodhouse, Kimberley, author.
Title: An unexpected grace / Tracie Peterson and Kimberley Woodhouse.
Description: Minneapolis, Minnesota : Bethany House, a division of Baker Publishing
    Group, 2025. | Series: The jewels of Kalispell ; 3
Identifiers: LCCN 2024039016 | ISBN 9780764239014 (paperback) | ISBN
    9780764239021 (cloth) | ISBN 9781493450893 (ebook)
Subjects: LCGFT: Christian fiction. | Romance fiction. | Novels.
Classification: LCC PS3566.E7717 U537 2025 | DDC 813/.54—dc23/eng/20240826
LC record available at https://lccn.loc.gov/2024039016

Scripture quotations are from the King James Version of the Bible.

Cover design by Dan Thornberg, Design Source Creative Services

Baker Publishing Group publications use paper produced from sustainable forestry practices and postconsumer waste whenever possible.

25 26 27 28 29 30 31   7 6 5 4 3 2 1

Dear Reader,

What a joy to get to share one of our favorite places with you—Kalispell, Montana. This final story in THE JEWELS OF KALISPELL brings us to the McIntosh Opera House, which we've been looking forward to for so long.

When we were first doing research, one of the most significant events we found in Kalispell during this era was a performance of *Uncle Tom's Cabin* at the opera house, which brought in more than 1,100 people. It was so crowded, people were reportedly standing in the windowsills to see the show. (One article even went as far as to say that people were hanging from the chandeliers. While we doubt that was the case, it was too fun to leave out of this note.)

The big problem was that none of the websites featuring the show had anything about the date. Funny enough, I found an obscure book at a museum there in Kalispell and discovered an ad for the show on February 27 and 28 of 1903.

This find was *after* the series was already planned out, so we have taken a bit of artistic license with the timing and have the show in 1905 rather than 1903 to enable us to share this cool piece of history with you in our fictional story. (Please note that all descriptions of the troupe, their shows, etc., are purely fictional. The only historic fact is that *Uncle Tom's Cabin* was on stage at the McIntosh Opera House to a sold-out crowd.)

The current owner of the building, Gordon Pirrie, was so

very gracious allowing me entrance into the historic opera house. His son runs the businesses now and gave us a ton of historic information about the place. We owe them a huge debt of gratitude. Though ravaged by a fire, and the upstairs opera house out of commission, the place is still magnificent. With a little bit of imagination, you can see the plays and shows of old dancing across the stage and into people's hearts. I'm hoping that one day the money can be raised to restore this historic place.

I have to say, I'm astonished at how they jam-packed more than 1,100 people, plus the cast and workers, up there. But what a sight to behold that must have been for the people of Kalispell.

We are so thankful that you have joined us on this incredible journey through these pieces of history still standing in Kalispell, Montana. Thank you for loving these stories.

Enjoy the journey,
Kimberley and Tracie

Prologue

SUNDAY, MAY 19, 1895—KALISPELL, MONTANA

Waiting for the man she loved to return from Chicago was about as easy as felling a tree with a nail file.

A giggle at her own analogy threatened to escape Johanna Easton's lips. She'd have to make sure to tell Dad that one later. Wouldn't he get a kick out of it?

But now was not the time to burst into a fit of giggles, although the more she thought about it, the more she wanted to laugh out loud.

Johanna pinched her lips tight. Her fingers tapped her bouncing knee as she waited for Pastor Bennett to wrap up his sermon so she could head back to the upright piano and play the closing hymn. That would at least get her mind off Parker.

For a moment or two.

Dad's right hand moved from his lap and covered hers, pressing her fingers and knee to an abrupt stop. She straightened and shifted on the wooden pew, heat filling her cheeks. If he had noticed, there was a good chance that the rest of their small congregation noticed as well.

Pastor Bennett started to pray, so Johanna eased toward the piano.

Amens echoed through the small room as she took her seat behind the piano and played the last line of the hymn as an introduction.

Voices lifted in praise, filling the church up to the rafters.

> "All praise to Him who reigns above
> In majesty supreme,
> Who gave His Son for man to die,
> That He might man redeem!"

She poured every bit of passion she could into the accompaniment and let her fingers fly over the ivories. It was a good thing her church loved to sing because her robust playing crescendoed through each stanza. The congregation's boisterous voices echoed back and accepted the challenge, which only spurred her on all the more.

> "Blessed be the name, blessed be the name,
> Blessed be the name of the Lord!
> Blessed be the name, blessed be the name!
> Blessed be the name of the Lord."

She sang on as they conquered the second stanza. Finally the third drew them toward a conclusion.

> "His name shall be the Counsellor,
> The mighty Prince of peace,
> Of all earth's kingdoms Conqueror,

Whose name shall never cease.
Blessed be the name, blessed be the name,
Blessed be the name of the Lord!
Blessed be the name, blessed be the name!
Blessed be the name of the Lord."

With the final note, she pulled back from the piano, a bit out of breath. She clamped her hands tight together, doing her best to quell the urge to attack the keys once again. Oh, why couldn't the minutes pass faster? She needed to *do* something. It was the only way to get her mind off Parker.

Pastor dismissed everyone and strode toward her.

In the hubbub of chatter and folks shuffling out of their small building, the questions that had plagued her all morning kept coming back.

When would Parker arrive? Dare she ask the pastor?

The pastor leaned down to whisper in her ear. "We surely marched in double time on our final hymn, but I understand your enthusiasm. We're expecting our son any moment now." His grin was wide. "I told him it was fine to visit you first."

She sprang to her feet, not caring one whit who saw her anticipation and glee. "Thank you, Pastor Bennett. So very much." She gathered her things in a flurry then scurried out the door.

The sooner she got home, the sooner she would see the man she was going to marry.

Marry!

The very thought of Parker Bennett's return to Kalispell had consumed her. Daily she plotted and planned for how things would be. How she would dress and wear her hair. She'd put on her Sunday best—a pink sprigged muslin that was a little lightweight for May in Montana—and carefully set her thick, cinnamon-colored hair in a tight braid that she left to hang down one shoulder. This was how Parker liked it best. She hadn't even woven it with a ribbon because he had once told her the beauty of her hair needed no adornment.

At the buggy, Dad and Mom spoke with one of the deacons. Johanna climbed up and arranged her skirts, hoping they would take the hint that she was ready to go.

When Dad turned to her, he didn't climb up into the buggy. "Jo, we need to help deliver some food and lumber to a family that lost their cabin in a fire last night. They need shelter as soon as possible, so why don't you head on home."

Mom reached up and patted Johanna's knee. "Make up some biscuits and maybe a pound cake? One of the men will bring us home, so don't worry."

"Do they need clothing? And what about blankets?" Johanna moved over to grab the reins.

Dad held the bridle of one of the horses while Johanna settled on the seat. "Probably both, dear. Word is getting around, but the elders and deacons are meeting with the women's hospitality group now, so your mother and I will be a while. Hopefully we'll return in time for the social this afternoon. Sorry to be so scattered, but we'll be home later." His gaze was serious, but the light in his eyes stirred her heart. "Love you, daughter."

She nodded. "Love you both. I'll get started with the baking. I'm hoping Parker will stop by. Pastor Bennett told me he'd encouraged him to come see me first."

Mom had already been called away, but Dad grinned. "I'm sure he'll be right over once he finally gets to town. You're as pretty as a picture, Johanna. You make your mother and me proud."

Her cheeks warmed. "Thank you, Dad. That means more than you know."

With a flick of the reins, she urged the horse and buggy out of the church's grassy side yard and toward home.

While they didn't live far from the church, the drive home gave her mind plenty of time to flit from helping the family in need to Parker and then back again.

She hated to risk her dress, but since there was no telling when her folks would get home, she needed to see to the horse. She parked the buggy beside the small outbuilding Dad used as a workshop.

The old gelding was more than ready to be led to his large, roomy stall. "You're a spoiled one to be sure, Mo." Even as a younger horse, Molasses had never gone anywhere in a hurry unless forced to. She and Parker used to make jokes about how a short drive to church could take hours if Mo had his way.

Parker! Her nerves were all aflutter once again. Ever since she was a little girl, she'd dreamed of marrying a preacher. Situations like the one today only strengthened that feeling of calling and purpose.

To be a pastor's wife meant serving and helping with the ministry of the church . . . reaching out to the poor and needy. Being available with a kind word and practical help for the suffering and the lonely.

And she could use her gifts of music to add to the services.

It was meant to be.

Three years ago, when her family first came to Kalispell, they had visited the little white church where Martin Bennett preached. At fourteen, she'd been smitten with his son Parker immediately. As Parker had been with her. They spent hours preparing duets to sing together in church, pored over the Bible with other young people, and brought meals to the widows and elderly.

Little wonder, then, that the entire town anticipated a wedding when Parker returned from seminary.

Parker. *Her* Parker. Soon to be a preacher like his father.

The Bennett men had a legacy of five generations of preachers. Every male family member had followed the calling. Parker's older brother had already taken a church in eastern Montana.

Soon, it would be their time.

The smile that lifted her cheeks lifted her heart as well. Patience had never been her strong suit, but she had people she could help in the meantime.

It might have been easier had Parker been better at correspondence, but writing was never his favorite occupation. And while she sent him at least one letter every week, she could count the letters from him over the last two years he'd been away at seminary on her ten fingers.

Not that she was upset with him about it. That was the grand thing about love—she understood his strengths and weaknesses.

"There now, you dear old boy." She made sure Mo had plenty of fresh hay and water. "I'm off to plan my future!"

Johanna hurried from the barn, although it could hardly be called that. She picked up her pace, and before she knew it, she had hiked her skirts and was making a run for the front door.

This was the happiest day of her life!

As she rounded the corner of the house, narrowly missing a large flowering lilac bush, she lost her footing and went head over heels. She landed flat on her back, stunned. Then something overshadowed her, and she gazed up into the eyes of Parker Bennett.

"That was quite the welcome home."

Johanna did her best to jump to her feet, but the heel of her boot caught in the hem of her skirt and refused to give way. She struggled and fell again, but this time Parker was there to take her in hand. As he helped her to untangle herself, Johanna could only burst into laughter.

"Here I had planned to be perfectly coiffed and gowned to impress you and leave you filled with love at the very sight of me."

He chuckled and pulled her into his arms. "Oh, Johanna. I was already filled with love for you."

Their gazes locked, and Johanna warmed from her toes to the top of her head.

This.

She'd waited and longed and dreamed of this moment for ages.

Parker pressed his lips against hers, and the ground felt as if it fell away and she floated up to the clouds in his arms.

Parker Bennett inhaled a few calming breaths before approaching Johanna at the church social. There wasn't a cloud in the sky, and the mountains in the distance clung to their shrinking cloaks of snow as the brilliant sun warmed the valley.

Taking slow, tentative steps, he prayed for help. Nothing had gone as planned since he'd arrived home in Kalispell. His intentions to tell Johanna the truth had unraveled.

Dad had been in constant motion helping the victims of the fire, and after Parker had kissed Johanna, he'd been so overcome with his feelings for her that he'd chickened out and raced home saying he needed to see his parents, but he'd be back for the social.

He'd lectured himself the entire way home, calling himself the biggest of fools, but then Dad rushed him into the house to change. "We need you, son. There's much to do before nightfall."

Unfortunately, he had his own hopes of things to accomplish before nightfall, and none of it had anything to do with tearing off burnt wood and rebuilding a cabin. There was so much he wanted—needed—to say to Johanna.

He could only pray she'd understand.

His plans to tell his family first had flown out the window as he'd prayed over his Bible this morning. The need to speak with Johanna pressed on his chest like an anvil.

She deserved to know the truth.

Surely their love was strong enough to face the trial ahead.

He'd helped Dad for as long as he could before telling his father that he must speak with Johanna. Today.

After a quick cleanup in the wash basin and a change of clothes, he raced to the church.

He spotted Johanna reading a story to a group of children. They sat on the green grass around her completely engrossed in the tale. The smile in her voice drifted to him on the breeze as she lowered her pitch for a character in the story. His heart constricted. She looked so carefree and beautiful, full of joy and light.

He prayed that joy would remain after their conversation.

Sweat slicked his palms as she looked up and caught his gaze. Her lips lifted, and their gazes connected.

The anticipation in her eyes was all he needed.

She still loved him. Of that he was certain.

He leaned against the one tree in the churchyard and listened to her finish the story.

Story.

For thousands of years, story had captured people's hearts and minds. Maybe that's why he loved it so much. But how could he convey what was in his heart to the woman before him?

Yes, he'd loved her since they'd met as teens. But they'd grown up. Matured.

What would happen when he shared his heart?

He blinked and found the children all gone. Johanna stood in front of him, her red hair parted down the middle and braided into a long plait that cascaded over her left shoulder. He'd always loved it like that. Had tugged on that braid hundreds of times.

The memories rushed into his mind like the waves on Lake Michigan washed over the shore. So many memories together. Would there be more?

He swallowed, but the lump in his throat only grew. Now was not the time to chicken out.

"Hi." Her voice was hushed. Not at all the dramatic and lively voice that had captured all the children's attention.

"Hi." He studied her for several moments, simply content to see her once again. But then his heart threatened to pound out of his chest. "I've got something important to speak with you about." He swallowed and grabbed her hand. "Will you take a walk with me?"

"Of course." Her cheeks tinged pink, and she ducked her head.

Their steps were accompanied by the fading sounds of the church social behind them. Once they were out of earshot of the rest of the congregation, Parker stopped and turned to face her. Inhaling a deep breath, he offered one last prayer to the Lord for help then plowed on ahead. "I don't know how to tell you this, so I think it's best to spit it out."

Her face fell, but she didn't look away. "All right."

Fighting the urge to forget all about honesty and pull her into his arms, he blurted it out. "I'm not returning to seminary. I've joined the Franklin Traveling Theatre Troupe and will be touring the country as we perform several Shakespeare plays." His breath left him in a whoosh, but the look on her face forced him to finish the rest as fast as he could. "I came home to ask for your hand and see if we could have a wedding in a few short weeks before we need to pack up and be on the road."

She blinked several times, but the shocked expression remained.

Parker glanced around and then took both of her hands. "I know this is a big change, but . . . will you still marry me?"

The blinking continued, then she put a hand to her heart. "I think I need to sit down."

This was not going as he'd hoped. Of course he'd bumbled up his words, but what choice did he have? He searched around him and found a relatively large rock. After guiding her to sit, he crouched down in front of her.

"It's a shock. I know. You've always dreamed of marrying a preacher, and I always thought I wanted to be one. But God has done some major work on my heart and mind as I've been studying His Word."

Her eyes widened and looked . . . sad.

He needed to explain. At least try. "One of my professors is convinced that the next wave of evangelism will come through the arts—more specifically, the theatre. Chicago has a bustling theater district, and we visited several plays in smaller theaters as part of our class. It was so inspiring. They played hymns and even prayed before some of the productions. It seems that more and more writers are creating what they are calling morality plays, and audiences are eating them up."

She shook her head and looked down at her lap. When her chin came back up, there were tears in her eyes. "But how did you get involved—I mean, why do you want to . . . act? All this time . . . you've said nothing about it."

It was a fair question. As far as she knew, this was coming out of the blue. "Well . . . I'm a bit embarrassed to admit this, but I was in a school play acting out the Christmas story when I was ten years old. Ever since, there's been this . . . itching inside me to do something different."

"But you're so good at preaching. The dramatic sermons you did for the children—I've heard you. You're so animated and engaging . . ." A bit of understanding entered her eyes, but she closed them and shook her head again.

Was he losing her? Was there a chance she wouldn't marry him now? He inched forward and grabbed her hands in a tight grip. Somehow she needed to understand how important this was to him. "Professor Clement taught on the passage in Exodus 28:1–8. Where the Lord puts a spirit of skill into each worker to help build the tabernacle and create the priests' robes for glory and for beauty. Don't you see? There are so many ways to reach the lost. God has given each one of us different talents so that we will use them for Him.

"You said it yourself, I'm animated and engaging. That's because God has given me that gift. The more plays we went to see, the more I longed to be on that stage and use my skills for the Lord. I don't believe this is something that is simply a flying fancy. For two years, I've been laying this at the Father's feet. Asking for His guidance. Asking for His will."

More tears pooled in her eyes. Not the sign that she was convinced.

"The power of storytelling has been used since creation.

Stories, art, the stage, music—all of these are mediums that can be used for His glory to reach people right where they are. You're a musician, you know how much it touches people's hearts and lives."

"But I'm not about to join a traveling troupe and jaunt off around the country playing in saloons and dance halls."

What? Where on earth was she getting an idea like that? "Hold on a second. I didn't say we were going to be performing in places like that."

"It's the same thing." Her back stiffened, and she swiped at her face. "We talked about getting married before you left, Parker. I promised to wait for you. Right here. In Kalispell. This is our home. We never talked about traveling around . . . we never talked about you *not* being a preacher."

His heart felt like it was being cut into two pieces. "So that's what it comes down to? You don't love me anymore because I don't want to be a preacher? Or because I'm asking you to leave Kalispell?"

"That's not what I said." A frown creased her face. "I love you, Parker. I told you I always will. But God has given you a gift . . . to *preach.*"

He squeezed her hands and softened his tone. "Jesus spoke in parables, Johanna. He ministered to people through story and word pictures. The apostle Paul understood Greek culture and the power of story. He was able to minister to the people in Athens because, yes, Jesus sent him, but God used his background and education to help them understand."

"But how is acting out Shakespearean plays the same?"

Maybe if he had been better at putting his thoughts on paper, he could have gradually shared all of this with her. "Look—" He tightened his grip on her hands. Somehow, he had to convince her. "Last year, we traveled to New York City, and I met Reverend Walter Bentley. Who is also an actor. He came over from England as an actor but felt God calling him to preach. Rev. Bentley encouraged me to follow God's calling. He still acts. In fact, he's so supportive of the theatre that he's thinking of putting together a Church Actor's Guild. To further the gospel."

Pulling her hands back, she shook her head and blinked. Then reached into her skirt pocket, pulled out a hankie, and dabbed at her eyes.

He looked down at his empty hands, his face burning. Never had she reacted to him like this. Like she didn't want to be near him. But that couldn't be. It was a simple misunderstanding. Surely she understood his heart—she loved him. And he loved her. They'd been planning on getting married for two years now. The whole town expected it—not that it mattered—and he wanted to marry Johanna more than anything else. All this time, he'd thought that she felt the same.

"Parker . . ." She sniffed and kept her gaze on her hands. "I . . ."

She looked up.

And he knew.

His stomach plummeted. No. No . . . she wouldn't do that to him—to them. She loved him.

Bolting to her feet, she shook her head. "I can't marry you. I'm sorry . . . I just . . . can't."

She turned toward the church gathering, but he reached for her arm and stopped her. "I'll always love you, Johanna. Always. Please . . . don't go."

Tears slipped down her cheeks as she stared at him. "I love you too."

But then she turned and walked away.

FIVE YEARS LATER
SUNDAY, APRIL 8, 1900

Cora Bennett tapped the envelope against her gloved hand and paced the room.

For weeks, she'd been weighing whether to give the letter to Johanna. As the maid of honor in Johanna's wedding, Cora had done everything in her power to find out if her dearest friend was still in love with her brother.

Oh, Parker.

Her older brother had written on a regular basis, and Cora had scoured the newspapers looking for news of him. Even though her parents had been disappointed in his choice to leave seminary and join the troupe, they were proud of their middle son. He had performed in some of the largest theaters in the country. Chicago, Boston, New York, Washington, DC, Atlanta, and Dallas.

All to high acclaim.

The first few years were filled with Shakespearean plays in which he moved up into lead roles almost immediately. No one could deny his talent.

But her family greatly missed him. He hadn't been home to visit but once. Probably because it was hard to see Johanna. She'd broken his heart by not accepting his proposal and following his dream.

To her friend's credit, Johanna had followed what she thought was God's calling on her life as well. To marry a preacher.

Which she would do today.

If . . . Cora didn't find a reason to give her the letter.

Cora had no idea what was inside the missive, but she knew

her brother was still in love with Johanna. He'd begged her to pray about showing the letter to his once-betrothed. If, and only if, she admitted that she wasn't in love with, or had any doubts about, Gerald St. John.

Gerald.

Cora and Parker's father had taken the preacher-in-training under his wing in hopes that Gerald would one day take Martin Bennett's place as pastor of the church.

He was an amazing man. A great match for Johanna. As much as Cora wished Johanna could be her sister-in-law, she couldn't fault her friend for falling in love with Gerald.

He wasn't as magnetic and vibrant as Parker, but he was steady. Reliable. Loyal. Father said he would be a great pastor and shepherd for their little church flock.

Her thoughts pinged in every direction as she weighed all the options. But this wasn't getting her anywhere. She either confronted her friend now or forever held her peace.

Opening the door, she gulped a deep breath, stuffed the letter in the small satin drawstring purse around her wrist, and lifted the hem of her bridesmaid dress so she could hurry down the hall.

Padding along the carpet runner in her stockinged feet, she looked in all directions to make sure no one else was around and could interrupt them. She lightly tapped on the door. "Johanna?"

"Come on in." The singsong voice sounded all too happy.

Was this the right thing to do? Of course it was. Cora bolstered herself and turned the knob.

Johanna sat at a small dressing table putting the final pins into her upswept coiffure. She turned and studied Cora from head to toe. "Don't you look beautiful. You've always looked so nice in blue. I think that gown is perfectly suited to you."

Once the door was shut properly behind her, Cora leaned against the door. She should thank Johanna for the compliment, but this was much too important to wait. "First, let me say that I love you, dear heart. I've never had a friend like you and would never wish to do anything to harm that relationship. But"—she swallowed hard—"I would be a terrible friend if I didn't ask this."

"Heavens, Cora." Johanna's bright smile beamed across the room. "You know you can ask me anything. It can't be as bad as all that."

All right. She could do this. "I want to make sure that you are certain about marrying Gerald. This is a huge step, and I don't want you to be hurt. Are you one hundred percent positive? Do you love him with *all* your heart?"

Johanna stood up in her well-worn dressing gown and glided over to Cora. Taking her hands, Johanna smiled even wider. Her eyes sparkled. "Yes. I'm certain. I'm positive. I love him with all my heart, and I couldn't be happier."

Cora studied her friend's gaze. "No doubts?"

"None whatsoever."

She held her tongue even though she wanted to argue that she should have doubts—Parker was her true love, right? But the longer she stared at Johanna, the more the truth hit her.

Johanna would marry Gerald St. John today.

Cora forced her brightest smile and hugged her friend. "I wish you both all the happiness in the world and pray for God to richly bless your union."

"Thank you." The clock chimed, and Johanna's eyes widened. "Gracious, would you help me into my dress? I let the time get away from me."

"We can't have the bride late for her wedding!" Cora

matched her tone to her friend's enthusiastic one while her heart pricked and burned with a sense of failure.

Parker's letter would never be read.

And his heart would be broken once again.

1

Johanna Easton St. John's heart overflowed as she smiled at her precocious daughter. "Let's try writing your name again."

"I can do good, Mama. Watch me." The child, who looked so much like her mother, picked up the pencil and began to write while speaking about each letter. "Dis one is a *E*. *E* for Emily." Her marks were backward and looked more like the number three than an *E*. But that could be corrected over time. The child was already leaps and bounds ahead of other children her age—especially in her speech. "Then *M* like Mama." She narrowed her eyes and made a nearly perfect letter.

"Very good, Emily," Johanna pressed a kiss atop her little girl's head. "What comes next?"

"*I!*" She hurried to draw the letter. "Then *L* like love. God is love!"

"That's right, sweetheart." They worked on Bible verses all the time even though Emily was still little. Johanna's mother had always said it was never too early to learn the Word of God.

Johanna ran a finger down the sleeve of her daughter's dress, feeling the tightness of the fabric around Emily's adorably chubby arm. It would have to be let out again. How was she to keep up with her baby's growth spurts? Though she wasn't a baby anymore. Not really. She'd be three in July. A few short months away. The shoes Johanna had purchased for her two months ago were already too snug.

"And last is *Y*." Emily made short order of the work and then dropped the pencil. "See, Mama? *Emily.*"

"Very good. You're getting better and better writing out your letters."

The child beamed. "I wanna show Daddy."

Johanna forced the smile to remain on her face. This was a part of the routine as well. She helped Emily down from her chair then handed her the piece of paper. Emily never walked anywhere, she ran. And this occasion was no exception. She took off in a blaze and raced to the front room.

"Look, Daddy. I made my name."

Johanna fought back tears as she joined Emily at the front of the house. The child stood at the little table in front of the window, holding her paper up to the silver-framed picture of her father.

"I made it for you." She looked back at Johanna. "Can Daddy come back and play . . . just a little bit?"

Oh, the questions of a child.

Crossing the room, Johanna took a deep breath, praying for wisdom. How was she to explain Gerald's absence to Emily for what felt like the one-hundredth time? The poor girl was too young to remember the handsome man who doted on her. He'd been as pleased to be father to a daughter as he would have been to any son.

Johanna lifted Emily in her arms and hugged her close. "One day, we'll get to see Daddy again."

"In heben?"

"Yes, in heaven."

Emily smiled and patted her mother's damp cheeks. "And then we play?"

Hot tears burned her eyes. "Yes, and then we play."

WEDNESDAY, APRIL 5, 1905—BROOKLYN, NEW YORK

The last vestiges of his father's belongings had been destroyed. He saw to that himself. A smile ticked up one corner of his mouth. How he'd enjoyed watching every last paper burn, along with any remorse he might have felt had Dad cared two figs about him.

James picked up the large round paperweight off the desk. The orb felt smooth and cool against his skin as he rolled it between his hands, his blood heating. The old man was as miserly in death as he'd been in life. Determined to keep his only living son from what rightfully belonged to him.

But James wouldn't be outsmarted. Not by Dad. Or that nosy Judge Lewis.

He slammed the paperweight back on the desk. *Why* had his father left the bulk of his money to Johanna, of all people? It was unfathomable. Dad and the woman had never even met each other. Maybe Dad had gone out to Kalispell for the wedding? It was out of character if he did.

No. Dad had left Johanna James's money out of pure spite.

Gerald had been on worse terms with Dad than even he was. His move out to that backward railroad town had been motivated by not tainting himself with the lives of sin and greed that colored their lives in New York City. Or so he said.

James gritted his teeth. Gerald had found himself a pretty, albeit pious, wife. Had a darling daughter.

And then dropped dead.

The news had taken James by surprise. Though he and his brother had never been close, they survived Dad's negligence together. Grief choked his throat. All that God talk. All that Bible reading. All that so-called right living, and what had it gotten his younger brother?

A pine box and a widow.

A widow ignorant to the fact that she was now very wealthy.

Well, she had to make it out to New York City first. And he wasn't going to let that happen.

Though Judge Lewis had tried his best, he hadn't been able to prove that the will James had in his possession wasn't valid. It was the last piece of James's plan, and it was perfect. Now everything was in place for him to return to Kalispell.

He paused. The thought wasn't as dreadful as he anticipated. He shouldn't want to be there. It lacked everything that made New York City exciting. Theaters. Cigar rooms. Dance clubs. Gambling halls. The hum and hustle of people trying to carve out a life for themselves though they were a speck of life in a sea of millions.

Kalispell had none of that. But one could trust most of the people there. Folks were welcoming, eager to accept newcomers into their society. The fact that upon his arrival there three years ago he'd become a generous benefactor of the town hadn't hurt either.

But it wasn't enough. Not yet.

So he would return to Kalispell and the role of doting, decent, reformed brother-in-law.

At least, that was the goal.

James strode across the room to the small gilded tray holding various liquor bottles. He poured two fingers of whiskey and tossed it back. Warmth seeped over him, leaving a trail of relaxed muscles in its wake.

If everything went according to plan, by this time tomorrow, there would be no evidence that James St. John ever lived in New York City. He would be untraceable. *They* wouldn't be able to find him. He'd created a new life for himself.

All he had to do was wait.

Patience wasn't his greatest strength, but he'd come this far. Laid the groundwork.

The time was ripe for him to harvest all he'd sown. Especially now that his former boss was also dead. Another hindrance gone.

He rubbed his hands together and surveyed the activity on the sidewalk below the brownstone. Merchants hawked their wares from wagons, harassing any passerby to purchase apples, flowers, or pots and pans. The wind whipped down the street, tugging the bowler hat off the head of a tall gentleman, sending him running after it.

Turning from the scene with a chuckle, he gave the study a last look. Once he locked up the house, it would sit empty and rot. Unless he had a new family to bring back to it.

Everything depended on Johanna.

The bell rang, and the hair on his neck stood on end. Who even knew he was back in town? Had they found him? No. It couldn't be. But then again, the Camorras were relentless. James headed for the door and opened it an inch, his pulse throbbing in his throat. "Yes?"

"Mr. St. John." Judge Lewis stood there. A smug look on his face. "I heard you were in town."

How? If the judge knew . . . could *they* know?

Pushing the thought aside, he squared his shoulders, leveling the meddling man with a glare. "Good evening, Judge. How nice of you to stop by. I'd love to offer you something, but I was checking up on Father's home, and there's nothing of substance here."

"I didn't come for a social call, but thank you." The shorter man didn't step over the threshold, simply clasped his hands over the bulb of his walking stick. "Your father was a good friend. Sadly, the last few years of his life we didn't see each other often—our schedules were too prohibitive of that— and that's why I allowed the will that you brought forward to stand."

"Thank you, Judge. It was good to mend fences with him that last year." James bit the inside of his cheek, tears stinging his eyes. The metallic tang of blood soured in his mouth. But at least the grimace of pain on his face was real.

"I hope that's true, I do. But I wanted to remind you of the terms of my probate ruling."

"That's not necessary, sir. I remember."

"Humor me." The judge raised his eyebrows. "Disbursement of the estate will not happen until both parties appear. Originally that was you and your brother. Then you told me of your brother's death—I have yet to see the death certificate, by the way—leaving a wife and child. Why haven't you brought her forward? Is it really that difficult to find her?"

James gripped the doorknob to keep from planting a facer on the old codger. "It's been a grueling search, sir, I—"

The judge banged his walking stick on the porch. "Before you say another word, James, let me tell you that I had a private detective find her. She's in Kalispell, Montana." A bushy salt-and-peppered brow rose on his forehead. "Astonishingly where *you've* been living for nearly three years yourself. Care to explain?"

His palms began to sweat. Why didn't people know when to quit? He would give the judge one last chance to back off. "I've been protecting her, sir. She hasn't wanted to travel. When Gerald died, she had a month-old baby to care for, and she was devastated. The child has been unwell."

A moment of silence engulfed them as the judge considered this turn of events. "But you've told Mrs. St. John of the inheritance?"

"Yes, of course."

The judge tapped his walking stick again. "If she's knowledgeable of the whole situation, I don't understand why she hasn't come." He pointed at James. "You're here. Why isn't she?" The man narrowed his gaze even further. "My detective reports that she lives meagerly with her father—it doesn't make sense that she wouldn't do whatever was necessary to come for the inheritance that would make life for her and her child better. Especially if there are medical bills to be paid for a sick child."

James let out a sigh. Change of plans. "Perhaps we should discuss this in the house, rather than on the stoop in front of all the neighbors." He stepped back and opened the door, allowing the older gentleman to pass by him. He shut the door, the click echoing through the empty foyer. "As I said, the child has been unwell, making travel impossible. Not only that, my sister-in-law despises big cities. She's afraid of them, in fact."

The judge's scoff seemed to boom in the cavernous space. "I cannot help her fears, however if she intends to claim her inheritance, she will have to do as I've instructed. How do you intend to convince her?"

"I can't answer that, sir."

Another penetrating glance from the Judge. "Perhaps I'll send her a telegram myself."

Now that would ruin everything. James reached out and grabbed the man's walking stick. One hand wrapped around his collar as he turned the official around and pinned his back against the front door. He pressed the gold ball of the cane under the judge's thick jowls, keeping his chin tipped upward.

The judge grabbed at James's hands, but to no avail. All bravado disappeared from Judge Lewis's face. His eyes were round. His breath came out in shudders, but it didn't stop him from talking. "You need to know, James, that I have legal assistants on my staff as well as two other judges that are always briefed on all my cases. You can't make this go away by getting rid of me. I only ask that you think about that for a minute."

James grinned. How little this man understood him. Eliminating obstacles was his specialty. "I shall take that into consideration. For now, please join me in my father's study. We should drink to old friends." He hauled the man away from the door, shoving him up the staircase, the thick carpet on the treads muffling their struggle. "But I feel I should warn you . . . the stairs in this house are steep. I warned my dear father of that. Such a pity that he and his good friend should die the same the way."

⟡

SATURDAY, APRIL 15, 1905—KALISPELL, MONTANA

Taking the train into Whitefish rather than Kalispell altered Parker's plans a bit, but he'd finally made it home on the seat of a freight wagon a day or two ahead of the troupe. Snow dotted the landscape from a late spring storm, while the mountains were covered with glorious white. A stark reminder that their rugged terrain was not to be taken for granted.

Parker tightened his hold on the coat that the freight driver had let him borrow to offset the chill. His own coat was packed away in trunks that would be shipped into Whitefish with the theatre troupe. He should have remembered the unpredictable weather this time of year—anytime of year, frankly. Montana was well-known for its changeable weather, and he'd seen snow in Kalispell and the surrounding area come at a moment's notice all throughout the year. At least this latest snow had been light in the valley.

Parker gazed around the area as the driver brought the wagon into the north end of Kalispell proper. The fact that the town had dug in its heels to survive without the daily train was a testament to the good people and their love for this place they called home.

It was as bustling as ever, and no one would ever be able to tell that the town's livelihood had been threatened when they lost regular train service. When the main hub for the Flathead Valley had been moved from Kalispell, they were sure they wouldn't survive.

But clearly, they had.

The wagon rumbled into town, and several people did double-takes as they saw him, then smiled and waved. Given his status as a world-famous actor, they were no doubt surprised to find him atop a freight wagon, dressed in a well-worn coat and casual attire. His agent always preferred Parker make a grand entrance into town. A "celebration of his celebrity" was what they called it. This generally meant his arrival would be publicized in the local paper, with a few hirelings to go ahead of them to stir up a frenzy of excitement . . . just in case it didn't happen on its own. The train would then deliver Parker and the theatre troupe to the city, and a staged welcome would take place, with Parker usually receiving some sort of accolade given by the town's mayor. Now here he was, sneaking back into his hometown without any fuss.

He couldn't help but smile. He preferred it this way. By slipping in, he could observe the town like anyone else. See the people as they went about their business and hopefully blend in with the rest of the folks.

Voices echoed around him.

"Parker Bennett!"

"Look! It's Parker Bennett!"

So much for anonymity.

"So good to see you, Parker!"

Returning their greetings, his heart lifted. It was good to be home.

Life on the road with the theatre troupe wasn't as glamorous as he'd first thought it would be.

The shows had been inspiring and rejuvenating, but all the travel, the set up and tear down, the constant getting to know new cast members . . . it made him feel like he was fifty years old rather than almost thirty.

As he stared out at the mountains that begged for him to drop everything and take a long hike through the thick, lush grass and into the beckoning trees, it struck him that no other place had brought him this kind of peace. This contentment.

He really should come home more often.

But his schedule hadn't allowed it, and now that he was in high demand for shows, that wasn't going to change anytime soon.

Then . . . there was Johanna.

His heart twisted thinking of her. The old wound was as raw as ever.

Parker sure had thought they were in love. His heart verified his side of it. But she must not have been. At least not as deeply as he had been. Her rejection still stung.

He couldn't blame her, though. Life on the road would have been horrid for her. The first few years, he'd had to work himself to the bone to gain the respect of the troupe. His acting skills bumped him up the ladder faster than he'd hoped, but the intense schedule kept him exhausted. It was no life for a young married couple or a family. He'd seen more than one couple part company after a few months of the chaotic routine. He would have hated to have to choose between his love for Johanna and his acting career. Frankly, back then he wouldn't have been able to. He hadn't been mature enough. Nor had he been mature enough to understand the blows that life could give.

Sadness settled afresh on his shoulders. He *had* made that choice, though . . . years ago. When Johanna turned him down, he left the love of his life and devoted himself to acting.

How many times in those early days had he stared at the ceiling of a room shared with six or seven other cast members, wide awake, wondering if he'd made the right choice?

Then there was Dad. Always supportive, but when Parker said he didn't feel called to be a pastor, Dad looked as if someone had punched him. Had his father forgiven him?

It wasn't until two years ago, when he landed the lead in *Everyman* in New York City, that things drastically changed for him. The press was constant in their requests for interviews, and when his first manager died in an automobile accident, he'd hired Alfred Richards, his current manager. Richards was a bit flashier than Parker was used to, going on and on about big plans and high hopes for his acting career. Including the silver screen—movies.

Part of the reason he was here.

Not only would their troupe perform many great Shake-speare plays in Kalispell for the next three weeks, but they were preparing to bring *Uncle Tom's Cabin* back to the stage in its full glory.

Ever since the movie came out in 1903, the Tom shows, as they were called in the industry, were back in demand. But not only minstrel shows or shortened little bits. No, people wanted the whole thing.

Just like the book.

Since none of the Tom shows had ever ventured to Ka-lispell, and Parker had his pick for the New York City's troupe tour, he chose to come home and stay for a while.

After their time here, the schedule would once again be full of travel to Idaho and Washington and then down through California. But oh, how he needed this breather. Time to con-template how much longer he wanted to do this.

Alfred wanted to transition him into movies, and several wealthy investors were sending representatives to watch a few of Parker's performances at various locations along the way. The idea was . . . intriguing. Parker had spoken at length with a man who worked in the rather new world of film. It would be great to get in on something like that at the beginning. The movie-set routine offered a different kind of world.

However, the stage was Parker's home, and the troupe . . . his family.

Oh, he loved it. The years had been good to him. But he wanted a different kind of family now. A wife and, in time . . . children. A family he could rely on rather than compete with. A family with whom he could share his good times and bad. Most of his theatre friends preferred the good times alone. They were a superstitious bunch. They didn't understand

Parker's passion for God, nor did they want to. Still, he had done whatever he could to live the life of a God-fearing man. And his optimistic hopes of sharing the gospel with people had come true with the success of *Everyman*, but . . .

Now what?

"You haven't said much since we left the train station." Carter Brunswick—owner of the flour mill and the freight service—lifted an eyebrow in his direction. "You still sore about the nickel I won from you in the sixth grade?"

Parker laughed and turned toward his friend. "Nah, I wasn't sure what kind of response I'd get. You know, being an actor and all."

"You mean, being a *famous* actor." Carter's face grew serious. "Does the reason have anything to do with the fact that you haven't been home in years?"

"Ouch." It would have hurt less if Carter had punched him. "But you're probably correct. I'm sure that has something to do with it."

The wagon rolled to a stop, and Carter slapped him on the back. "Well, it's time to get over that and face the fact that you are here. Home. You sure you don't want me to bring you to your folks' place?"

"Nah." Parker looked up at the West Hotel. "I'd like to get cleaned up before I go."

"Suit yourself. I'll see you soon. Don't hesitate to stop by if you need anything."

Parker hopped down with his bag. He tossed the heavy coat up to the driver. "Thanks, Carter." He tipped his hat as the wagon moved on.

Carter sent a two-finger salute over his shoulder. "Good to see you home."

Parker walked into the hotel and spied the woman manning

the reception desk. "Why, Mrs. Montgomery, you look as pretty as the last time I saw you."

The silver-haired woman grinned up at him. "Parker Bennett, you'd best not be using those acting skills on me, young man. I still remember you as a gangly boy delivering telegrams with trousers two inches too short."

Laughing at the picture that gave him, he shook his head. "My very first public role." He removed his hat and gave her a little bow. "I told my manager that he should book my room here. Did he make the reservation?"

"That he did. Nice fella—a bit slick, but I'm guessing most of the city folk in your line of work are." She flipped the registration book to a new page.

Parker chose to let the words slide off his back. Hopefully none of the people here would think that of him . . . would they? He took the pen from her and filled in the line with the date and his signature.

"I figured you woulda been staying at home, since you're here for so long, but I thank ya for your business." She handed him a key. "Room seven. It's got the best view. Just for you." With a wink, she turned the book back around to face her and shifted her spectacles up on her nose to read.

"Thank you, Mrs. Montgomery. I appreciate you taking such good care of me. We in the theatre keep strange hours with our rehearsals and such. And what with my sister's wedding and all happening soon, I didn't want to get in Cora's or Mama's way."

"You're a considerate young man, Parker. And I've never known menfolk to know what to do with themselves in the middle of wedding planning." She walked out from behind the counter and gripped her skirt in her fist, lifting the hem an inch to make it up the stairs. "Let me show you to your room."

She led the way and opened the door. "I'll leave you to settle in."

"Thank you again." Parker gave her a smile and closed the door as she padded off down the hallway.

It took him all of five minutes to get settled in. The room was nothing special. In fact, by the standards set in other cities it was shabby. He could only imagine what his fellow castmates would say about the accommodations. Still, it contained a bed and nightstand, along with a dresser and a single chair. What more did he need?

He walked to the window and looked out on the promised view. It was good to be home. Even though it had been years, his return felt as comfortable as putting on an old pair of slippers. The air was so much more breathable. The temperatures more desirable. The people . . . Well, the people were special here—a link to happier times.

He shook his head. He was happy now, wasn't he? He had the career he'd wanted and the opportunity to use it for God's glory. So why did coming home make him feel as though there was still so much missing in his life? The question sent him bounding back down the stairs. It was time to go see his mom and sister.

He covered the distance in quick, determined steps that caused people to step out of his way. He gave waves when they recognized him or offered quick greetings but remained focused on reaching his mother's house. This was something he had looked forward to for far too long. As he reached the last block, his stomach decided it wanted to twist into knots.

What would it be like without his dad there? When the telegram about his father's passing had reached him in Europe last spring, Parker didn't perform for three days. There wasn't time to get home . . . besides, he couldn't see his dad one last time. Couldn't have a heart-to-heart talk by the fire.

Dad was gone.

A truth that had taken several days for him to digest. His emotions had all come to the surface, and avoiding people had been the best choice.

But now? He was headed home. Letters from his mom and sister had been steady, but how would his family receive him? Would they even really want him here?

No matter. He lifted his shoulders and attempted to shake off the depression trying to weigh him down. Shoving his hands into his pockets, Parker took purposeful strides down the street. When he reached Third Street, he turned northeast, and a spring entered his step.

It didn't matter how much time passed, he couldn't wait to see his family.

Taking the steps of the porch two at a time, he smiled.

The door boasted a sign. "Welcome Home, Parker!"

He was wanted.

He lifted his hand to knock, but the door whooshed open.

"Parker!" Cora surged toward him and wrapped her arms around him. Giggling, she squeezed, pulled back, squeezed, pulled back again, and then went in for one more hug. "You weren't about to knock, were you?" She patted his shoulder. "Silly goose." In a flurry, she moved inside.

Parker followed. "Well, I didn't know what kind of madness might be happening over here. You know, with a wedding and all that." Why did he feel sheepish all of a sudden?

"Is that Parker?" Mama's voice sounded from the kitchen and she came barreling around the corner, dishtowel in hand. Her eyes widened, along with her smile. "It *is*!"

Parker smiled despite the immediate realization that she had aged considerably in the years of his absence. How old was she now? Would he lose her soon, too? He forced the thoughts aside with a swallow.

After another round of hugs, they all moved into the parlor and sat down. Cora offered him coffee off of a cute little rolling cart that held pastries and other goodies.

The coffee was tempting, but he couldn't risk it. "Could I bother you for some tea instead? Coffee tends to make my voice a bit hoarse."

"Let me put the kettle on to boil. I'll be right back." Cora scurried back into the kitchen, the perfect picture of a hostess. She had grown into a beautiful woman.

Time had changed them all.

Mama turned to him and held his gaze. "Let me look at you." Her hankie flew up to her mouth, and her eyes filled with tears.

"Mama, I'm sorry . . ."

And he was. For leaving. For not being there when Dad died. For not visiting in years.

What kind of son *was* he anyway?

"Don't you apologize. You've done a much better job corresponding these past few years than you ever did when you were in seminary." Her smile was bright despite the tears. "And I'm grateful for that. It has been wonderful to hear what God has done through your plays . . . but . . ."

He frowned. "But what?"

Mama reached for the paper beside her and passed it to him. "I *am* a bit concerned about where you are headed."

Parker took the newspaper, and the headline on the front page caught his eye: "Famous Actor and Playboy Returning Home to Kalispell with Appearances at the Opera House." He scanned the article as his stomach sank. His new manager

43

had a reputation of making his clients stars, but he was also known for his sleazy way of doing things.

Parker folded the paper but didn't give it back. "My new manager likes to be flashy with the press."

"Flashy? Is that a nice way of saying that he lies?" Mama stiffened. "Or is that depiction of you accurate?"

"Depiction? What does it say?" Maybe he should have read the whole thing.

"Basically it states that you are a famous actor with a new, wealthy socialite on your arm every night and that you are quite the partygoer." One of her eyebrows shot up.

He opened the paper again and read a little more. "Good heavens, that isn't true!" It was one thing for Alfred to arrange for this kind of wild publicity in the city, but here? Why would the man do such a thing?

"Perhaps you need to set things straight with your manager, then. Do you really want someone like that promoting you like *this*?"

But he'd worked so hard to get to this point. "This is what the press likes to print about those of us in show business. It's not true, Mama. It's another way to help sell tickets." As soon as the words were out of his mouth, the excuse tasted bitter. He held up his hand. "I can't believe I even said that. It's not about selling tickets—"

"No, Parker, it's about your character. Are you telling me"— she pointed to the paper in his lap—"that *this* kind of stuff has been printed about you before?"

He couldn't be false with his mother. "Not to this extreme, at least not that I know of, but I usually don't have time to read the papers."

"And this started with your new manager?"

It was like he was ten years old all over again. He nodded.

Character.

Something his father had drilled into him his whole life. A man should conduct himself with integrity and upright character.

Her face softened. "I'm sorry, I shouldn't have brought this up at the beginning of our visit. But needless to say, I'm worried about you and what this means for your reputation."

Cora came back with a kettle full of hot water and some tea leaves. "I hope this will be good. I've got some honey from the Nickels too."

Mama's face lit up, and she smiled at her daughter. "Thank you, dear. Now why don't you tell your brother all the news, and ask him your most important question." She patted Cora's cheek.

His sister practically bounced up and down on her chair. "First, Parker, let me say thank you for arranging for your troupe to be here so you could come for my wedding."

"You're welcome." A bittersweet ache constricted his chest. Cora had grown up while he was away. Ten years tended to do that to a person. Gone was the awkward youngster. Now she carried herself with a gentle grace. No more skinned knees and grass stains on her dresses. Instead, she was about to be a married woman.

Thank God, he'd made it back in time. "If I hadn't pulled some strings while I had the chance, they might have had me back in Europe for the next three years."

Cora's bright smile widened. "Well, thank you again. It means the world to me. And I would like you to walk me down the aisle when I marry William Landry."

All the air left his lungs in a whoosh. Normally, he was good at keeping his emotions in check, but this? "I . . . well, that is . . . I . . ."

The lump of tears in his throat grew at an alarming rate. He swallowed, fighting the wave of grief pressing hard on his chest. This was a happy day. Yet his father's absence felt like an open wound.

Summoning every bit of his stage training, he took a sharp breath and smiled. "I would be honored."

Cora walked over to him. "Thank you, Parker. I'll feel like Dad is right there with us." She bit her lip as she sat next to him on the settee. "But there's one more thing that might make it a bit . . . uncomfortable."

"Oh?"

"Johanna is my matron of honor, and her daughter, Emily, is my flower girl."

"Oh." He sank back into the couch. Just hearing Johanna's name brought a flood of memories. He picked at a string on the couch. Did Johanna know what Cora was asking him to do? What had her response been?

He glanced at his sister. Her bottom lip had disappeared between her teeth, and the small furrow between her brows was deep. He straightened. No matter how he felt, or how Johanna felt, it didn't matter. They were adults. He'd missed far too much of his sister's life to come back and mess up her special day over feelings that should have died a long time ago.

"It won't be a problem, Cora." He reached over and squeezed her hand. "I promise."

If only he could convince his heart that was true.

2

Johanna wove the ribbon through the hat she was making for Mrs. Conrad and hummed the chorus to "When We All Get to Heaven."

The lively hymn had become a favorite the last few years. Not only did the rhythm of the music help her work fast, but the lyrics had been a balm when Gerald died.

> "When we all see Jesus, we'll sing and shout the
> victory."

The truth felt almost too big to comprehend. While she was still on earth, Gerald was living the reality of seeing Jesus face-to-face.

Tears blurred the hat in her hands.

She set it aside for a moment, releasing a breath. She pressed her lips together in a thin line as she inhaled through her nose, determined to push back the temptation to cry. There was no time for tears.

With a firm nod, Johanna picked up the creation again, examining it for flaws. Mrs. Conrad asked for something fashionable, but not too embellished, to wear to the opera house for its opening show.

The base was a black straw hat with a wide brim, perfect for all the trimmings women loved these days.

Johanna poked and tugged the folds of white chiffon, making sure each tuck was secure to the crown of the hat. Satisfied the construction was sound, she picked up the large ostrich tip and ran her finger over the soft feather, relishing in the texture.

Looking at the hat once more, she stuck the feather in the back and picked up her needle. With fast, even stitches, she secured it to the back, so it dipped and bobbed dramatically over the chiffon. The shades of black, white, and gray were stunning. Even if she did say so herself.

Finally, she attached a bit of black velvet band around the base of the hat to keep the straw from scratching Mrs. Conrad's scalp. Another black velvet band trimmed the base, while folds of chiffon and ostrich tips hid the crown.

It was one of Johanna's finest creations. Even Gerald, with his preference for the understated, would have found it perfectly acceptable.

Oh boy. The tears were threatening again. She tied her thread and snipped the length off, placing the finished hat on the mannequin head. Then she set to cleaning her worktable, fighting the tugging temptation to sit in the corner and cry.

What on earth was wrong with her today? Though she still ached for Gerald, the deep grief of a few years ago had subsided. Or so she thought. Was this normal? There had been days, months even, when grief stuck to her like a shadow, but she felt able to live her life.

So why was today so stinking hard?

She stuffed ribbons in one box and laid the extra ostrich tips in another. Velvet scraps and buttons found their respective bins. When everything was in its place, Johanna sat at her desk and smoothed her hands over the polished surface. With an active toddler, quiet moments were so rare. She almost forgot what silence sounded like.

A beam of sunlight filtered through the small window on her left, dancing across the picture of Gerald on her desk.

Picking the picture up, she traced the angle of his cheek, the curve of his chin. A soft laugh escaped as she spotted the small cowlick curling his hair. He never could tame it, but it only added to his boyish charm. How she'd loved running her fingers through it, trying to help him smooth it on a Sunday morning before they left for church.

She clutched the picture to her chest and finally let the tears fall. It was hard to believe August would mark three years since his death.

The memory flooded her, making it hard to breathe.

One moment he'd been practicing his sermon in the pulpit while she prepared the hymns for Sunday at the piano. The next . . . he was on the floor.

Doc said it was a cerebral hemorrhage. "A tragic death for one so young."

And it was.

Gerald hadn't made it to his thirtieth birthday. Their daughter Emily was exactly one month old, and they'd celebrated their second anniversary a few short months before.

A sob escaped. She leaned forward, clutching his picture. It felt as though her heart would tear in two with the memories of that first year without him. Her parents had been a gift from the Lord. They helped with Em as much as they could, letting her and her baby stay with them. At the time the thought of going home without Gerald there had been unbearable.

But then the bills came due.

Her husband had provided life insurance for her, and once the check came, she bought the shop, fully intending to live above it with Emily.

But Johanna's mother had taken ill, so they stayed with Dad to help since they'd been so wonderful taking her in when her days were the bleakest. Selling her little home with Gerald had been bittersweet, but it had been for the best.

Losing Mom so soon after Gerald . . . A fresh wave of tears bubbled up and out of her. Dad seemed to age ten years overnight when Mom slipped from them. Still, he hadn't shied away from sharing story after story about Mom. How he'd courted her. Their wedding day. Walking with the Lord. Watching Kalispell grow and flourish and become home. He kept her memory alive and well, honoring her whenever he could.

Dad's example helped her see that packing memories of Gerald away in a tight box wouldn't help her grieve. She learned to talk about her husband, finding relief in sharing her stories. How he'd made her laugh. Why she loved his gentle nature. What an amazing pastor he had been to their small congregation. The overwhelming joy of finding out a baby was on the way.

With a watery smile, Johanna put the picture back on her desk and tugged her hankie out of her sleeve. She wiped her face clean, the thought of her daughter easing some of the ache. Her boisterous almost-three-year-old was the light and joy and focus of all their energy, driving away the clouds in their house of sorrow.

Whenever Johanna needed some extra time in the shop, Dad was gracious in taking care of Emily. Even with the limp from his injury at the lumbermill the year before, he could keep up with her pretty well. What he couldn't do was work a regular job any longer. For a man of his integrity and beliefs, that was another huge blow. Johanna had watched him slip into a stupor of uselessness in the months that followed. The only thing that seemed to help was time with his grand-daughter.

That was when Johanna decided she would engage her father to help. It gave him a purpose once again, and little by little he had recovered some of his joy. Watching over a child might not be a typical job for a man, but Dad knew he was needed again.

St. John's Millinery for Ladies had been popular from its inception. Johanna was creative and skilled with a needle. After years of making her own hats, making them for others came naturally. She invested in all the popular ladies' magazines to keep up with trending fashions, but after a time those were nothing more than templates for popular size and shape. The good Lord continued to give her creative ideas, and so she supported her little family with the income from the millinery.

It was a good situation for all of them.

The clock chimed, and she started. "Gracious." She'd been reminiscing for far too long. She needed to get home.

Laying aside her things, she stood, brushed the remaining threads and pieces of ribbon from her apron, then slipped it over her head and placed it on the hook by her desk. She wrapped her shawl around her shoulders then pulled on her gloves, going through a mental checklist. Finally, she turned off the lights, locked the door, and turned toward home. Everything was in its proper order, just as she needed it to be. Especially given her order at home was about to be disrupted.

Gerald's brother was stopping by this evening. He had entered their lives after Gerald was gone. Oh, he tried to be the fun and doting uncle, but his presence only made Johanna miss her husband more, so she kept James at a distance. Perhaps that needed to change as well. James was part of the family. And Emily enjoyed his company.

Gerald had rarely spoken of either his brother or father. Probably because he'd left home on uneasy terms with them, telling them that their choices and greed weren't honoring to God.

Deep down, Johanna understood that Gerald had chosen to serve God as a preacher because of his family's choices. He'd been so adamant about the love of money leading to destruction. While she respected her husband's stance, sometimes it did come across as harsh and unyielding. Something she never said to him, of course. A godly man holding himself to high standards wasn't something to criticize.

However, James had been gracious to them over the past couple years. He'd softened around the edges a bit and settled into the life of a smaller town. Perhaps losing his brother had helped him see the error of his ways?

Besides, he said he had exciting news, and who couldn't use a bit of joyous tidings after a long week?

Then tomorrow was Sunday, and it would be good to catch up with Cora about all the wedding plans.

Celebrating with her friend helped her to remember to look forward and not back. Ever since Parker left, she'd gotten closer and closer to Cora. Both had suffered from his departure, passing from heartbreaking loss into a beautiful friendship that focused on more good than bad. When Johanna fell in love with Gerald, Cora was there to cheer her on, despite admitting that she'd always hoped Parker would return home to take the pulpit and marry Johanna.

But by the time Gerald entered the picture, Johanna had packed away her feelings for Parker in a neat little box at the back of her heart. She chalked up the experience to girlish infatuation, although fully accepting that the love she had felt for him was real. She told Gerald everything about Parker, never wanting there to be so much as a shadow of the past to come between them. Gerald in turn had told her of a young woman he had once cared for in New York. Laying out the past for each other had only drawn them closer and ensured there would be no jealousy or memories to haunt them.

Now the only negative feelings nudging at her were that she'd had too little time with Gerald.

What a lifesaver Cora was after Gerald died. She stayed by Johanna's side day and night for weeks. Getting up with the baby, changing her, bringing her to Johanna to be fed. Bringing cool compresses to help with her eyes swollen from hours of crying. Singing to Emily, telling her silly stories, and showing the newborn that she was loved and cherished during a deep time of grief. It had been Cora who suggested Johanna move home to allow her parents to fill the void. Emily needed them as much as Johanna did, and it would serve them all well as they dealt with the new life that they would face.

And now, Cora had found her true love.

William Landry was perfect for Cora. Johanna couldn't be more happy.

Her feet stilled, and she stopped in the middle of the street. Wait. What day was it?

Cora told her last week that Parker and his theatre troupe would be coming to town soon. For several weeks.

At the time, Johanna hadn't thought much of it. People spoke of Parker on a regular basis, and she'd gotten good at letting it slide right on past. He wasn't here after all.

But still . . . regret over her rejection of his proposal haunted her.

Oh, she loved Gerald. God had clearly ordained for the two of them to marry. She would love him forever.

But as a young, almost eighteen-year-old, she'd rejected another man she had loved all because he wasn't going to be a preacher. What did that say about her? At the time, her convictions were so fierce and deep. However, she knew now she hadn't been fair to Parker. Hadn't listened to *why* he felt God was calling him in another direction. Even now, her cheeks pinked with the recollection of her stubbornness all those years ago. It wasn't as though marrying a preacher would have made her any holier.

How rigid and self-focused she'd been back then.

Picking up her pace again, she prayed for peace over the situation. There was no sense in rehashing everything. She'd made a mistake. She could admit that. Yes, God had worked through it and brought her Gerald and a love so deep and beautiful it still moved her. But she had hurt Parker—probably his entire family, if she were honest. It wasn't something to ignore.

Not any longer.

Perhaps when he was here to perform, she could apologize for her actions, and the weight resting on her mind would ease.

Yes. That's what she would do.

With a lift of her chin and a squaring of her shoulders, Johanna rounded the last corner toward home. She wasn't eighteen anymore. Ten years had passed. They had matured and lived a lot of life. The least she could do was face him and apologize.

When Johanna made it home, Emily was at the screen door and greeted her. "Mama, Mama, Mama!" She hopped from one foot to the other. "Unca James is here, and he's got candy." Red drool dribbled out the corner of her mouth, something large bulged in her cheek.

Johanna flung the screen door open and stepped inside. "Emily, what did I say about sweets before dinner?"

Em blinked hard, and tears pooled in her eyes while her lips worked toward a pout, but they couldn't close around whatever it was that James had given her. "I's sorry, Mama. I foh-got."

"It's okay, sweet girl." Johanna pulled off her gloves and tucked them in her pocket. "Why don't you spit it in my hand and we can have it later?" Or never. What was that man thinking?

Her daughter's chin quivered as she obeyed.

The candy was huge as it plopped into Johanna's hand! One wrong move, and it would have choked the small child for certain. Her mind swirled with all the horrible scenarios that could have happened. Her husband's brother might be some hoity-toity lawyer, and he might have the town wrapped around his pinky finger with his persuasive speech and charm, and he might have a big house and fancy horseless carriage— which was useless here most of the year—to flaunt, but really! *She* was Emily's parent. How dare he do such a thing without asking permission?

All the negative remarks Gerald had made about his brother rushed to her mind. *Selfish. Greedy. Only concerned with climbing the ladder of wealth and societal recognition.*

Granted, Gerald hadn't said much more than that, but it was enough to fuel the fire of her anger.

"James!" Her shout echoed through the house.

Each second he didn't appear, the heat within her rose.

Why had she ever thought it was a good idea to allow this man close to her child?

Gerald even admitted once that their father had disowned his eldest son for representing shady clients.

That was it. James St. John wasn't trustworthy.

End of story.

Johanna took her daughter's hand. "Dad?" She frowned. Where was he?

"He's upstairs lying down." James rounded the corner with a slow stride and easy smile. Well. How nice that he had such a lack of concern for her urgent call to him.

If blood could boil, hers surely would. She clenched her teeth against words that threatened to explode from her mouth. If Emily weren't at her side, she'd release them in all their fury.

James leaned against the banister as if nothing in the world was wrong. His blond hair lay slicked back, and his mustache was oiled into curlicues at the ends. His hair and eye color might be similar to her precious Gerald, but that was where the similarities ended.

"Why is he lying down? And why didn't you come when I called? We need to discuss the rules about what you are allowed to give to my child." The words tumbled out, and she tugged Emily closer to her side, willing her own fingers to stop trembling.

James shrugged and stepped closer. "He simply appeared worn out when I arrived, and poor Emily was climbing all over the furniture." He tweaked her daughter's nose. "Unlike a proper young lady, you little scamp."

If she hadn't been frowning before, she certainly was now. Her eyes narrowed so much, she could barely see him through her lashes. "She's not yet three, James." How dare he speak to her daughter that way? Was this how city men behaved? "If we're talking about *proper*"—she held out her hand with the offending stickiness—"why on earth would you give this to a young child? One, it's right before supper time. Two, she's too small for such a treat. She could have choked on it!"

James looked at the gooey red mass in her hands, his mustache twitching. Was he trying not to laugh? "Oh dear, I do apologize for upsetting you, Johanna, but there's no need to be so melodramatic. Sweet little girls need a sweet treat every once in a while, and I obliged since you can't afford them."

Her chin lifted. If he made one more insinuation about her financial situation, she would bar him from her house. "We aren't a charity case, James. Gerald provided for us just fine." She moved into the kitchen, deposited the candy in the trash, and dropped her hold on Emily. "And God continues providing."

James didn't argue, but his jaw tightened a fraction before shifting back into that all-too-eager smile. "I believe we've started off this evening on the wrong foot. Speaking of providing, I want to share my surprise with you."

The stairs creaked, and Dad's voice echoed. "Not without me. I told you not to say anything until I was here." He joined them in the kitchen, grumpy and a bit disheveled, and sat down at the table.

Johanna's shoulders sagged as she and Emily rushed toward him. She squeezed his shoulders. "Hi, Dad." She kissed his cheek then sat in the chair next to him. *Thank You, Lord, he's here.* No one was better at helping her calm down than Dad.

But with the way her blood was pumping, that would be a mighty big challenge.

Emily climbed up into his lap and leaned her head back on his chest.

Dad melted and kissed the top of her head. "My day is complete with my two best girls here." He winked at Johanna, then turned his attention to James, his expression hardening. "Go ahead, James. Let's hear this news."

"Well"—he nodded toward Dad—"since Mr. Easton can no longer work at the sawmill after his injury and you've been putting in such long hours at the shop, Johanna, I took it upon myself to contact several businesses with whom I am well acquainted."

"About what?" Prickles inched up Johanna's spine until the hair at the nape of her neck felt like it stood on end.

James held up a hand and lifted his chin. "Allow me to finish, please."

Her jaw ached from clenching it so tight. How did that man see anything with his nose so high in the air? Who was he to scold her?

Dad cleared his throat before she said anything.

All right, all right . . . She was probably riled up about the candy. Her thoughts from earlier rushed back. James was family whether she liked it or not.

Lord, help my attitude. "Fine. Please, go on, but I need to get this mess off my hands." She glanced at the clock. Her stomach was rumbling, and she needed to feed the family. She stood, went to the sink, and washed her sticky fingers, praying the cool water would cool her temper. As she dried her hands, she studied James's face. He was more than a little pleased with himself.

Mama had always warned, "The devil never comes at you with growls to frighten, but with smiles to enchant."

As if reading her mind, his grin grew, which made his mustache turn up as well. "Sears, Roebuck, and Co. would like to manufacture your hat designs and put them in their catalogs. Think about it. You won't have to slave in the shop anymore. Simply design the hats, send in the sketches and even pictures, and they will take care of the rest. They will require new designs for each new season—a minimum of at least twenty. I'm told that the legal contracts will be drawn up within the week, and once I look over them to ensure that you are getting your fair share, you can sign and you'll have a steady income. You won't have to leave your father and daughter. Isn't that wonderful?"

Johanna's jaw became limp for a moment, and then she snapped her mouth closed. All the ill feelings she'd had toward her brother-in-law pushed to the back of her mind. Could he really have done something so incredible? For her? "I'm flabbergasted . . . Are you certain? How do they even know I can design what they want?"

"Oh, I took care of all that. I sent them pictures of items from your shop."

Without her permission. Again. Still, if this was true, she couldn't hold it against him. The opportunity would be an answer to prayer. Dad couldn't keep up with Emily for too much longer, and it was harder and harder to bring her little girl into the shop. "I don't know what to say . . ."

"Thank you is all I require. It's the least I could do. You are my last living family, and I promised my father and brother that I would always look after you."

Johanna folded her arms against her chest. Was he telling the truth? He made everything sound so sweet. All tied up with a pretty ribbon. But still, she hesitated to give him her trust. If only Gerald were still here so she could ask him if it were true. But then, if her husband was still alive, she wouldn't be needing James's help at all.

Dad didn't say a word. His gaze remained fixed on the top of his granddaughter's head. She'd love to know his thoughts on the matter, but he'd share them once James was gone.

Besides, he told her time and again that she could make her own decisions.

James stood and headed toward the door. "Walk me out, please, Johanna? I have something else I wish to say."

"All right." She patted her daughter's head. "I'll be right back, and we'll eat supper." She followed James to the door and walked him out to the porch trying to untangle her knotted-up thoughts.

He kept one foot on the porch and stepped down with the other. Turning, he faced her.

Leaving the front door wide open, she stayed in the middle of the porch and gave the tall man a nod. "Thank you for thinking of me for this opportunity. It would be wonderful to have more time to take care of my father and daughter."

"The deal with Sears wouldn't be necessary if you would agree to marry me, Johanna. I can move all of you into my mansion, and neither you nor your father will ever have to worry again. You'll have plenty of servants to take care of all your needs and a doting husband to make sure you never want for anything."

The onslaught of words was accompanied by him reaching out for her hand.

She jerked away, taking one large step backward. Was he playing some sort of sick joke? *Marry* him? How on earth had he come up with such an absurd idea? She linked her hands behind her back and looked him in the eye.

His hand was still suspended in the air, that silly smile pasted on his face.

Her stomach clenched. At the moment, she had no desire to ever marry again. But if she ever did, James would be no-where on the list!

Oh dear . . .

She bit her lip.

That was rude. Gerald might not have trusted his brother, but he still had loved him.

Even so, no matter James's reasons for asking for her hand, she needed to make her own heart clear. "Your offer is extremely kind and generous, James. But I must refuse. I loved your brother with all my heart, and I don't think I will ever love or marry again."

She turned on her heel and walked back into the house, closing the screen, then the big door, then made sure the latch was in place. As she walked back to the kitchen, the urge to wash her hands overpowered the rumbling in her stomach. A shiver raced up her spine.

Marry her brother-in-law?

Ew. Not ever.

His teeth ached and his jaw felt as if he'd been punched. It had taken every ounce of strength to not react to Johanna's rejection. And that faff about never marrying again.

He'd just turned, maintaining as calm a demeanor as he could, and walked back to his house.

James snorted as he shoved his key into the lock of his mansion. The door opened before he could even turn it, and Mrs. Simpson gave him an odd look.

"It's not locked, Sir." His housekeeper raised an eyebrow at him.

"Whyever not? Are you inviting the thieves in?" He pulled the key and shoved it into his pocket. "Bring me coffee and something to eat. I'll take it in my room."

The woman didn't even wince. "Yes, sir."

He stormed upstairs. In the moment, asking Johanna to

marry him had seemed like the best decision. The most logical. Quick and easy. Everything would fall into place.

But no. The revulsion on her face danced in his memory. How dare she! He was ten times the man Gerald had been. *He* could actually provide for her. Tenfold if they married and the inheritance entered his coffers.

She was just like Gerald. Self-righteous and every inch the hypocrite. Of course she didn't want to marry him. But she had no problem considering the sweet little deal he'd gotten her with Sears.

He frowned. Perhaps it had been unwise to lead with that. He pressed his thumb and index finger to the bridge of his nose. It was impossible to think straight with throbbing temples.

Johanna would see reason. She had to. He dropped his hand and continued down the hallway toward his bedroom. A woman as beautiful as that wouldn't stay single for long. And he *had* to ensure it was *his* ring on her finger in marriage. Whether she liked it or not.

He tugged his tie off his neck as he entered the master suite and threw it on the bed. His jacket followed. Spring was blooming in Kalispell, and though the mornings were still chilly, there were days like today when the sun was merciless. Thankfully, Mrs. Simpson had opened the windows.

Plopping down in the overstuffed chair, James crossed his legs and steepled his fingers. What he wouldn't give for a stiff shot of whiskey. But right now he needed his thoughts ordered and clear.

He replayed the afternoon, pausing at each place where his plan should have worked.

He hadn't missed the frustration and almost anger she had with him as he interacted with Emily. As if he wanted anything to do with the little brat. She was merely a means to an end.

However . . . gratitude showed in Johanna's expression when he offered her the Sears job.

So ensuring the safety of her precious daughter and her dear father could force Johanna into almost anything. Maybe the little girl was a bigger piece in his plan than he'd originally thought. It would serve him well to spend a bit more time mulling that over.

For now, Johanna had his entire focus.

Her need for stability was understandable.

The St. John family had been impoverished all his growing-up years. He scoffed. His father's obsession with invention and tinkering, leaving nuts and bolts everywhere. There was that invention to mop floors without hands. And his father's idea to create something that toasted bread on both sides at the same time.

None of it ever came to fruition. It only left them further and further in debt and forced them into squalor.

Enough!

James stood and stretched. There was no fruit in dwelling on the past. He'd become a lawyer. Put himself through school and amassed the wealth he'd so desired. Never mind that some of his tactics to gain his fortune had been less than savory. The end result had been satisfying.

He picked up his jacket and shook out the wrinkles before hanging it on the hook on the door. The fine tweed of the jacket bespoke its expense. It was a far cry from the thread-bare coat he wore to school as a young boy. A shudder shook his frame. The stinging wind and slapping sleet of a New York winter on his cheeks were as real in that moment as they had been seventeen years ago. The wet snow seeping into his back. Frozen toes poking through patched and repatched boots—

Goosebumps rippled up his arms, a breeze tickling the back of his neck.

He shook his head and ran to the window, slamming it shut. He rubbed his hands down his arms, easing the chill. If only it were as easy to wipe away the horror of his past. He'd overcome poverty and a childhood in New York's slums, risen to wealth, and been prepared to shove every success in Dad's face.

But then his father had to go and ruin everything. He'd robbed James of the pride of his own achievements by one-upping him.

One of his stupid inventions actually caught on. Who on earth could have conceived that his father would become wealthy over some silly invention? It was a ridiculous notion. More than one of their neighbors had made fun of the senior St. John over the years.

But his silly old man and his even sillier friends ended up richer than Midas.

The world was so unjust.

It didn't matter now, though. His father was dead. All his attempts to cut James off during his life had been ineffective.

Or would be, once he convinced Johanna to marry him.

It was ridiculous that his whole future rested on the emotional whims of his brother's widow. But he couldn't afford to be choosy. Not when he was so close to what he wanted.

Judge Lewis's replacement was waiting for him to produce the heiress of the St. John fortune. If James and Johanna weren't married when that happened, all would be lost. Or at least half. And that wasn't acceptable. That inheritance, *all* of it, was rightfully his.

Landing back in the chair, he let out a long sigh. He rested his elbows on his knees, pushing his hands through his hair. A bad habit that mussed his usually perfect style.

No matter. Mussed hair would be the least of his worries if he couldn't get his hands on this money. He'd been a fool to think altering the will to add himself back in would make things right. Judge Lewis had known better than almost anyone how bad the blood had been between him and his father.

And Dad had never been one to relinquish a grudge.

Not even on his deathbed.

But Judge Lewis was out of the picture now. Granted, James had to speed up his timeline in case the old coot hadn't been bluffing that night at Dad's house about others knowing the facts of the will.

But no matter. He could deal with that. The Camorra gang, though . . .

That was the real threat. Representing them had brought him lots of money. But now he owed the gang. Big time. And they weren't the kind of people to forget that. No, he would have to be careful until he had enough money to ensure his security and put an end to those who would see him dead.

James sat up and smoothed his hair back into place. The clearest path was to marry Johanna. And if she wouldn't come willingly, he would show her how foolish it would be to refuse him. After all, he could be quite convincing.

He straightened. Yes. Convincing. How quickly would the young widow change her tune if her precious daughter was threatened? Or if her father had a little accident? He rubbed a hand down the side of his face. Of course, those threats wouldn't fit the image of the reformed family man he'd been portraying.

But they didn't *have* to come directly from him . . .

James tapped his fingers together for a moment. Yes, his plan was coming clear. He made his way to his desk, smiling. Johanna would learn the error of her ways soon enough.

3

Marvella Ashbury nodded at several friends as she gripped her husband's elbow and they exited the church. Her little town was thriving and handling the loss of the railroad hub with grit and their heads held high.

With Parker Bennett's theatre troupe in town, they were sure to show everyone else how well they were handling these tough times.

Thoughts of Parker turned her attention back to Johanna St. John. The woman was a miracle worker with hats and had endured such loss in her young life. Marvella couldn't hold back a smile.

Perhaps there might be a chance for things to spark back to life between the sweet widow and the actor.

"I know that look, my dear." The Judge chuckled in her ear. "Who have you set your sights on this time?"

"Whatever do you mean?" She batted her lashes at him.

"Don't play coy. Matchmaking. You're up to it again. It is plain as day on your face."

No sense in telling the man that he was correct. It might

go to his head. Instead, she turned her gaze to the streets of Kalispell. Where James St. John drove his automobile out in the streets for all to see.

Repugnant man.

She lifted her chin a fraction. "Contrary to your opinion, my love, my thoughts are quite different."

"Oh?" Her husband waggled his eyebrows at her. "Please enlighten me."

"It's Mr. St. John. Something about him has never sat right with me. He's only accepted one of our dinner-party invitations in all the years that he has lived here. I do believe he thinks he's better than everyone else in town." She squinted at the man and then turned back to her husband. "He seems . . . shady."

"Hmm."

She stopped in her tracks. "That's all you're going to say? *Hmm*?"

Her husband tugged her along, and she acquiesced. "Your observations are astute, my dear."

"Oh? So he *is* shady?" She knew it!

He put a finger to her lips. "Not so loud, darling." The Judge's head searched the area around them. The man's eyes rarely missed a thing. One of the things she loved about him. "I'll simply say that I have had my doubts about him for some time, but I can't put my finger on it. At least he seems to practice the law in an honest manner."

"That's it?" Well, that wasn't what she'd hoped to hear. "I don't trust him."

"Which is probably wise, Marvella."

Rarely did he ever use her name rather than a pet name. Which only proved he was serious about the matter.

"I don't either."

A knock at the front door had Johanna wiping at her bleary eyes and then patting her hair as she hurried to answer it. After such a long night she was sure to look a fright.

When she opened the door, Cora's smile greeted her but was replaced with a frown in the blink of an eye. "Is everything all right? When I didn't see you at church this morning, I was worried." Her brown eyes held concern. "And rightfully so, it would seem."

Johanna welcomed her friend with a hand toward the parlor. "I was up all night with Emily. Stomachache."

"Goodness, is she sick?"

She closed the door and followed her friend to the parlor, yawning as she went. "Forgive me. No, I don't think she's *sick* sick. I think this is a case of too much candy."

Cora pulled off her gloves as she sat, her brow creased in deep furrows. "Candy? You never give her candy. Did your father?"

Johanna plopped down beside her friend and rubbed her forehead. Her head ached as if it were the pin cushion on her worktable poked and stabbed by giant hat pins. "Gerald's brother came to the house yesterday afternoon while I was still at the shop." She groaned and leaned against the back of the settee. "You would *not* believe the size of the piece of candy in Em's mouth when I got home!"

Her words gushed out, fueled by a gnawing frustration she hadn't been able to shake since her encounter with James. "*Then* I found out that he'd given her a sack before that. A sack. *Full.* Of course she ate it all."

She flopped her head back against the couch. Just thinking about yesterday made all the anger stir inside her belly again.

"I guess Dad was tired and had gone to lie down, and James offered her candy. It was a treat and from family, so she didn't really know better. She's not even three, for pity's sake!"

Cora laid a hand on her knee. "I am so sorry."

"So all night long, she moaned and groaned and cried while she was curled up in a ball with her hands on her tummy. Neither one of us got much rest, I'm afraid, and I couldn't bear to wake her to go to church this morning."

"Completely understandable." Cora surged to her feet. "Let me get into the kitchen and brew some coffee. It looks like you need it."

Johanna was so tired, she didn't argue. "That would be lovely." Leaning forward, she felt a hand on her shoulder and looked up.

Cora pushed her back. "Sit. Rest your eyes for a few minutes while I get the coffee and something for you to eat. Is your dad around?"

"No. He went to sit with a friend who isn't doing so well. One of his men from the mill who had a heart attack. Dad planned to read the Bible to him and give his wife and children a chance to go to church."

"Your dad is a good man."

"So was yours." Johanna smiled. "We were beyond blessed to grow up with godly fathers. I never let myself forget that."

"Me neither. Now rest while you can. I'll have that coffee for you in a quick minute."

A rich scent caused her mouth to water. Johanna licked her lips. Then her eyes popped open.

Something smelled wonderful! Coffee and savory beef. Had she left food on the stove? Blinking several times, she focused her gaze.

The parlor. She sat up and rubbed her eyes. She must have fallen asleep on the couch. Where was Emily?

Working her way to the kitchen, Johanna forced the cobwebs from her mind. She was still so groggy. What happened to her youth when she could easily survive on a couple hours of sleep?

It was long gone. That's what happened to it. It disappeared with motherhood, grief, and managing a house and a business. And those things, while blessings, also brought the fine lines on her face and the dark circles under her eyes that mocked her so often now from the mirror.

Her daughter's sweet little voice, accompanied by Cora's richer alto, erased Johanna's dismal thoughts. They were singing a silly song about flowers.

Johanna's heart swelled as she pushed open the door to the kitchen and saw Em standing on a chair beside Cora. Aprons tied around their waists, flour on their faces and hands and every surface around them.

Lifting a hand to her mouth, she giggled. "What's all this?"

"We maked you dinner." Emily's face beamed. "But no candy." Her brow scrunched as she waggled her index finger as Johanna had done the night before.

Goodness, but she would have to be careful. Emily was likely to imitate almost anything.

"Oh good." She put on a serious expression. "I wouldn't want a tummyache."

"It's almost ready, so why don't you go get freshened up, and Miss Emily and I will have it all out on the table by the time you get back."

"Did Dad ever come home? I should probably round him up while I'm at it."

Cora shook her head. "He's come and gone. He went down

the street to help plan out the Mitchells' new barn. I could tell he was itching to get to drafting it, so I told him I'd save him a plate."

"Thank you." Johanna headed up the stairs to her room so she could wash her hands and face and make some sense out of the tangled mass of hair that was sure to be sticking out in every direction by now. Sometimes she forgot about what Dad did before the accident at the mill. Even with his limp and his age, he was a master at drafting buildings. His skills at the mill all these years went far beyond cutting logs and scoring planks. The entire Flathead Valley knew that if they needed drawings for a building, they could come to him. It would always be exact and not too fancy. And sometimes it brought in a little money.

Money . . .

She frowned. Her least favorite topic.

Rather than dwelling on all the negatives of James's visit, she had to admit he had brought a glimmer of hope. It had been kind of him to set things up with Sears, Roebuck, and Co. They were known nationwide—maybe even in other countries. It was hard to imagine what kind of requests they might get for her hats.

The contract from them couldn't come fast enough. She and her family had been surviving, but oh! Wouldn't it be lovely to *thrive*? After everything Dad had done for her—was doing for her now—it would be wonderful to give him the chance to rest a bit more. Or work on projects he loved. Or even retire.

He should be visiting all his mill buddies rather than spending his days corralling a rambunctious toddler.

As much as she hated to take any favors from James, it was the right thing to accept the contract.

She hurried down the stairs and walked into the dining

room to a feast. The smells wafting up from the table made her mouth water again. "This looks fantastic, Cora and Emily. Thank you."

Em beamed up at her. "I helped smash the potatoes."

"Did you now?"

"She was a huge help." Cora spooned some potatoes onto Johanna's plate and passed it to her. "I didn't do all that much, however. Your leftovers were easy enough to find in the icebox."

"We got to pray." Emily held out a hand on each side.

Laughter bubbled out of Johanna. "You are right, sweet girl."

Em closed her eyes once they were all holding hands and began, "Our Fadder . . . who art . . . in heben . . ."

Together, they said the Lord's Prayer with her little almost-three-year-old leading the way, even through some of the most difficult words. Last year, when Johanna had been reading through the New Testament to her daughter at bedtime, Em picked up on the fact that Jesus told his disciples, "When ye pray, say . . . " Ever since, she'd been learning the prayer and insisted they pray it before each meal.

The more Johanna thought about it, the more she applauded her daughter. It was such a good idea, and Johanna found herself paying more and more attention to the words.

Cora passed around the other dishes and smiled down at Emily. "I'm so proud of you that you can say the Lord's Prayer. It's been far too long since I've heard it spoken."

"Why?" Emily held up her fork, waving it in the air like a flag. "Jesus said it."

"That He did." Her friend chuckled. "But people seem to say it less and less."

"Why?"

Her child's favorite question.

Cora grinned and ruffled Emily's silky ringlets. "Can't get much past this little one, can you?"

"Not a thing." Johanna scooped up a bite of the beef. It was so tender, her fork had no trouble slicing through it. She relished the meal almost as much as the afternoon nap her friend had given her.

They ate in companionable silence for several moments until Cora set her fork down on her plate. "There's something I need to speak with you about, and I don't think I can wait any longer."

"Oh?" Johanna scooped another bite of mashed potatoes into her mouth. She'd been hungrier than she thought.

"Parker is here with the theatre troupe. I know you know that already, but . . . in case you haven't heard, they're staying for several weeks. I asked him to walk me down the aisle, since our father isn't with us any longer. The last thing I would want is to make you to feel uncomfortable in any way, but I love you both so much, and it would mean the world to me if you were both there and a part of this celebration." The anguish in her friend's eyes couldn't be missed.

"Oh, Cora. Parker is your brother, and this is your special day. You shouldn't be concerned about me." But her stomach balled up into knots all the same.

"Why not? You are my dearest friend in all the world."

All of a sudden, she wasn't hungry anymore. Johanna set down her fork and then lifted her napkin to her lips. Stalling. "To be honest, Cora . . . I hadn't thought about Parker being at your wedding, because I didn't expect him to stay very long. Not that I have a problem with it. I'll be fine. It's been ten years since Parker and I . . . since . . . well . . ."

Her tongue wasn't cooperating. This was silly. She was a

grown woman with a child. "It doesn't matter. My time with Gerald was the happiest of my life. Parker and I are still friends—at least, I hope we are. And we both love you. That's all that matters." She pasted on a smile. "Don't you worry one more minute about the two of us."

Cora's shoulders sagged. "Are you sure?"

"Definitely." She forced the smile on her face to widen. How could she show her friend that all was well? "How *is* your brother? I'm assuming you've seen him?" Needing to do something with her hands, she picked her fork back up and pushed the food around on her plate.

"He looks wonderful and says he's doing well. Although, I can tell that our mother is worried about his reputation."

Johanna frowned. Parker never had an issue with his reputation. Though she had ignored most news about his career over the years, she would have remembered if she'd heard something untoward. "What on earth for?"

"Apparently his new manager likes to get the press to print outlandish stories so that the tickets will sell out even faster." Cora shrugged.

"Outlandish?"

"Oh, yes. Haven't you read the paper?"

As a matter of fact, she hadn't. There never seemed to be time. And Dad hadn't said a word. Perhaps she needed to probe him about it. "No, I've been too busy with everything around here, keeping up with Emily, and all the new hats at the store." Which reminded her, she hadn't told her friend about James's offer yet. But maybe she should hold off in case it didn't happen like he said.

"All the nonsense in the paper aside, I'm worried about him."

"Oh?" She glanced at Cora, who was dragging her own fork through her mashed potatoes.

Cora met Johanna's eyes and put down her fork, pushing her plate away from her. "He seems to have enjoyed touring Europe and especially playing the lead in *Everyman*. But all that did was make him more famous, and now he seems a bit . . . lost."

Johanna dabbed at her lips with her linen napkin. What could she say? *Should* she say anything? Perhaps it was best to listen for now.

Cora took a sip of water then continued. "He didn't really have much to say other than how busy he was with all the shows that had booked him." She looked at Johanna with a frown. "That zest for acting he once had, the joy that was always present when he talked about preaching the gospel through stories on the stage, seems gone. And I think he's lost sight of why he left seminary to pursue it."

A bit of Johanna's heart broke. This picture of Parker sounded nothing like the passionate, energetic young man who'd left his small town to share God's love with the world. But what could she say to Cora to comfort her? Would it be hypocritical to offer words of wisdom when she hadn't agreed with his decision in the first place?

Was she in part to blame for Parker's trouble?

Monday, April 17, 1905

Opera Block.

Parker stared up at the sign at the top of the two-story building and grinned. To perform in his hometown was a dream he'd had for many years. To see that dream come to fruition . . . it was almost too much to put into words.

He crossed the street, entered the building, and took the stairs up to the second floor.

Set creation was in full swing for *Uncle Tom's Cabin*, and the crew had already brought in all the sets and backdrops for the Shakespeare plays they would be performing. All the materials were lined up against one wall, while the opposite wall was full of arched windows. The domed ceiling soared overhead—it had to be close to twenty feet. A balcony was at one end, the stage at the other.

The McIntosh Opera House was beautiful. It opened the year after he left home, and he'd kept track of all the happenings, thanks to Cora.

These were going to be the best shows Kalispell had ever seen. He would see to that.

If only he'd done this while Dad was still alive. So his father could have seen him on stage. Parker had always longed for his dad to be proud of him for the choice he'd made. Now Dad would never have the chance to truly know . . .

He swiped a hand over his jaw to force the thoughts away. Turning to survey the entire space, Parker caught sight of his manager making a beeline for him.

Alfred looked like he might bust the buttons on his waistcoat if he held in his excitement much longer.

Parker crossed his arms over his chest and waited for the man to reach him. "Good morning, Alfred. You look pleased with yourself."

"Indeed I am, Parker." In a flurry, he flicked open the paper. "It's the afternoon edition. The editor gave me a copy to show you."

A bit of dread filled his stomach. What had Alfred done this time?

LOCAL BOY MAKES IT BIG

Great. Just what he needed. Touting his fame to his hometown.

Parker read the article.

Oh no . . . it was so much worse than that. The more he read, the more he wanted to throw it *and* his manager out the second-story window. Back in New York, this wouldn't be a big deal. People knew they couldn't believe everything that was in the paper. But here? This was his home. The townsfolk lived and breathed the news in the paper. What did Alfred think this would accomplish?

According to what was written, famous local boy Parker Bennett was now linked as a romantic interest with Yvette Lebeau, a French actress who was to be an upcoming co-star.

What made it even worse was that whoever wrote the piece spoke with Yvette—or Alfred had spoken for her—and in response to the inquiry about their romance she was quoted as saying, "I think it's marvelous. I've had my eye on Parker for more than a year now. He's incredibly talented, famous, and rich. What more could a girl want?"

Parker shoved the paper into Alfred's chest.

Either his manager had ignored him, or he was a complete idiot.

Alfred grinned. "You should make some public appearances together to encourage the story."

Clearly it was both.

His manager was practically vibrating. "This is going to be *gold* for your career once we make it to California and then back East. Yvette has tons of fans in her own right, which will bring you even more devotees. This is what we need to take you all the way to the top."

Parker glared at him. "I'm not interested in Yvette, and I'm not going to make public appearances to feed your ridiculous stories." He stormed across the hall and down the stairs while Alfred chased after him.

What in the world would Mother think of *this*?

It was simple. He'd wanted to come home and perform. Maybe a little part of him had wanted to show his success, that he hadn't chosen the wrong direction for his life. That all his hard work had paid off.

But this was terrible!

"Parker!" Alfred tugged on him. "There are investors all over the world waiting for the right new talent to bring in when they start up new film companies. Edison's company will be small peanuts. You have no idea how big of a deal this is. I do. You need to listen to me about this. The future isn't going to be the stage for long. It will be the screen. You wait and see."

Parker stopped in the middle of the boardwalk and stared down at his shoes. He shouldn't be worried about what his mother thought, but what the *Lord* thought. "I need some time alone to think all this through." He pinned Alfred with a glare. "But I do *not* appreciate these kinds of methods."

He strode away before he said something he would regret.

Changing directions, he headed toward the edge of town. He needed fresh air and quiet, and lots of it. Rehearsal began in forty-five minutes. He had always been early, but not today. Alfred could stew about him storming off, the cast and director could start without him for all he cared.

With long strides, he reached the edge of town and headed toward the mountains in the east. It had been far too long since he'd gotten away from the hubbub and talked to God.

He'd prayed before every rehearsal and performance. Anyone who worked with him knew to expect him to gather people in prayer.

Then he'd been cast in *Everyman*. No one had been more

surprised at his rise to fame than he. And fame brought re-sponsibilities. People pulling at his time and talent. At first, each party had been the opportunity to talk about why *Everyman* and other morality plays were a wonderful chance to share the true good news of the gospel.

Every time he did so, though, he'd been laughed at. Mocked. Told to shut his mouth.

In a way, he had. After all, his performances could preach the gospel loud enough. As his professor had suggested.

When had he last shared the gospel from his heart with someone? Three years ago? His brows dipped. Four? His face dotted with sweat. He couldn't remember. How had he allowed this to go so far?

In the middle of a pasture, he stopped and stared up at the sky.

He was famous.

But rather than being fulfilling, it was . . .

Empty.

How could he be otherwise? He was so far from the man he was raised to be and the truth he believed.

All the articles he'd ignored came rushing back to mind. Articles describing him as a womanizer, a partier, the typical rich actor who only cared about his social status.

Dear God . . . is that who people think I've become?

And then an even more terrible thought hit.

Is that who I am?

4

She was on a mission.

Marvella Ashbury quick-stepped her way down the boardwalk, practically dragging Sir Theophilus by his leash toward Johanna's millinery shop.

Outside the millinery, she checked her reflection in the window and straightened her hat. Then she picked up her little white dog, unclipped his leash, and stuffed it in her large pocket as he licked her chin. "Be on your best behavior, Theophilus. We have much to do."

He gave another lick and then a short yip.

"Good boy. I have a nice treat for you in my pocket if you behave."

Another yip.

She nodded and entered the shop. "Good morning, ladies." Cora Bennett and Johanna Easton St. John were both bent over a hat creation, surrounded by ribbons, flowers, lace, and tulle. "It appears you are busy-busy this morning."

Johanna pulled a needle through the hat she was working on and looked up with a wide smile. "Good morning, Mrs. Ashbury, how lovely to see you." She set her project down and stood. "I presume you are here for your new hat?"

"Yes, dear. And I must say, I have been looking forward to this."

The lovely young widow turned toward the back of the shop. "I'll be right back with it."

"Such a shame what happened to her husband." Marvella turned to Cora. "And so young too. Now mind you, I didn't know them very well since the Judge and I attend under Pastor Woody—wonderful man, we are so thankful for his teaching over the years—and we love our church, but I'd always heard wonderful things about your father's preaching and then Gerald's." She lifted her shoulders as she took a big breath.

Sir Theophilus whined and wiggled his backside, his little black eyes fixed on the tulle in Cora's hand. Marvella pressed her beloved dog closer to her side.

No need for a scene today.

"Pastor Woody and my father used to meet for coffee and prayer once a week." Cora continued the delicate work of stitching tulle around the brim of the hat in her hands. "He loved those times of fellowship."

In all her years in Kalispell, and as one who made sure to know all the goings-on in her town, this little revelation was a bit of a shock. "I didn't know that. One would think Pastor Woody would have told us."

Cora shrugged a bit, glanced up for a second—her eyes sparkling—and then went back to work. "I don't think they made a big deal out of it. It wasn't for show, but a way for the two men to pray for each other's needs, encourage each other in the Word, and discuss the best ways to reach the lost in Kalispell."

Fascinating. She would have to discuss this with the Judge when she got home. "What wonderful men we have had in our pulpits—"

"Here we are." Johanna came through the curtain that separated the back of the shop—presumably storage—from the front. "I apologize it took me a moment, but I had to find a hat box large enough." She brought the creation to Marvella.

With a hand to her chest, Marvella shook her head. "My, my, my, you have outdone yourself. It's glorious."

Johanna set the box down and held the hat out. "Let's try this on, shall we?"

Marvella handed Sir Theophilus to her with one hand and took the hat with the other. "Oh my, it's heavy."

The young widow worked to get the wiggling dog settled in her arms. "The bigger the hat, the heavier it usually is."

Marvella walked over to the mirror, removed her hat, and then lifted the new one to sit on her head. The wide satin ribbons formed into loops and bows and flowers at the top were different shades of peach—exactly as she requested. Tulle encased the entire outside of the wide-brimmed straw hat, with a piece of tulle to tuck under her chin as well.

Tipping her head back and forth, Marvella tested the hat. Then wiggled from side to side. Then hopped up and down twice.

Johanna stepped up beside her and looked at her reflection in the mirror. "Is something wrong, Mrs. Ashbury?"

"Not at all, dear. Simply testing out how this will do for automobile driving." She narrowed her eyes and wiggled her upper body several times. Nodding, she removed the hat. "I do believe I would like a bit more to hold it on." Seeing the question in the milliner's eyes, she continued. "How about some matching ribbons—perhaps two on each side a few inches apart?—that I can tie. The Judge has indeed bought one of those horseless carriages, and I find I must be able to keep my hat in place."

"I see." Johanna handed Sir Theophilus back to her and took the hat back. "I've got the perfect ribbon. It might take a day or two for me to get it finished with all the other projects I'm working on."

"Not a problem, my dear. So long as it gets done." Marvella handed the dog to Cora, who had to jump up from her chair to catch the animal, and then turned back to the mirror to replace her hat from earlier. "Hat pins simply won't cut it anymore, I'm afraid. Not with all these fancy machines, which go entirely too fast. They will be the bane of our existence in no time." She adjusted her hat and pin and then fluffed her hair around her ears. "Why the Judge insists on such a contraption, I don't know. It's ridiculous and expensive, not to mention the fact that I will have to secure an entire new wardrobe with hats that will endure the travel. We will be going for another drive later today, so that I can see for certain what is needed."

She turned back to the two young women and smiled. Reaching for Sir Theophilus, she positioned him in her arms and then reached into her pocket for the promised treat.

"Let me know if you'd like to purchase another in a different color, and I'll order the supplies if I don't have them." Johanna waved at Marvella and took her seat again.

"Wonderful. I do appreciate you, dear. But it wouldn't be necessary if he wasn't so insistent on an automobile. An automobile!" She opened the door. "Men. What were they thinking?"

As the door closed behind Marvella, Cora was finally able to release her pent-up laughter. "Oh my goodness, Mrs. Ashbury is one of my favorite customers." But the giggles wouldn't stop.

"Those automobiles, they will be the bane of our existence." Johanna laughed along.

"When she started wiggling and jumping in front of the mirror, I thought for sure she'd gone daft." Cora winced. "I'm sorry. That was disrespectful." But remembering the picture of the Judge's wife bouncing and wiggling this way and that in front of the mirror induced another round of laughter. She covered her mouth.

"Once she explained herself, I had a hard time keeping a straight face myself." Johanna looked back down at the hat in her hands, a soft smile on her face.

Cora studied her dear friend for several moments. "It's so good to see you laugh and smile."

The comment brought Johanna's startling blue eyes back up to connect with hers.

"It's been a tough few years, and you have handled them with grace and courage." Cora couldn't bear to hurt her friend. "I'm thankful for the opportunity to laugh with you."

The shocked look slowly disappeared, and Johanna glanced down again. "It has been hard. I won't deny that—but you're right. Laughter is good for the soul."

Conversation stalled, and Cora lifted up her friend in prayer. She couldn't imagine how hard it would be to lose a husband. Losing her own father had been more difficult than she'd ever imagined.

Perhaps she could try to bring some more laughter and light-hearted fun back into her friend's life.

She'd be lying if she said she hadn't thought about Parker and Johanna reigniting their first love now that he was back in town. But that wasn't something she would ever say aloud. What she *could* do was pray for the Lord's will to be done.

Someone out the window caught her eye, and Cora glanced

up—and her mouth dropped open. The most glamorous woman she'd ever seen was walking toward the shop. Perfectly coiffed blonde hair and an outfit that must have come from New York or Paris declared the woman didn't belong in Kalispell, Montana. It was often said that a fashionable ensemble made the woman wearing it, but in this case the woman clearly commanded the gown. The lavender-colored fabric draped her in such a way that it was obvious the dress had been tailored to perfection. And was that exquisite lace of French origin?

When the woman entered the store, Cora covered her shock with a smile and greeted her. "Good morning. How may I help you?" She still couldn't take her eyes off the woman's outfit. From the hat on her head to the lace-trimmed hem, it was absolute perfection.

"I'd like to see if you can fashion a hat for me that will match a new dress I have coming." The woman had a slight accent. French?

"Mrs. St. John can design something perfect for you, I'm sure." Cora led her to Johanna. "She's one of the best milliners in the country."

Her friend stood and nodded. "Is there something in particular you are looking for? I'm sure I can make something that will match your vision."

Brown eyes that looked as hard as earth before the rain scanned the small shop. Cora suppressed a shudder. She'd always considered brown eyes warm and friendly, but this woman's gaze seemed the opposite of both those traits.

"Well, we shall see about that." The woman touched ribbons and flowers on the worktable. "I usually have my hats created in Paris. It seems unlikely that you can manage something as elegant. I have a certain special someone to impress, so it needs to be the absolute pinnacle of fashion. Best you've ever done."

"Of course. I will do my very best." Johanna slid her gaze to Cora, and it was hard to miss the pleading in her eyes.

This woman was . . . interesting, to say the least.

The lady sniffed. "I'm in town with the theatre group, but what you don't know, what most of the troupe doesn't know, is that a representative of investors for a potential new film company is coming to see us."

"For motion pictures? That's great to hear." Cora bit her lip. Did Parker know about this? How exciting for him! But her heart sank a bit. Would that mean that he wouldn't come home for years and years again?

The woman turned to the mirror and checked her reflection, tilting her head side to side. She put a handkerchief up to the corner of her mouth and lightly wiped at the red lipstick. "Now, perhaps you understand the importance of this hat I need you to create. My manager is arranging a picnic for us to see whatever picturesque place is north of here in the mountains"—she waved a dismissive hand—"and it's imperative that everything be perfect."

Cora took notes as the woman rattled off her requirements for the hat. It would probably end up being the largest one Johanna had ever made.

Johanna gave the woman a warm smile. "Could you perhaps have the dress brought over so that I might match the color?"

The actress rolled her gaze heavenward and heaved a sigh. "*Oui.* I suppose if I must."

How Johanna maintained her smile was a mystery to Cora, but she did it. "It would be to your benefit. I would hate to disappoint you."

"Very well. I'll send my maid over with it this afternoon. I'll need the hat delivered to the West Hotel for Yvette Lebeau. By the end of the week."

"I'm sorry, we don't do delivery, Miss Lebeau." Johanna arranged several items for their guest to inspect. "But you are welcome to pick it up in a week."

The lady huffed. "I forgot we are in a backwoods town." Derision laced her tone. "Perhaps I'll ask Parker to pick it up for me, then."

Cora didn't miss the way Johanna's eyes snapped to attention. Of course, she'd done the same thing at the mention of her brother. "You know Parker Bennett?"

Miss Lebeau turned to her with a regal smile. "But of course. He's my co-star"—she leaned closer—"and soon to be much more."

Their table inside the Kalispell Just Peachy Eatery was front and center with the best window view of the mountains.

Parker had hoped that his invitation to his mom and sister would be well received. It was nice to spoil them since he hadn't been back home in so long. To his pleasant surprise, his sister's fiancé had also joined them. Parker found he very much liked the man.

"This is lovely, Parker, thank you." Mom dabbed her napkin to her mouth.

"Yes, thank you." Cora grinned and dipped her spoon into whatever chocolaty concoction she'd ordered for dessert. "I can't say how long it's been since I've eaten here."

William Landry—her fiancé—patted her hand. "Perhaps I should bring you here sometime."

The lovesick look she gave William lifted Parker's spirits. Landry was a banker and a good man. He loved the Lord, and his love for Cora was evident in every look and kind word between the couple. Judging from the look on his mother's face, she was pleased as punch with her soon-to-be son-in-law.

"Have you seen Johanna yet?"

Good heavens! Where did his mother's question come from? He picked up his water and took a sip, measuring how to respond. "No, I haven't. How is she doing?"

A couple stopped by their table. "Mr. Bennett, we saw you in Chicago where you performed *Everyman*." The woman put a hand to her throat. "It was the most moving program we've ever seen."

"Yes"—the husband chimed in—"stellar performance. We are looking forward to seeing many more the next couple weeks."

"Thank you." He gave the couple a smile. They were genuine in their praise, but there were times it simply rang hollow. Why did it feel that way? Where was the joy he'd always felt before? He nodded to the couple and took another drink of water to avoid further conversation.

As the couple walked away, Mom had one eyebrow raised at him. "That's the third group of people to talk to you during lunch. Does this happen often?"

He shrugged and put his glass down. "Some. Yes."

"Guess that's what happens when you're famous." William chuckled. "I know that the talk of *Uncle Tom's Cabin* has been all the buzz about town. Well, that and your relationship with that French actress."

If they hadn't been in public, he would have groaned out loud. "That is all publicity and nothing more. Miss Lebeau and I are merely coworkers and not at all interested in each other."

Cora's eyebrows took their turn at rising.

He knew that look. He better change the subject and fast. "How are the wedding plans coming along?"

"Wonderful and on schedule." Cora's face radiated utter happiness. "My dress is complete, and the flowers have been arranged. And now that you've agreed to walk me down the aisle, I feel certain that everything will come together beautifully."

William stood. "I'm sorry to bring such a lovely time together to an end, but I must get back to the bank." He reached inside his coat as if to get his wallet.

Parker waved him off. "This is my treat, William. I won't hear of you paying a cent."

The man smiled. "Then I will buy our meals next time."

"It's a deal."

"Let me walk with you." Cora stood and took hold of William's arm. "Johanna is swamped in the shop, and I need to get back and help her."

The cute couple left, and Mom eyed him. "You don't seem happy, son."

"You never have been one to mince words, have you, Mother?" He leaned forward a bit so their conversation would be a little more private. "It's not that I'm not happy, Mom. Honest. But I have been doing a lot of contemplating since I've been back."

"Would you like to talk about it?"

The tension eased from his shoulders. Mom had always been a great listening ear. Perhaps sharing would ease some of his agitation. "I love acting. It's not only been a wonderful way to see the world, but I've had the opportunity to share God with people. I know the reputation the theatre has, but as with every setting of life, it is what one makes of it."

"I wish I could have seen you in *Everyman*. I've heard it's a wonderful play." Mom's warm smile made him feel a bit lighter. The fact that she wanted to see him in anything after all of Alfred's stupid articles was a blessing.

"It is. And that was probably the greatest time I had of sharing God with others. Even other cast and crew. But things have changed. My schedule has gotten busier and busier. I thought rising to the top would give me an advantage, but instead people expect certain behaviors and tolerate little else. It hasn't been the same for a while. I was lucky to get them to arrange for us to be here. Believe me, it wasn't easy to convince anyone that Kalispell was the place to start our tour."

"I can imagine." Mom poured cream into her coffee. "But clearly you've used your skills of persuasion, because here you are." She gave him a wink.

He chuckled. "It's true. And while it's a blessing to be back home, it's also feels like a curse. Especially when it comes to those articles. *You* know I'm not that man, but there are so many new people in town who don't know me. That those articles are their first impression of who I am as a person . . . " He rolled his mug between his palms, unable to look Mom in the eye. "Those articles make it difficult to be myself off stage."

"So this reputation has been created for you, and sharing your faith now would rip at those fragile threads." She took a sip of her coffee. "You know . . . your father would say that you'll never be happy living a lie."

The words struck hard. And they were true. But how could he change when he didn't know what the next right step was?

"Fancy meeting you here." Yvette's smooth voice came from the left and, with it, a deepening sense of dread in his gut. "Won't you introduce me to your lovely lunch companion?"

Parker bit back a sharp retort. It would be far better for

everyone if Yvette stayed away from his family, but he couldn't be rude. "Yvette Lebeau, this is my mother, Mrs. Martin Bennett."

"Mrs. Bennett," Yvette gushed, "how lovely to meet you. Thank you for allowing me to interrupt your meal."

"Lovely to meet you as well." Mom glanced from her and back to him, her expression inscrutable. He needed to get out of this situation and fast.

Yvette sidled up to Parker, her red lips twisting into a pout. "Do you know the time? We really should be getting to rehearsal, Parker. Please escort me?"

He stood and straightened his jacket. "I need to walk my mother home."

"Parker, don't worry about me. I can make it home on my own." She gave Yvette a final look before standing and patting his forearm. "If you need a listening ear, I'm always here for you."

He leaned down and kissed her cheek. "Thanks. I love you, Mom."

"*Allons-y*, Parker, we don't want to be late." Yvette tugged on his arm.

As they walked out the door, Yvette slipped her hand into the crook of his elbow. They were met by two men from the newspaper, pencils poised over their pads.

Questions flew at them, and Yvette was quick to respond while sidling closer and closer to him. It took all his self-control to not push her away. And the whole time, his mother's voice echoed in his mind . . .

"*You'll never be happy if you're living a lie.*"

5

Parker walked up to the director while the actors on the stage struggled with their new assignment. "Mind if I leave for a bit? I need some fresh air." He kept his voice low.

"Be back in two hours. I doubt we will have moved past this horrid display of mediocrity, but there's always hope." The man rolled his eyes and crossed his fingers. "Thank heavens *you* are part of this troupe, or I would have to run away to Timbuktu."

Parker gripped the director's shoulder. "I'll be back." He stepped away with long, quick strides. He couldn't argue with the man's words. His direction was impeccable, and the harsh lecture he'd given the cast had been needed. It was far too easy for people to get lazy in their speech nowadays, and that would not do in a Shakespeare play.

At least he had a few moments to himself.

Especially after that display at lunch.

Mom's words kept coming back to him. Was he living a lie? In the world of the theatre, it wasn't wrong to work his way up to the top . . .

But *how* he did so . . . that could be wrong.

Very wrong.

Yvette's behavior and the press's questions had made him cringe and want to take a bath.

Especially since his mother saw a lot of it.

Shoving his hands into his pockets, he walked the streets of downtown Kalispell—around one block and then another—until his feet brought him to the street where Johanna's millinery shop was located.

That hadn't been his intended destination. At least, not originally.

But he still hadn't spoken to her.

It had been ten years. Yes, he would always care for her. But would he always feel rejected? Unworthy?

From what his sister told him, Johanna had found true love, and that was all that he could hope for her.

Their young love was water under the bridge. He'd followed his passion to share the gospel through theatre. She'd married a preacher.

They'd each gotten what they wanted. Now they could at least be friends.

But coming back to Kalispell had wrenched open a long-closed door in his chest. Nothing felt quite right anymore. He hungered for that same passion for his faith that he'd left town with. He longed to spend time with his dad—but he was gone. And his best friend had rejected him.

Everything was simply . . . catawampus.

Like he was up on stage, in costume, with an overflowing crowd in the opera house, and yet he couldn't remember one line. Not one word. No other cast members were present.

Just him.

On an empty stage.

And a room full of people waiting for him . . . pressing closer and closer . . . and looking angrier by the moment.

He shook his head of the image and glanced through the window in front of him.

Johanna stood alone in her shop with her back to him. Her shoulders hunched, arms wrapped around her middle, and her head dipped low.

The weight of whatever burden she carried seemed to press down on her. Gone was the young girl who'd been overly optimistic about everything. Before him stood a woman who carried the scars of life. Grief. Loss. Pain.

Now wasn't the time to see her. Not when she seemed burdened enough. And not until he sorted his own thoughts out.

Parker slid his gaze from the window and walked away.

His teeth were going to fall out of his head.

James shifted in the driver's seat of his brand-new automobile, knuckles whitening around the steering wheel. What a fool he'd been! Driving from Whitefish to Kalispell after the automobile's delivery from Buffalo seemed like a good idea thirty minutes ago. The roads were nice and firm from baking in the spring sun.

What he hadn't anticipated were the rocks. And the massive amount of dust. Goggles might protect his eyes, but the rest of him—indeed the whole auto—was covered in thick Montana dirt.

His surprise was ruined.

Instead of his sister-in-law *ooh*ing and *ahh*ing over the enclosed body of his 1905 Pierce Great Arrow Suburban, with its cherry-red wheels and spokes gleaming in the sun, all she would see was travel wear and tear from this crazy drive.

Which wouldn't do at all. He hadn't gone to all this expense to *not* impress her.

His Oldsmobile Runabout was beautiful and luxurious, and very few people in Montana had even seen a motorcar, much less ridden in one. But that hadn't impressed her. In fact, she'd quickly declared it unsafe for a small child with its open seating and curved dash and declined ever going for a drive with him.

So he'd bought another automobile. Which was now filthy.

No matter. His house was located on the outskirts of the town. He could park the new auto around back and have several of his servants clean it until it shone once more.

He'd have to change and get cleaned up himself. Then he'd have that new man he'd hired as a driver take him over to Johanna's. That would surely impress her.

He wrenched the steering wheel, rounding a curve. Pain throbbed from his temple down to his neck. There was no way he would ever drive this stretch of road again. The state should be ashamed of itself for leaving its roadways in such disarray. Perhaps he should contact the governor's office and file a complaint.

He made one more turn and let out a breath.

Finally.

Kalispell sprawled before him, a welcome sight. He drove to the outskirts of town and shifted to make a right-hand turn.

AHHOOOOOGAAAAH!

He jerked the steering wheel sharp left and slammed on the brakes, feeling the pegs of his driving shoes pressing into the bottom of his foot. Dust clouded around him for a moment, then a breeze cleared his vision.

The blast of another automobile horn was a shock to be sure.

Who else even owned one in Kalispell? He jerked his head

around and spied none other than Judge Ashbury driving a beautiful Cadillac Model B with his plump wife and her little dog beside him on the black leather seat.

The Judge tipped his hat. "A fine day for a drive, Mr. St. John, isn't it? But I suggest you keep your eyes on the road."

Black spots danced before James's vision, and heat surged up his neck.

Mrs. Ashbury had a hand to her chest, her eyes wide. "Indeed, young man. You nearly scared us to death."

The Judge's bushy eyebrows rose as his head bobbed up and down. "You wouldn't want to get in an accident because you weren't paying attention. These machines rely completely on the driver's expertise"—he patted the steering wheel—"unlike a horse, which could still navigate without us at the helm."

How *dare* this man lecture him about driving an automobile!

James opened his mouth to spew his thoughts on the matter, but the little mutt in the pudgy woman's arms began to bark and yap up a storm. The Judge waved and drove on, leaving James in his wake.

James pounded the steering wheel with the heel of his hand. He'd never liked judges, but most of the time he'd managed to work with them. Most were eager, ladder-climbing politicians, willing to do anything to serve their own ends, especially in an election year.

Judge Ashbury was, unfortunately, not that kind of judge.

It had made James's time in Kalispell a bit more difficult to navigate. He couldn't schmooze and bribe his way into the man's good graces, which had meant he had to do things aboveboard here. How tedious.

He shifted the gears of the car and pressed the gas pedal, easing into the right-hand turn before his long driveway.

He needed to keep an eye on Ashbury. And his nosy wife. What was her name? Minerva? Arabella?

Whatever her name was, he'd seen both of them hanging around Johanna's hat shop and home. He'd been around Kalispell long enough to know the kind of power they wielded. It would be unwise to deal with them as he had others in New York.

Hmm. The Ashburys would be a challenge to eliminate, but if the need arose, he would not shy from the task.

He maneuvered the vehicle around back and parked it beside the large barn that held his horses and carriages.

Two men came running out of the barn to greet him.

"I want three more men with you, scrubbing this automobile clean from top to bottom," he barked. "It must be done in two hours, and I want it to shine. If there is a single scratch, every one of you will pay."

They nodded and scrambled around the car as he stalked into the house.

A little more than two hours later, he stood in front of the beautiful automobile in a clean, pressed suit, his hair slicked back with pomade. The afternoon sun glimmered off the auto's shiny paint.

The man he'd hired as driver stood by the vehicle in a gray suit and cap. The perfect picture of a wealthy man's driver. James climbed into the enclosed back of the vehicle, and his driver closed the door.

"We'll be off to Mrs. St. John's house, Edgar."

"Good, sir." The man nodded and eased the vehicle into a slow meander down the driveway.

The town of Kalispell rolled by, and James couldn't help but notice how many people stopped and stared at him. His mouth tipped up into a grin. Yes. Keeping looking, peasants.

There were advantages to breaking free of the big city. Here, he could be royalty if he wanted.

He leaned against the seat and pretended to ignore the gawking crowds.

An afternoon drive and perhaps a little charm should soothe Johanna's ruffled feathers. And if he had to placate the toddler as well, so be it.

As they pulled up to Johanna's house, he tapped on the glass in front of him. "Press the horn."

Edgar did as he was told, and James exited the back of the vehicle and stood next to it.

The front door opened, and Johanna appeared behind the screen. A deep *v* furrowed between her eyes as she met his gaze. "James?" She opened the screen and wiped her hands on her apron.

"Let's go for a drive! Isn't it beautiful?"

The frown turning her mouth downward wasn't what he expected. "You bought *another* automobile?"

Frustration clawed the back of his throat. She acted like he had some sort of contagious disease. Forcing a grin, he unhooked the latch of the gate and walked up the path to the porch steps. "I did. Since you don't believe the other one is safe for Emily to ride in, I purchased one fit for a family." He cleared his throat. A change of tactics was in order. "Look. I know I sprung the offer of marriage on you the last time we spoke. That was wrong of me."

Johanna's blue eyes softened a fraction. "It was indeed unexpected."

"And perhaps I went about winning Emily over in an inappropriate way as well." He dropped his gaze from hers for a moment, hoping the play of contrition was persuasive.

"She was sick for two days," Johanna shot back, but her retort lacked heat. She was melting.

"I apologize, Johanna. Rest assured, I come bearing no gifts or offers except to take two delightful ladies for their first automobile ride." He gave Johanna a wide smile as she pushed the screen door open and took a couple tentative steps his way.

"A ride?"

"Nothing dangerous or fast." He held up his hands. "I just thought—"

"Unca James!" Emily's squeal cut him off. She darted around her mother and launched herself off the top step into his arms.

"Em!" Johanna's scolding voice didn't stop the child in mid-air.

Air whooshed from his lungs as her small body slammed into his chest. He rocked back on his heels, clutching her close so they didn't fall. This was the welcome he'd hoped for. Proof his candy trick hadn't been wasted on the child.

"Young lady, you come here right now."

Emily pulled back and looked into James's face, her eyes wide. "Oops." She wriggled down out of his arms and turned to her mother, her head hanging low.

James watched Johanna bend down to her daughter, her voice a furious whisper. A moment later, the toddler turned. "I sowwie, Unca James. That was bad."

James shuffled his feet. "All is forgiven. Now. Are we ready for a ride?"

Johanna's hands landed on Emily's shoulders as the little girl squealed. "Thank you, James, but we have to decline. Emily's behavior has shown she is not ready for a treat such as this. Perhaps another time."

No. No, no, *no*. She was not going to ruin his plans again. "Surely we can overlook this small transgression. Show a little grace? I had the car cleaned up for the two of you. And it's such a lovely day."

Johanna shook her head. "Not today. I'm sorry. It's already been a long day."

James frowned. She didn't *look* sorry. "Johanna, what's the harm in a little ride?"

She ignored him, instead leaning back down to Emily, giving some instruction to her daughter. The little girl walked back into the house, her sniffles echoing into the front yard.

Johanna straightened and looked at James, her arms wrapped around her waist. "I appreciate what you're trying to do." Her voice was even and kind. "But I can't have you show up and offer all sorts of fancy and exciting things."

His brow dipped low. "What is wrong with fancy and exciting?"

"They're not stable, James." She blew out a breath, and wisps of her hair blew off her forehead. She looked heavenward for a moment then dropped her hands to her sides and offered a small smile. "Thank you for your apology. I can appreciate that it was difficult to do. I hope we can remain friends. I do desire for Emily to have her uncle in her life."

James shoved his hands in his pants pockets. He could feel his nostrils flaring, his patience stretching thin. "That's what I'm trying to do."

"In your own way, yes."

The woman was impossible. "But?"

Johanna spread her hands wide. "But Emily is an impressionable little girl. She needs steadiness. Consistency. Not bags full of candy and fancy cars." She bit the corner of her lip. He could see the struggle rippling across her face. "I know the spirit behind the offer is right, but I would much rather you show up and have dinner with us. Or come to church. Or even watch Emily for an afternoon. Not show up on a whim whenever it fits your flights of fancy."

James pursed his lips for a moment. "Fine." The word burst out of him.

Her eyes widened a fraction. "Please don't be angry."

He huffed a laugh. "Make up your mind, Johanna. You don't get to dictate how I feel. I have tried for the last three years to have a presence in my niece's life. And you've constantly rebuffed me. As if my efforts are subpar to your perfection."

"That's unfair!" She fisted her hands on her hips. "You are twisting my words and my meaning. I—"

He slashed a hand through the air. "You're no different from Gerald. Unless someone meets your high and holy standard, they aren't good enough to be in your life." Heat poured through him. No more of her silly, self-righteous games. He took a step toward the porch, leaning forward so she would not miss his meaning. "But perhaps I have had it wrong all along. Perhaps I need to be more concerned about Emily. And how you are raising her."

Two bright red spots stained her cheeks. "What are you insinuating?"

James straightened and shrugged. "Nothing. Merely that as Emily's uncle, I have a vested interest in making sure she is being well cared for. I'm here to help, Johanna. And you would do well to consider that. I bid you good day."

He turned on his heel, leaving her with his veiled threat hanging in the air. If she was unwilling to bend to his offer of peace, so be it. But when he was through with her, she would regret her refusal.

He would ensure it.

TUESDAY, APRIL 18, 1905

The scent of her shop in the morning as she opened the door always made Johanna smile. Never in a million years could she have foreseen herself making beautiful hats for the women of her hometown, but the job, and the ability to create, fulfilled her in a way she hadn't anticipated.

Yet there were days she hated how much time she had to spend away from Emily. Especially when things were as busy as they were right now.

This morning, Em had gazed at her with big, sad eyes and hugged her tight. "Do you hafta go, Mama?"

It nearly broke her heart.

She shook off the melancholy and surveyed the room. This shop was so bittersweet. Gerald's death had made its existence possible. Yet the Lord had helped her grow the shop into a thriving business. A lone tear slid down her cheek. In a way, each hat she created felt like beauty rising from ashes. Gratitude for the Lord's provision filled her soul. He had been so gracious to her small family.

Sending a prayer of thanks heavenward, she made her way to the back of the shop. The sun was blazing through the windows at the front. There were over thirty-five orders to fill, with several more coming in each day as the women purchased tickets for the next few weeks of shows at the opera house.

Good thing she had ordered plenty of extra supplies, because she probably would use up every last bit of them.

She took a seat behind the U-shaped table where she liked to work. Cora would be coming in about an hour from now, which meant Johanna could design and plan out what to have her friend work on. With Cora's help, they should be able to knock out a good number of the orders today. By day's end, she might have to make yet another order for supplies if the demand kept up.

She glanced at the watch on her shirtwaist. If she didn't take more than fifteen minutes to eat her lunch, that gave her nine hours to work and allowed her to leave at four this afternoon. Dad was sure to be exhausted by then, and Em would be ready for her mama.

Tomorrow morning she could bring her daughter to the shop for a bit and have her play with the box of scraps.

If she could get through the next six weeks, and if the contract with Sears came through by then (*Please, God*), then she could breathe. At least where work and finances were concerned. It still wouldn't resolve the issue of Parker.

She hadn't really allowed herself too many memories of him. Years ago, after he left Kalispell, Johanna had worked hard to put aside any thought of him. It hadn't been easy, but when memories of him came to mind, she prayed and memorized Scripture to help her put aside the past.

Now, with him back, she would have to see him from time to time. His image came to mind—those warm brown eyes in particular. Johanna had lost herself so many times in those eyes. From the first moment they'd met, she'd known Parker was someone special. He'd felt the same way about her. At least that's what he'd said. She had no reason to believe he wasn't telling her the truth. One thing about Parker, he was always good at being honest with her. He hated lies as much as she did.

Which was why she had told Gerald, in great detail, about her feelings for Parker and all the plans they made and prayed about. She assured him it was in the past and that her feelings for Parker were no longer an issue. The past was in the past.

And it had been.

She had loved Gerald with all her heart. He had been a good husband and friend and fulfilled her calling to marry a pastor. Never once did she fear he might upset her idyllic home with thoughts of traipsing all over the world.

But then he'd died. And there wasn't anything she could do to bring back the beautiful life she'd cherished.

Gazing around the shop, Johanna's chest ached again, as it had yesterday afternoon. For three years, she'd done everything she could to heal and move forward in God's grace. Marriage proposals had come to her from dozens of men in town, but that hadn't been the answer.

The ache would still come, and she'd have to fight for all she was worth to keep it from overwhelming her. Most days she clung to joy from the Lord and could feel His presence.

But then there were moments like right now . . .

When nothing felt safe and secure anymore.

6

James opened the drawer to his mahogany desk and searched for the file on the Newton case. This one would bring in a pretty penny.

A knock at the door preceded his legal assistant, Reginald. "Mr. St. John. This packet arrived for you from New York. Would you like me to go through its contents?"

"That would be fine." His gaze went back to the file, then snapped back to the packet. "Wait. New York?"

His assistant was halfway back out the door. "Yes, sir."

James held out his hand. "I better handle that."

"Of course, sir." The thin-as-a-rail man laid it on his desk. "Anything else?"

"No, thank you. Please close the door on your way out." Just in case he needed to make a phone call.

He looked at the thick packet for a moment, and his thoughts raced. This had to be from the judge. No one else knew he was in Kalispell.

No one.

They couldn't find him here. Those idiots wouldn't think to look outside Manhattan for him, let alone in a place like

Kalispell, Montana. At least, he didn't think they would. But what if they did—?

Stop it! Paranoia would get him nowhere.

He was so close to victory he could practically see his bank account filling with wealth. He took a deep breath and let it out slow. Plucking his silver letter opener from his desk drawer, he ripped open the package.

The thick packet was from the desk of a Judge Masterson. The man who took over after Lewis disappeared.

The penmanship on the top sheet would rival that of John Hancock.

> Mr. St. John,
> Judge Lewis's cases have now become mine since he is taking a leave of absence.

Is that what they were telling their clients? It was laughable.

> Lewis kept me abreast of your father's will(s) and the probate decision he'd handed down. As I have reviewed everything, I believed a thorough investigation was needed. Through this investigation, I found the man who wrote your father's previous will. He didn't know the man who prepared your father's latest will, but he did fill me in on what he knew of the situation.

James narrowed his eyes. Was that a veiled threat?

> As you are aware, Judge Lewis decided, upon reading the new will, that it was prudent to require both beneficiaries to be present in New York before distributing the estate. When your brother died before he could come, I understand that

you then were tasked with bringing your brother's widow to New York.

Judge Lewis was concerned with how much time this took, as the charities your father listed in his will have had to wait for their disbursement as well.

This brings me to the papers you have received with this letter. Because of the discrepancies between the two wills and the time that has passed, I have made a new ruling in this case to clear it up once and for all. The state of New York is due taxes, and the rightful beneficiaries shouldn't need to wait any longer.

Unless you appear in my chambers with Mrs. Johanna St. John—the heir to your brother's estate—within ninety days of the date on this letter, the entirety of your father's estate will be divided between the charities in his will.

A packet has also been sent to Mrs. Johanna St. John, thanks to Judge Lewis's attention to detail in finding your late brother's location and address.

Please see the included legal documents for your perusal.

> *Respectfully,*
> *His Honor,*
> *Judge Masterson*

Why, that meddling man!

Had James known that his brother would die right after his father, he would have done things different. At the time, it seemed logical to keep everything as his father had it—with the exception of adding himself back into his father's good graces. So the estate should have been divided between the two sons.

James had paid a hefty sum to retrieve the first telegram sent to Gerald, and then he'd paid to have another telegram forged and sent to the judge stating that the St. Johns had moved away with no forwarding address. It should have worked. The fortune should have been his.

But when Gerald died, everything became difficult.

He'd had to move to Kalispell to ensure no telegrams or correspondence from New York reached his sister-in-law. At least, not until he figured out another plan.

Having his assistant pay a man at the post office to direct anything of a legal nature for Johanna to James's office had done the trick.

At least, it should have.

He would love nothing more than to throw something that would shatter to pieces. But he couldn't do that in the office.

He stormed toward the door and yanked it open. "Reginald"—he kept his voice calm—"has anything of any importance come for my brother's wife?"

His assistant pulled open a drawer. "As a matter of fact, yes. This came yesterday." He handed over another thick packet.

He should throttle the man for not showing it to him sooner. "Thank you. Please do not disturb me unless it's an emergency."

"Yes, sir."

James walked back into his office and closed the door. He ripped into the packet and saw the duplicate documents from Judge Masterson.

He tossed the file into the fireplace and lit a match.

Once there was nothing left but ash, he poured himself a drink and pulled out his calendar. The packet from the Judge was dated fourteen days ago.

That left him with . . . roughly seventy-six days to convince Johanna to marry him, get her to New York, and appear before the Judge. They'd need a week of that time for travel. He glanced at the calendar. That barely gave him until the end of June to court, marry, and secure his wife.

And his future.

Parker left the theater at half past three and headed for Johanna's shop. It was time to see her.

Rehearsals had gone off without a single hitch, and shows were scheduled to start on Friday. The director loved Parker's idea of doing several showings of *Everyman* to transition from Shakespeare to *Uncle Tom's Cabin,* so that had been added into the schedule.

Now Mom would get to see the show that propelled him to the top . . . and perhaps she would gain a greater understanding of his passion for sharing the gospel through acting.

Last night, though, he'd had a nightmare like the image he'd wrestled with yesterday afternoon. It wasn't until the crowd disappeared in the dream that the stark reality hit him. He'd lost his focus. Oh, he might say that he still wanted to share the gospel through acting, but he wasn't living that out.

His focus had been on climbing the ladder of success. In fact, he'd been lying to himself—thinking that he needed to get to the top so he could share with more people. But Mom was correct.

He was living a lie.

This morning, he'd been awake for hours tossing and turning. But it wasn't until he got down on his knees that things changed. He'd prayed for over an hour after spending half an hour in the Word. For the first time in years, his mind was clear. And so was his conscience. A deep chuckle erupted out of nowhere. He probably looked like an idiot, walking down the street and laughing to himself. But he couldn't contain his relief. Or joy.

What was that verse about rejoicing with joy unspeakable? It was exactly how he felt in this moment. Parker searched for the reference, but it wouldn't come. He'd have to look it up later. And memorize it.

The first thing he had to do was admit to himself that he'd never felt called to be a pastor. That had been everyone else's expectation of him. Not that he didn't love preaching. When Dad trained him and gave him opportunities in the pulpit, it had been a thrill. But deep down . . . the tug toward working in the theatre, the joy of using the talent God gave him, the people he'd encountered, such as Professor Clement and Rev. Bentley—

All of that affirmed God leading him in this direction.

As for getting off track? That was all his own doing. His own neglect. What God would decide to do with him now, he had no idea, but he'd left it all at the feet of his heavenly Father this morning.

The weight he'd been carrying for months had lifted, and even though there were several more not-so-fun things he had to tackle in his life, he was prepared. He'd put on his armor.

For now, he would take it one day at a time and do his best to keep his focus where it needed to be.

When he reached the millinery shop, the door opened, and Johanna exited. When she caught sight of him, she blinked rapidly.

"Oh . . . ah . . . hello, Parker." Her momentary discomfort made him pause. "Ah . . . if you were hoping to catch Cora, she left already." Johanna turned and locked the door. Was her hand trembling?

"Actually, I came to see you. I didn't want you to think I was avoiding you."

A hint of pink colored her complexion as she turned and met his gaze. That combined with her long, silky red braid hanging over her shoulder and the blue ribbons in her hat— ribbons the exact shade of her eyes—made the butterflies from over ten years ago launch in his insides again. She was as lovely as he remembered. In fact, more so. The years had taken her from a pretty girl into a beautiful woman.

Rarely had he ever seen her speechless . . . until now. All she did was stare at him, and time seemed frozen.

Then the blinking returned. She pointed down the board- walk. "If you'll excuse me, I'm on my way home. I'm sure Dad has had his fill of his granddaughter's antics by now." She hurried away.

Oh no, you don't. He fell into step beside her. "May I walk with you? I'd love to see your dad . . . meet your daughter."

She took four steps before answering. "Of course."

Twenty more steps. Parker did his best to stay in stride with her, but the silence was killing him. For years he'd reminisced about the easy camaraderie between them. He loved the way she took his hand and laced her fingers through his. Or how she would laugh when he made a silly joke.

Now she wouldn't even look him in the eye.

Pushing a hand through his hair, he took a steadying breath.

All of those memories were the past. They'd both lived ten long years of life since. *Lord, I need Your help. I want to be a good friend to Johanna and not bring the past up between us.* He glanced at her profile. Her jaw was tense, eyes glued firmly ahead. He searched for safe territory to help her feel more comfortable. "What's your daughter's name?"

"Emily."

Even from the side, he could see her smile. "Cora says she's three years old?"

"Almost. In July." Johanna shook her head. "And she already thinks she's in charge. She loves to learn. Loves to get into absolutely everything. Dad won't be able to keep up with her too much longer. Almost-three-year-olds are exhausting."

The more they talked about little Emily, the more relaxed Johanna seemed. Within minutes, they were at the Eastons' familiar home. The house he'd come to call on hundreds of times in the past.

She walked up the steps to the porch and opened the door. She hesitated then turned toward him, tipping her head toward the house. "Come on in. I'm sure Dad will love seeing you."

The running footsteps of little feet thundered toward them. "Mama!"

Parker was barely in the door when the little girl launched herself into Johanna's arms.

"I missed you!" Johanna held her daughter close, then pulled back and tucked Emily's hair behind her ears. "Were you a good girl for Grandpa?"

"Sure I was." A chubby hand pointed to him. "Who's that?" The whisper was louder than her voice had been.

Parker chuckled.

"This is my friend, Mr. Bennett. He's Miss Cora's brother."

"Miss Cora's brudder!" Emily squirmed out of Johanna's arms and surged toward him. Before he could brace himself, she'd thrown her little arms around his legs.

"It's nice to meet you, Emily." He regained his balance and crouched down in front of her. Goodness, up close she looked like Johanna in miniature. Her hair was a little different tone of red, but her eyes were the same striking blue. "You can call me Parker, if that's okay with your mom."

"Can I, Mama?"

Oh, my. How could anyone deny that sweet little voice?

Parker watched emotions flicker across Johanna's face. It had been too long since he'd seen her to decipher them all, but there was one he couldn't dismiss.

Sadness.

The same look he'd seen when she'd turned down his proposal.

And once again, he'd put it there.

"Well, if it isn't the famous Parker Bennett!" Dad's voice boomed through the sitting room.

Johanna caught Parker's wince as he stood, but he covered it with a warm smile for her dad. The two men shook hands, and Johanna bit her lip as Dad limped to the large chair he loved so much and eased into it with a sigh. Had Cora told Parker about Dad's accident?

"Come, sit a spell. You're not too busy for old friends today, are you? Stay and chat a while. Johanna should have dinner ready soon. She put a roast in the oven earlier today, and I've been tending the oven to see it cooked properly."

"Of course I'm not too busy. In fact, I told Johanna I'd love a visit with you. If that isn't an inconvenience?" Parker glanced at her, an eyebrow lifted.

She pried Emily from off Parker's legs and gave both men a smile. "Please stay awhile. I'm sure Dad would enjoy hearing about your adventures. I'll put a pot of coffee on. And dinner should be ready in about twenty minutes."

"Oh, don't go to any trouble on my account."

"It's no trouble. And nothing fancy. Pot roast and vegetables." She couldn't keep the edge out of her voice. Who knew *what* Parker liked anymore, with all his travels and elegant meals.

And beautiful women.

She frowned. Why, that actually sounded like jealousy bouncing around her thoughts. Heat filled her cheeks. She needed a moment alone. Or some fresh air. Anything to be out of the same room as him and gather her thoughts.

"I wanna stay with Parker, Mama!" Emily wriggled in her arms, as if desperate to escape and cuddle up with her new friend.

"Not now, dear one." She adjusted her daughter on her hip. Gracious, when had this child gotten so heavy?

Dad waved a hand. "Leave her here, Jo. She won't get into too much trouble with us men watching her. You'll need two hands to manage things."

She glanced down at Emily, who gave her a giant grin. Well. She wouldn't win this battle. "All right. But you be a good girl, Miss Em." She tweaked the toddler's nose and couldn't stop her smile when Emily let out a loud giggle.

Once on the floor, Emily ran over to Parker and climbed up in his lap. She folded her hands and tucked them under her chin, giving their guest a wide grin. "Hello. I'm Emily Staind John!"

Parker's laughter filled the small room, and the sound evoked a thousand memories. Johanna bit her lip, fighting the rush of tender emotion within her heart. How many times had they sat in this room together and she'd made him laugh, just like that?

The thought was too much.

She mumbled her excuses and practically ran into the kitchen. The swinging door smacked behind her several times as it came to a standstill, then she walked to the sink and pressed her palms against the edge of it, trying to slow the beat of her heart.

Gerald had only been gone three years. Three years! She had no business letting old feelings for someone else bubble to the surface. Tears slid down her face, and Johanna swiped them away.

Stop it! You are not a silly, immature girl anymore!

Parker Bennett had no business in her heart. Not when Gerald had loved her so well and true. Had adored his daughter in the short time he'd known her.

Lord, help. The prayer was short, but sincere. How on earth would she navigate Parker's presence back in her life?

Seeing him with Emily, how gentle he was as she snuggled in his lap and chatted away, filled Johanna with a strange mix of grief and gratitude.

Perhaps she should have been more intentional with Emily, telling her about the wonderful man her father was. How much he loved her. The joy that had seemed to light Gerald from within when Johanna told him they were going to have a baby.

Gerald would have been an incredible father to their little girl.

She had told Emily about him on many occasions, even making sure to keep a photograph of Gerald prominently displayed for the little girl to see every day. Often, when Emily prayed at bedtime, she asked God to tell her Papa hello. Still, Johanna had never stressed his importance in their lives. She'd never wanted to make Emily miss what she'd never known. Was that wrong?

Oh, what a muddle her feelings were in!

Johanna pulled herself out of her thoughts and went through the motions of putting dinner together. Thankfully she'd decided early in the day to make a roast with vegetables. She had figured it would provide enough leftovers so she could make vegetable beef soup for a second meal. Now as she looked at the small roast, she remembered Parker's appetite. He had always been able to put away a lot of food. Would this even be enough for him? Oh, wait. There were the rolls Cora made on Sunday, as well as several jars of peaches on the pantry shelf.

She'd make do.

Fifteen minutes later, the table was set and the food ready to serve. Johanna walked into the sitting room to announce supper and stopped short.

Parker's jacket was folded neatly on the couch. He was in his shirtsleeves and kneeling on the floor with Emily, the pair studying a tall, yet very thin tower of blocks between them. With slow movements, he was putting one more block on their structure, and the look on Emily's face was pure adoration.

"What do you think, Mr. Easton?" Parker asked as Johanna entered the room. "Do you think our building is structurally sound?"

"Son, I told you to call me Daniel." Dad scooted to the edge of his chair and studied the blocks, stroking his chin.

"Forgive me. Daniel." Parker grinned. "What do you think?"

"Pawpaw! Tell us, tell us!" Emily clapped her hands together.

Johanna's heart melted. She wouldn't trade the bond her daughter and father had for anything.

"Well, you two," Dad drawled. "I don't think it would survive an earthquake. But it looks mighty fine."

Emily giggled and kicked her legs, sending the blocks flying everywhere. One hit Parker square in the forehead, his head jerking back from the force.

Johanna rushed forward. "No ma'am!" She put her hands on the little girl's legs. "You know better than that. You've hurt Mr. Bennett."

Tears welled up in Emily's eyes, and her bottom lip pushed

forward. Her little shoulders trembled, and Johanna braced herself for the wail that was about to erupt.

"It's really nothing, Jo."

She jerked her gaze in Parker's direction. There was a small red mark that should fade in a half hour. But still, Emily needed to learn her manners.

Ignoring the man next to her, she focused her gaze back on her daughter. With two fingers, she tipped Emily's chin up until they were eye to eye. "What do you say to Mr. Bennett?"

"I sowwie, Pawker."

Parker looked back at Emily and tapped her nose with his index finger. "All is forgiven."

Johanna let go of Emily's chin and gave her a squeeze. "That's a good girl. Now it is time to clean up these blocks. Can you do that for me?" With Emily's nod, Johanna stood and turned back toward the kitchen. "Good. When you're finished come to supper."

Parker's hand on her wrist stopped her progress. "Jo, I—"

The heat of his touch warmed her skin, sweet and familiar. All at once she was seventeen again and in love with the handsomest boy in town.

She swallowed.

Hard.

Oh, good heavens. It was true. There was no sense in lying to herself. The love she'd once felt for Parker was still in her heart. It had roared back to life at the very sight of him.

And now he'd touched her. Smiled at her. Wormed his way into her daughter's heart.

Johanna yanked her hand from his grasp. No matter how much time had passed, she couldn't consent to anything while he was still an actor. Perhaps as a young woman she'd judged him too harshly. She could own that.

But she had to live in reality. Feelings were fragile. Changeable. What was real was that her dad and Emily depended on her to be responsible in every area of life. Especially her heart. She couldn't ignore Gerald's memory or chase after flights of fancy with her childhood love. She definitely couldn't traipse all over the country with a theatre troupe and a three-year-old.

Without another word, she went back into the kitchen and did her best to even her breathing. She squared her shoulders and picked up the coffee pot.

"Please help me, Lord."

She made her way into the dining room. Dad came in a minute later, and Parker followed, ducking through the doorway with Emily on his shoulders. The little girl let out a giggle as Parker slid her from her perch into the chair Johanna had pulled out.

Johanna poured coffee for Parker and Dad, then returned the pot to the stove and took up a pitcher of lemonade. Emily's favorite. Once Johanna was seated, Dad offered grace.

It was easy enough to busy herself with helping Emily while the men talked. Dad asked Parker countless questions about his travels and acting, and Johanna was all too happy to let them fill the awkward silence. With any luck at all, maybe she wouldn't have to say much. After all, Dad and Parker used to be able to talk for hours.

She busied herself with buttering a piece of roll for Emily after cutting her meat and vegetables into small pieces. The child was surprisingly good at feeding herself, but always seemed to inhale her food so fast that Johanna doubted she chewed it at all. Hence the small pieces were important. Even so, more than once Emily had to be chided to slow down.

"You don't need to eat so fast. No one is going to take it away from you."

Emily giggled and leaned toward Parker. "Pawker can share."

He laughed and pretended to come toward her plate with his fork. Emily burst into squeals of laughter.

"Emily!" Johanna's eyes widened at her daughter, who immediately sobered. But then she could feel the men staring at her.

"I'm sorry. I didn't mean to sound so harsh." She looked at her daughter and smiled. "Mama's tired. It's been a long day."

"I'll say it has. You left at the crack of dawn." Dad speared himself another piece of roast. "I tell you, Parker, Jo works harder than anyone I know."

Parker met her gaze, and Johanna wished she would melt into the floor. A look of concern mingled with worry was not an expression she wanted to receive from Parker Bennett. The boy she'd once known would try to right the wrongs of the world . . . at least her world. Would he try to do that now?

Emily chattered about the cat that lived next door and how she wanted a kitty, too, so Johanna took the opportunity to jump up and retrieve the coffee.

Another fifteen minutes later, every last one of her nerves seemed frayed. Why was she so on edge? This was her home. Her family. And it wasn't as if Parker was a total stranger.

Dad pushed back and patted his stomach. "That was a mighty fine dinner to cap off a pleasant visit, daughter." He smiled at her, a twinkle in his eye.

That never boded well.

"Yes, thank you for dinner, Johanna." Parker nodded in her direction.

Words were stuck in her throat. She knew she was being an ungracious hostess, but she couldn't bring herself to acknowledge his thanks.

"I have an idea." Dad smiled. "Why don't you put Emily to bed, then come and sing a duet or two with Parker? You always sounded lovely together at all those hymn sings at church. It would be like old times."

Johanna's skin prickled with the heat of Parker's gaze on her. She worked to keep her jaw from falling open at Dad's obvious maneuver. It was clear he would not aid her in keeping her feelings at bay.

"Perhaps another time, Dad. As you said, I must put Emily to bed, and my throat is scratchy after conversing with so many customers today." She pushed back from her chair and picked up her daughter. "It was lovely to see you, Parker. Dad can show you out when you two are done."

"Wait."

Taking a deep breath, she halted her attempted escape, turned back, and lifted an eyebrow at Parker.

"I, uh, I have something for you and your dad." He reached into his pocket then coughed. "One moment." He left and reappeared, his jacket in his hands. Pulling a white envelope out of the pocket, he handed it to Dad. "Tickets to see *Uncle Tom's Cabin*. Vouchers, really. Whichever time you have free, I'd be pleased if you'd come see it."

Dad took the envelope and opened it, pulling the vouchers out with a flourish. "That's kind of you, son. Johanna hasn't had a night to herself since Emily was born. A night at the opera house might be a nice treat. Don't you think, daughter?"

Johanna shifted Emily on her hip and gave Parker a nod. "Thank you. We will do our best to make it. Good night."

She scurried out of the kitchen and up the stairs to the small washroom to ready Emily for bed. Once her daughter's sticky face and hands were clean and she was dressed in a fresh nightie, Johanna settled in the rocking chair for their nightly reading and lullaby.

"I like Pawker."

Emily's innocent declaration was like a knife in Johanna's heart. "Yes, I know you do." She began to rock.

"Do you like Pawker?"

Johanna swallowed the lump in her throat. "Ah . . . well . . . yes. Parker is a very nice man."

Emily smiled up at her. "Can Pawker come back . . . and play?" The smile changed to a yawn.

"We'll talk more about that after you've had some sleep."

Emily snuggled her head against Johanna's neck. She let out a soft sigh, and soon the even sound of her breathing signaled she was asleep.

But as Johanna continued to rock, humming Gerald's favorite hymn for their daughter, all she could think about was the sound of Parker's laughter and the familiar feel of his hand on hers.

And the fact that her daughter was as enamored with the man as she was.

7

WEDNESDAY, APRIL 19, 1905

James waited outside the shop's entrance and checked his pocket watch. Johanna should be arriving at any moment.

At 7:45 a.m. sharp, she rounded the corner and caught sight of him.

She stopped in front of him but didn't move to unlock the door. "Good morning, James. To what do I owe this visit?"

She was guarded, but welcoming. At least as welcoming as Johanna ever was with him. He'd change that soon enough. He handed her a packet of papers. "This has arrived from Sears, Roebuck, and Co. I've taken the liberty of going over the legal documents, and everything is in order. Take your time reading over them, and feel free to ask any questions when there's language you don't understand."

She relaxed a bit. "Thank you, James. I appreciate you setting this up for me. Emily needs more and more of my time, and this will give me that opportunity."

"You are most welcome. You know I would do anything for you." He inched closer. "Think of all that I could give you and Emily."

123

Stiffening, she stepped back. "I already told you my feelings on the matter, James. Please don't bring up marriage again."

He snorted. "Whyever not? You're young and in need of a husband. Emily needs a father who can direct her after the fashion of her father . . . my brother." He was nothing like his weak-willed brother, Gerald, but James didn't let that stop him from reminding Johanna that he was the closest thing she had to the deceased love of her life.

She shook her head and fidgeted with the packet. "Emily is . . . ah . . . doing fine. I tell her stories about Gerald every day."

Her halted speech made James study her more closely. Was she nervous? He inched forward again. "You seem upset. What has you troubled, my dear?"

Johanna settled her glance on the papers in her hand. "I'm not troubled. A lot has been happening what with the theatre troupe in town. I've had a great many orders to create, and . . . well . . . I've been busy."

"I see. The opera is in town. Is this about the famous actor, Mr. Bennett, about whom I keep hearing so much?"

Her gazed snapped to his, fire in her blue eyes. "No. Why would you say such a thing?"

Ah, he'd touched a nerve. Perfect. He should have known that golden idol of the stage would somehow worm his way into Johanna's life again. "I wonder if the famous Parker Bennett is the reason you're holding me at arm's length. I know what transpired between the two of you before you married Gerald."

"How *dare* you bring that up!" Her eyes narrowed to slits. "You know *nothing* about my time with Parker."

"You still feel something for him, don't you? Was my brother a second choice? A stand-in? Did you think about your precious Parker while in my brother's arms?" Perhaps he was laying it on thick, but he had no choice. He had to move fast if he was to have her in New York in time.

Tears filled her eyes. "You are cruel and hateful to say such a thing. I loved your brother with all my heart."

"Lies. I see the truth now." Time to go in for the kill. It wouldn't endear her to him . . . at least not yet, but he had to sever any feelings she had for the notorious actor.

"Mr. Bennett is a man of the world, who has no doubt had countless love affairs. He's certainly not worthy of my brother's widow and child. Think of how he would corrupt you, and then my niece!" His words were having the desired effect because she'd gone from fiery to fearful. "Let me be clear, Johanna. Your best choice is me. I would be willing to forgive this slip of your moral compass in light of a future together. But if something were to, say, start up between you and Parker Bennett again, I would feel obligated to protect my brother's child from such an evil world."

She lifted her free hand, then glanced around and lowered it. "If we weren't standing in full view of others right now, I would slap you. I demand that you leave and not return until you can be more civil and respectful. I would never to do anything to cause Emily harm, and neither would Parker."

James's nostrils flared. This defense of that actor was untenable. "Let me remind you that I'm a well-respected lawyer. The entire town admires me and knows I always get what I want." He backed off and relaxed, pasting on a grin so the onlookers would see him being gracious and kind. "Who do you think people would believe?"

He let that sink in. He'd never lost a case in Kalispell. "Because I'm a gentleman, I will give you some time to come to your senses and realize your best, and only, option is to marry me."

"I needn't marry *anyone* now that I have this contract." She held up the papers.

His smile only broadened. "A contract to which I can easily put an end. Remember, I was the one who arranged it in the first place. You need me, Johanna. Without me, you have no future. No family. No *child.*"

Marvella couldn't wait to get her hands on the new hat. She entered the millinery shop with Sir Theophilus on his leash and a coffee cake in her hand.

Out of all the people she'd met in all the cities and grand places they'd visited, Johanna St. John was the most talented designer and creator of women's hats. Johanna was the first one *ever* to do exactly what she envisioned.

As the bell jangled over her head, Marvella scanned the shop. Usually, Johanna was there to greet her from the large table where she worked. Well, she was probably in the back getting supplies. "Yoohoo! Johanna, dear!" She set the baked good down on a table. "I brought that cinnamon coffee cake you love so much."

The curtain shifted, and Johanna appeared. Her eyes were red-rimmed as she dabbed at her face with a hankie. "Forgive me, Mrs. Ashbury. Let me get your hat. It turned out beautifully, if I do say so myself." She scurried back behind the curtain.

Marvella marched over to the table and waited for the young widow to return.

As soon as Johanna came back with the hat box, Marvella took the box from her hands and set it next to the coffee cake. Then she wrapped her arms around the young woman. "Now, now, dear, whatever is the matter?"

A lot of sniffles and sobs were pressed against her shoulder. Then Johanna pushed away a bit. "I'm so sorry. I didn't mean to fall to pieces. I couldn't bear it if I soiled your dress."

"Nonsense. I don't believe for a moment that God gave me this ample figure to not comfort those in need. I'm not worried a whit about my dress. Sir Theophilus drools on me at least once a day."

The younger woman sputtered a slight laugh.

Marvella gave her a smile and patted her cheek. "Good. There now. Sit. Let's hear all about it."

Johanna mopped up her face and then tilted her head at her. "I couldn't bother you with my concerns, you have so much on your shoulders already."

"Ridiculous notion, my dear. I have the right amount on my shoulders. With God as bearer of my burdens, I neither struggle nor strain. I am blessed to have Him as my stronghold and refuge. I know you have Him as well. Now I'm not leaving until you tell me what's upset you so." Theophilus barked at her feet. "Sir Theophilus agrees. We have no other pressing matters. You have often blessed me, now allow me to return the favor. Is it your husband? Do you miss him terribly?"

The unique blue eyes of the redhead before her sought her gaze and studied her. "It's true, I miss Gerald every day. But I've been past the worst of my mourning for some time now."

That was good to hear. Grief was such a terrible burden for a young woman, with a toddler and an injured father to boot. "Well, then. Is it our famous actor? He hasn't hurt you, has he? Or is simply seeing a long-lost love difficult?"

Johanna blew her nose and set down the hankie. "Mrs. Ashbury, if I confide in you, you must promise me that you won't speak of this to anyone. Not a soul. Promise?"

She reached across and squeezed the widow's hand. "You

have my word, and you know by my reputation that is as good as gold."

Sighing, Johanna placed her hands in her lap and stared at them. "It has been a challenge to have Parker back in my life, but he's not so much the problem as Gerald's brother. James St. John has threatened to take Emily away from me. He fears I am endangering her with the company I keep."

Well! If that didn't confirm her suspicions about that slick city lawyer. She had told the Judge that man was up to no good in their town. And now to put one of her sweetest friends into such a state? It wasn't to be borne. "Dear, you have a stellar reputation, there's nothing to worry about."

"But, Mrs. Ashbury, he's a lawyer, and he's never lost a case." Her wide eyes filled with tears anew.

She patted the young woman's hand again and shook her head. "He's no match for *my* husband."

"He also wants me to marry him."

So that was his game. Marvella smacked her lips together. "And *there's* the crux of the matter. Some men don't know how to accomplish anything without bullying. Believe me, he's all bark and no bite."

Sir Theophilus barked as if on cue.

"Isn't that right, my sweet little boy?" She used her gushy tone to the little dog.

Johanna leaned back in her chair, her shoulders relaxing. "You really think I shouldn't worry?"

"Not over this, dear. The good Lord tells us that we can't add a day to our lives by worrying. And rest assured, if anyone came after your sweet baby, we would all rise up and fight for you." She nodded. "I think it's best that we speak to the Judge about this."

"Oh, I don't know." She threaded her hankie through her

fingers, not meeting Marvella's gaze. "Won't James get furious that I went to your husband?"

"And what if he does?" Marvella lifted a finger. "Who gives a fig what he thinks?"

"All right. I'll pray about it. But I'm hesitant to bother your husband with something so small."

"Small? You and your daughter are not a small matter." She watched the younger woman for several moments.

But Johanna stiffened her spine and offered a weak smile. "You came here to see your hat."

Marvella could take a hint. She stood to open the hat box. "Now, let's see this beauty."

The bell jangled, and Johanna popped out of her seat and rushed toward the door, most likely eager for a change of subject.

"Mrs. St. John." The French accent drew Marvella's curiosity, and she turned around to see who it was.

Ah. The actress she'd heard so much about. She was a beauty, there was no doubt about it. At least the papers hadn't exaggerated *that*. Still, there was something in the woman's manner that was cold. Marvella could see it in the stiff way she discussed something with Johanna.

"Allow me to introduce you to one of our city's most distinguished ladies, Mrs. Marvella Ashbury." Johanna nodded to her. "Judge Ashbury's wife and the leader of many women's organizations in town."

"It is a pleasure." The woman curtsied.

"And this is Yvette Lebeau—the actress."

"A pleasure indeed," Marvella countered.

Miss Lebeau moved a bit closer and eyed Marvella's automobile hatbox. "I see you have commissioned one of Mrs. St. John's creations. I should dearly love to see what you have purchased."

Was that a challenge in the French beauty's tone? The tilt of her chin and slight narrowing of her eyes betrayed the woman's feelings of superiority. Well, this young miss clearly had no clue whom she was dealing with.

With deft movements, Marvella tugged the box's strings and lifted the top off it. Her breath caught. Johanna had fashioned her vision to perfection. She opened her mouth to tell the milliner that, but was cut off by a *tsk* from Miss Lebeau.

"This is a lovely hat, Mrs. St. John. But it's a little small and commonplace for my tastes." The woman looked at Johanna with a stiff smile. "I'm anticipating the need to attend a wedding here, and I need something . . . grander."

It was a good thing Marvella was above such petty games, or she'd give the young woman a piece of her mind. But she made sure to take mental notes as she listened to the visiting woman give details to Johanna.

"It must be exceptional, as am I. My fans will expect glamour and elegance. It is my trademark, no? The hat must be *parfait*."

Marvella glanced at Johanna. The widow's lips tightened for a moment before releasing a slow breath. "Perhaps you might bring in the gown and allow me to see the fabrics used like you did with the other dress and hat I made for you. I can attempt to match the lace and ribbon."

"No, that will clearly be impossible. The gown was created in Milan. You will have no chance of making anything like it. However, for such a place as this, how do you say it, *frontier town*, I believe you offer my best hope. The other hat I purchased from you is quite serviceable."

Serviceable. Ha! What a hoity-toity way to say that she was a snob and thought everything and everyone was beneath her. Marvella hated to impose herself in another person's conversation, but she felt she must. "Mrs. St. John has made hats for the governor's wife, as well as other women of high status. You would be fortunate indeed to own one of her creations. As for a *frontier town*, Kalispell is nothing of the sort. We are an oasis of beauty offering many opportunities. Soon we hope to be the gateway to a fine national park, which will only serve to aggrandize Kalispell."

Why, the little snip was looking down her nose at Marvella!

"*Eh bien*, as I said, I suppose her to be the best I can hope for."

Marvella stiffened at the actress's bored tone, but remained silent. Women like that were so pretentious and self-serving. There would be no reasoning with her.

Miss Lebeau finished describing what she wanted Johanna to create and then left without so much as nodding Marvella's direction. So rude.

How dare that woman be so condescending to her friend! Well, Marvella could make up for it. "I am in love with your work, Johanna. I think I will order another hat for the automobile, and one more for Cora's wedding."

The milliner's gaze bounced between the door and Marvella, her blue eyes wide. "A-all right," she stuttered and grabbed her notepad and pencil. "What would you like for the wedding? And I need to know colors for the other automobile hat."

"For the wedding, it needs to be a light rose color to match my dress. I'll have my maid, Mimi, bring it over. I don't care what you decide to put on it—your taste is impeccable, and I trust you—but I have one request."

Johanna looked up at her. Was that a glimmer of fear in the young woman's eyes? "And that is?"

"That you make it larger and grander than Miss Lebeau's." With a chuckle, she winked. "I'm serious." She held her hands out beside her head to illustrate a big hat. "It *is* a special occasion, you know."

✧

Parker raced to the restaurant. Rehearsal had gone a little late.

He'd asked to speak to Alfred, so they were having a lunch meeting.

At least Parker could get this weight off his chest. He'd tell Alfred to stop with all the shenanigans. If he didn't, Parker would find another agent.

Plain and simple.

Parker entered the restaurant to find Alfred already seated. The agent waved at him, but as soon as Parker sat, Yvette appeared and took the seat next to him.

"It's wonderful to have this time together."

The packed room was not a place for a scene, so Parker sent Alfred a glare. But the rotund man refused to meet his eyes. Well, he wasn't going to sit here and be manipulated.

Before he could move, two reporters appeared at the table and hemmed him in.

What was going on?

"Thanks for the exclusive, Al." One of the reporters pulled out his notepad. The other gave the table a nod and took a seat.

Exclusive? Sweat prickled across Parker's forehead. He *had* to get out of there! "Excuse me." He stood and almost knocked his chair over. "Alfred, we need to speak today. You and I. Alone. It is imperative."

The man still refused to look at him. Coward.

"I'm leaving on the train in an hour, Parker. So it will need to wait until I return. There are more urgent matters to attend to at the moment."

Parker did his best not to grind his teeth. But now everyone was watching. It took every bit of control to not unleash his anger on his agent—the man who seemed to be holding the reins on his career. *His* career.

Well, no more.

"Forgive me for my abrupt departure, but I've forgotten to take care of something very important." He had no wish to publicly humiliate Alfred. But the man was no longer in his employ. Whether he liked it or not.

He ignored the questions aimed at him and had to wriggle his way around the table as it was crammed into the corner. Had Alfred arranged that as well?

As he made it out, he heard one of the reporters question Yvette, "Will you say yes if he asks you to marry him?"

Yvette's sultry laugh lifted to his ears. "He's handsome and brilliant, *n'est-ce pas*? Why wouldn't I say yes?"

The scowl he wore helped pave the way out of the restaurant. In a quarter of an hour, the entire town would be talking.

But that was the least of his problems. Alfred was a smart cookie. Trying to predict what else the man orchestrated for the next week was going to eat him alive.

"Parker?"

He glanced up and smiled. Carter Brunswick.

This man he could trust. Had done so since childhood.

A smile spread across Carter's face. "I was hoping to get a chance to see you again, but I knew you'd be busy."

"Carter, I always have time for you." The two clapped each other's shoulders.

"I read in the paper that you're here for at least three weeks, is that right? I'd love to invite you to dinner at my home one night . . . if you have the time. I would love for you to meet my wife, Eleanor."

Were *all* of his childhood friends married? He pushed away the intrusive thought. "That would be wonderful. Congratulations. Do you have children?"

Carter's eyes lit up. "We're expecting our first in the fall."

"Even more reason for congratulations." The words tasted bittersweet on his lips. These were things they'd planned for as young men. Wives, children, and vocations that would serve their families well.

Parker had failed on all accounts.

"Are you staying at the house or the hotel where I dropped you off?"

Parker shook his head. "At the hotel."

"I'll send you word there, then. It'll be great to hear about all of your travels and adventures. Sounds like you've lived quite the life."

His friend's words made his stomach roll. "Do me one favor." Parker couldn't disguise the disgust he felt. "Don't believe everything you read in the newspapers about me. Most of it's as much fiction as the plays I perform."

Carter chucked and placed a hand on Parker's shoulder, giving it a strong squeeze. "Don't worry about that. I know the real man and don't pay attention to the stories."

If only more people were like Carter.

Parker watched him walk away with a wave, leaving him alone with his churning gut. Carter had said he knew the real Parker Bennett.

If only he could say the same thing.

8

The scent of coffee filled Johanna's senses as she sat down at her worktable with the newspaper. Sleep had eluded her once again last night, so she told Dad she would go in early and come home early to try to take a nap. He said he'd handle breakfast and shooed her out the door.

But at 6:30 in the morning, she'd started drooping over the hat she was working on. Guess she wasn't very productive without coffee. Thankfully the café two doors down was more than happy to provide the rich, black liquid.

Her stomach rumbled as she held the steaming cup up under her nose. A slice of Marvella's coffee cake sounded divine right now. Mouth watering, she headed to the back of the shop and pulled it out of the cupboard. Yesterday, she'd been too upset to eat any of it. Well, today, she and Cora would enjoy the treat.

After taking a generous slice and wrapping it up again, she went back to her seat. She took a bite and almost moaned over the sugary goodness. The cinnamon flavor danced on

135

her tongue, and she released a sigh. Whoever invented this concoction should be applauded for all time.

Flipping open the paper, she reached for her coffee. The headline slapped her in the face:

Kalispell's Own Famous Actor to Wed?

Her eyes raced through the article as her stomach dropped.

The bell over the door jangled, and Cora entered. "Your father told me I'd find you here. How are you this morning, Jo? Is that Marvella's coffee cake? I'm famished." Her chatter halted as she came closer. "What's wrong?"

Johanna handed her the paper. "Your brother is getting married?"

Cora glanced at it and scrunched up her face. "Heavens, no." She waved it off and plopped down next to Johanna. "Parker has been perturbed with his new manager. The man has been setting up all kinds of ridiculous things for the press. It's all to sell tickets and keep people talking. Apparently that's the way it's done with theatre people, but my brother despises it."

"Then why doesn't he put a stop to it?" The Parker Johanna knew would never stand for such underhandedness. Had he really changed so much in ten years?

Cora shrugged. "Mama talked to him about it the other night, and Parker came by yesterday in a fit to speak to her again. But I wasn't privy to that conversation. Maybe there's a contract or something, and he has to figure a way out of it." She stood and headed toward the back.

Oh. That was reasonable.

But Johanna had met this Miss Yvette Lebeau. She was beautiful—on the outside, anyway. Her inside seemed cold as ice. Not at all the kind of woman Parker would fall in love with. "Cora?"

"Yes?" Her friend came back with her own cup of coffee and slice of cake.

"Is your brother bringing someone as a guest to your wedding?"

She took a bite. "No. He hasn't said a word about that. Why?"

"Because Miss Yvette Lebeau came in the shop yesterday saying she would need a hat for a wedding she would be attending. The only wedding I know of is yours. Maybe there *is* something more between her and Parker, and he's not had a chance to explain it to the family. I mean, why else would a woman spend the kind of money she is for a hat if she has no place to wear it?"

Cora set everything down and leaned close, forcing Johanna to look at her. "I've been doing my own research, Johanna St. John. Parker has absolutely no interest in that actress. None. She's as fake as they come. Probably playing into all this nonsense so she can get into those motion pictures she was talking about." She wiggled her eyebrows, "Besides, did you see the woman's hat? It was atrocious! So much for French fashion, I say."

Johanna laughed. "It was a bit over the top, wasn't it?"

"Those city people. They wouldn't know true fashion if it bit them on the big toe. If she wants to pay you outrageous money to make her a hat, then take it. She'll get a chance to finally see what a truly amazing design feels like." Cora took another bite of cake. "I am sad to have missed Marvella yesterday. This is delightful. And she always makes me smile."

Thinking of the older woman's visit warmed Johanna's insides. The care and concern she'd shown for Johanna—as well as the advice—was a true testament to the woman's love of God. And her love of knowing what was going on in everyone's life.

Johanna giggled.

"What's so funny?" Cora had almost finished the coffee cake.

"I was thinking about Marvella." Then she remembered the best part. "What's even funnier is that you and I have two more *massive* projects to work on."

"Oh? Massive, you say? I'm intrigued. Who are they for?"

"One is for Miss Lebeau, who said that Marvella's automobile hat was too small and commonplace—in front of Marvella, mind you. And then after she left, Marvella insisted that she needed a new one as well. But even larger than Miss Lebeau's."

Cora laughed so hard tears streamed down her cheeks. "Oh, I wish I could have been here to see that."

"Well, your wedding *is* coming up you know. It's not like you can be here all the time."

"Now I want to be, though. This is the most excitement we've had in a while. I can't wait to see what you've come up with for these two fine ladies." Her laughter continued.

Johanna pulled out the designs she'd worked on yesterday afternoon and placed them in front of Cora. But she couldn't keep from laughing. "Let the hat wars begin."

<hr />

FRIDAY, APRIL 21, 1905

James drummed his fingers on his desk and studied the article in the New York newspaper one more time.

Balling the paper in his hands, he grunted and then threw it across the room.

The Camorra gang had gotten to his man he'd planted in their midst. That was the only logical conclusion.

Now there would be no way for James to know what was going on inside. The coded messages in the newspaper would stop.

The last message he received said nothing about the Camorras knowing he was in Montana. The only positive thing about all this.

But he was running out of time.

He had to force Johanna's hand. Get her to New York. Get the inheritance. Pay off his debts. Then he could go wherever he pleased and leave all this stress behind.

Pain behind his eye began in earnest. These headaches were getting tedious. Another reason why he needed to eliminate all this stress. He wasn't about to give up now.

He was done playing nice.

The spring day had turned warm and sunny by lunchtime. Parker headed out to walk off his frustrations and get some much needed fresh air. He had no desire to be cooped up in the opera house or a dining room with other cast and crew members. Especially after all the buzz from yet another infuriating newspaper article.

Even though most of the cast knew it wasn't true—and Parker denied it to everyone—Yvette seemed to enjoy hinting around that it *could* be true. That they would become a couple. Even marry!

Ludicrous. Why would she do that? They'd had no connection before, and it didn't make sense that she would imagine one now.

What was worse, she'd only been with the troupe the past few months. Everyone in New York was talking about her being an instant success and a rising star, so why did she decide to leave New York City and travel here? Yes, their troupe was highly acclaimed, but why would she want to play second fiddle? Someone of her caliber would want to be the big star.

Not that he knew much about her résumé. In all actuality, he knew very little about her.

By the time he'd walked the Opera Block and then to the Great Northern Depot and back, he'd only used up fifteen minutes. Taking the same route again, his thoughts turned to the situation with Alfred. At this point, he would simply tell the truth to reporters and let Alfred go when he returned to Kalispell. The man was underhanded and only seemed to care about making his own name with reporters.

What good was an agent who never considered his client's wishes?

By the time he'd settled that in his mind, he'd finished another loop. And he still had another hour and a half before he had to be back at the theater. His eyes scanned the familiar landscape of his hometown. It had changed plenty in ten years, yet it was as familiar to him as his old room at his parents' home. An ache filled his chest.

How was it possible to be home and still feel homesick?

Part of it was missing his father. The other part was this unsettled feeling about his future. Parker shoved his hands in his pockets and started walking again. His feelings were too much in a muddle to sort out in under an hour. A distraction was necessary to lift his mood.

He could stop by the hat shop and see his sister. The wedding was coming up awfully fast. And then she'd be off on her honeymoon and return in time for his last performances. Then *he* would be the one leaving.

Again.

His feet headed south without any more thought on the matter. To be honest, he wanted to see Johanna too.

Ever since having dinner with her family, he had a hard time *not* thinking about her. More than anything, he'd love to be able to sit down and really talk with her. Just the two of them. Oh, he didn't have any grand dreams that they would rekindle their long-ago romance. But it sure would be good to find out how she was doing, what had changed, how she'd grown . . .

Oh, who was he kidding? Deep down he ached to know if she felt anything for him. Or could . . . in the future.

When he reached the shop, he grinned and opened the door. This was exactly what he needed.

"Parker!" Cora stood up and hugged him.

"Ow!" He pulled back and found the culprit. Her needle was now sticking out of his chest.

His sister covered her mouth, but it didn't hide her mirth. "I'm so sorry."

"Sure you are." He teased. "Now would you mind pulling this thing out? It appears to still be attached to thread that's attached to that monstrous hat you're working on, and I'd rather not drag it around all day. I don't think it goes with my costume for the show tonight."

Laughter from further into the store drew his gaze.

Johanna.

As their eyes connected, her joy radiated to him.

Oh what her laughter did to him.

"Hold your breath. This might sting." Cora brought his attention back to the large needle impaling him.

"I think I can handle it."

"Uh-huh." She winked, and with that, she yanked it out.

He flinched, and his hand instinctively pressed the spot. Bad idea because he immediately felt the damp warmth of what had to be blood. He pulled his shirt away from the skin and looked down. Yep. A nice little one-inch red circle marked the center of his white shirt.

"Oh dear." Cora bit her lip, but the tears in her eyes only proved that she was doing her best to hold back a tidal wave of laughter. "Let me grab a bandage." Giggles erupted as she walked away.

"Thanks for the sympathy, sis. Especially after you stabbed me."

Johanna's laughter grew along with Cora's. He loved it.

"It's just a needle." Cora came back with gauze and unbuttoned one button of his shirt, then shoved it over the wound and buttoned his shirt back.

"*Just* a needle? That thing is six inches long!"

"Isn't that a bit melodramatic?"

Johanna was still chuckling, and he was desperate to keep her laughing. The lightness between them was better than the awkward, heavy silence at dinner a few nights ago. He fixed a stern glare at Cora. "Nope, it's the truth, and I plan on milking it for all it's worth. My sister stabbed me. I have the bloodied shirt to prove it."

"Oh posh. It'll stop bleeding in a moment." She went to cleaning her weapon—well, needle. "Besides, I think it's only four or five inches. I could measure it if you like."

"We might need to do that. You know, so I can tell the police if they ask."

She rolled her eyes at him. "I stick myself with one of these at least once a day, and you don't hear me bellyaching."

"Same here." Johanna joined in, her smile wide and blue eyes bright.

It was hard to believe ten years had passed because his heart beat crazy for her in that moment. Like when he was a kid. He tried to shake the thought from his mind. "Why do you use such big needles?"

"It's what it takes to stitch through the hat, ribbon, tulle, flowers, whatever we're attaching." Johanna grinned at him and kept her eyes on him even as she stitched. "Sometimes we use smaller ones for more delicate work. But not today."

Now that took talent. And showed her experience. "The one you're working on has to rival some of the hats I've seen in New York City. Who's it for?"

She and Cora exchanged a glance and chuckled. "The Judge's wife."

"Mrs. Ashbury?"

"Yes." The longer Johanna stared at Cora, the more it looked like laughter might explode out of her.

He looked to Cora. "Want to fill me in on what's going on?"

But she apparently couldn't hold it in any longer and laughed louder than he'd heard in a long time.

He turned back to Johanna for help.

"You see that hat Cora is working on? That's for your friend, Miss Lebeau. They were both in here the other day. Yvette complimented a hat Marvella had ordered, then told me it wasn't grand enough and that she needed something bigger and fancier."

Cora piped up. "After she left, Mrs. Ashbury told Jo that she wanted one even bigger."

Both ladies laughed and laughed.

He didn't get it. It was funny, but not *that* funny. "What am I missing?" Maybe it was because he was a man. Or perhaps, and much more likely, he didn't understand all that frippery women trussed themselves up with. It was ridiculous. Why, more than once in New York City he'd almost lost an eye because a stuffed bird or flower from one of those monstrosities hit him in the face. Women really should be more careful when they were walking around in those things.

At least the pieces Johanna and Cora were working on seemed to be a bit more reasonable.

And sans stuffed birds.

"We've dubbed these"—Johanna held up her hat and nodded toward the one in Cora's hands—"the hat wars."

Parker joined in with the laughter and shook his head. Women and their hats.

The clock chimed, and Cora gasped. "Goodness, we have so much to do. I'm sorry, Parker. As good as it is to see you, you should probably go so we can focus. I need to get as much done today as possible, since the wedding is next week and I'm not sure how much I'll be able to help Jo."

He held up both hands. "I can tell when I'm not wanted."

Two voices lifted in insincere "Aww"s and then burst into more laughter.

"Well, at least I can leave you laughing. Johanna, if it's all right with you, I think I'll go see your dad and Emily for a little bit, since I've got some time."

Her face softened as she nodded. "They would love that. Please tell Dad that I'll be there soon. I forgot a couple things that I need for this hat, and I'd like to finish it today."

"I'll pass on the message." He shoved his own—much smaller, thank you very much—hat back on his head and waved to them both.

Back out in the fresh air, he headed east toward the Conrad mansion. A few paces past that was where Daniel lived with Johanna and Emily. It was a beautiful piece of property that Mr. Conrad had graciously sold to Daniel when they'd first moved to Kalispell. During the spring and early summer months, a creek filled at the back of the property from all the runoff in the mountains.

It had been like a second home to him after meeting Johanna.

He took the steps of the porch two at a time and knocked on the door. But no one answered. They must be in the garden in the back.

As he rounded the house, Parker's heart plummeted.

On a log stretching out over the full and rushing creek sat Emily.

All by herself.

9

You know, Johanna, he still cares a great deal about you." Cora could see the longing in her brother's eyes. "And I think you care about him as well."

"Of course I care about Parker." Johanna turned away and busied herself with folding pieces of tulle. "We've been friends since—well, I don't have to tell you how long."

A small seed of hope blossomed in Cora's heart. Her friend's admission was a huge step. "Caring is good. It's a strong foundation." But watching the frigid set of Johanna's shoulders gave her pause.

"A strong foundation for what?" Johanna didn't stop folding, but the tone of her voice held a sharp edge.

"To see if you could love Parker again." Cora took a step closer. "Perhaps it's because I've always felt that you were like a sister . . . you and Parker might not have been perfect for each other back then, but what about now?" She placed herself directly in front of her friend, but Johanna wouldn't meet her gaze. "You know I'm not saying anything against Gerald. He was a wonderful husband. But maybe you need to think and pray on it. When you sent Parker on his way—"

Johanna whirled around, two splotches of red in her cheeks.

"I never sent Parker away. I never wanted him to go anywhere! He *chose* to leave."

The vehemence in Johanna's voice caught Cora off guard. She'd pushed too hard. Said the wrong thing. Holding up her hands, she swallowed. "I'm sorry, my friend. I wasn't trying to insinuate you did anything to push him out of town. You are correct, Parker made his own choices." She leaned forward and touched Johanna's arm. "And I remember how we all reeled at his decision." She licked her lips, hesitating for a moment. Was she being a busybody? Perhaps. But she couldn't stand by while two of the dearest people in her life were hurting. And apart.

"Exactly, and just because he's back in town for a few weeks doesn't mean that we should be having this discussion. The issues are still the same as they were ten years ago—only now they're more complicated. I have a little girl. An ailing dad. The last thing I can do is chase Parker all over the world while he performs." Johanna turned back to the fabric, her jaw tight.

Cora pressed her lips together. "I know. And I'm sorry I've been so pushy, Jo. I want to see you happy. See Emily with a father who dotes on her." She paused a moment before pushing forward. "This afternoon, with my brother, you were laughing and sparkling and joyous. The sadness and shadows were gone. Parker brought that out in you."

A lone tear slipped down Johanna's cheek. Finally she met Cora's eyes, her chin trembling. "There's a lot more at stake here than you know. Please, just let me work through this on my own. I'll be fine."

Cora opened her mouth to question her friend, but she'd pushed enough for one day.

As she studied Johanna a little longer, the stark reality hit her that this wasn't about Parker. Something—or someone—had frightened the sweet mother.

But what . . . or who? The bell above the door jangled.

"Mrs. Bennett." Johanna's expression shifted into a smile. "What an unexpected surprise."

"Hello, Mom." Cora kissed her mother's cheek.

Mom beamed as she glanced back and forth between her and Johanna. "I have a gift for you. Since you've been working so hard and Cora's about to get married, I thought it would be fun to have a treat for you two."

"What do you mean?" Johanna's puzzled expression still held wariness.

"I have tickets for the two of you tonight at the opera house for the first performance of the troupe."

Cora released a tiny squeal and wrapped her mom in a giant hug. "This is so exciting! I feel like a child at Christmas!" But when she caught her friend's expression over her mother's shoulder, her heart sank.

What was Johanna so afraid of?

The walk home was only about eight blocks, but Johanna appreciated every minute out in the sunshine. Nothing could compare with Montana's blue skies and weather. It helped erase the rough conversation with Cora and her mixed-up feelings about Parker.

She glanced heavenward, mulling over what Cora said.

Did she hope that Parker was a part of her future?

She couldn't hope for that. Not with James breathing down her neck.

And yet . . . Her friend was right. God could do anything, even straighten out the mess that had become her life.

"Nothing takes God by surprise," her mother used to say.

God had never failed her, and even when there had been times of confusion or questioning why things had happened as they did, Johanna had always known God was there for her—that He would see her through.

Even though she had an incredible amount of work to do, she had a spring in her step. The gift from Mrs. Bennett was so generous.

If she and Dad used the tickets from Parker, she'd actually go to the opera house twice in one month, and she hadn't expected to go at all.

At least it gave her something to look forward to and a way to get her mind off James. Maybe Marvella was right, and she just needed to hash it out with the Judge.

Grief had to be pushing James to act the way he was. He seemed to care about her future and Emily's. Otherwise he wouldn't have gone to Sears in the first place. Once she signed the contracts and he saw that she would be okay, he'd relax. Wouldn't he?

In three short years, Emily would be old enough for school. Johanna already worked with her on her letters and numbers. It was her goal that Emily would be able to read and write before she even walked through the schoolhouse doors. The Sears contract would help her to do that. She had only to sign it and send it off.

All right. Her mind was made up. She would read through the contracts one more time this weekend, then sign them and send them off.

If Marvella and the Judge were at the opera house tonight, she would ask him if he would mind stopping by tomorrow.

Good. Decision made.

Life had been hard, but it was so beautiful to see God's

handprints all over the provision for her. And with the play to look forward—

Oh! The play! She hadn't even thought about what to wear or how to do her hair. She'd grown so accustomed to her work dresses and keeping her hair out of the way in a long braid. Besides, with her heavy hair, any upswept hairstyles gave her headaches.

Getting a new dress for the evening wasn't in her stringent budget. Nor was there time. There was her navy-blue dress—it wasn't that far out of fashion. And she would be comfortable, which was the most important thing. A little thrill shot through her. A night on the town with Cora.

She frowned. Why were all these people scurrying toward the Conrad mansion?

Dozens of people ran in the same direction. But once she reached the mansion, the crowd didn't stop there.

They were headed toward her home!

Lifting her skirts, she ran as fast as she could. Had the house caught fire? Had Dad suffered a heart attack? She pushed through people at the back of their little property and gasped at the sight before her.

About one hundred yards ahead, her daughter was standing on top of a log that was precariously situated over the rushing creek. The snow melt this year was intense and had filled their creek—which normally only had a few inches of water—to several feet deep.

She clamped her hand over her mouth. She wanted to scream but was afraid it would scare Em and send her careening into the cold water. An adult could withstand the depth and temperature . . . but a child?

Moving toward her daughter, she saw Parker only a few

yards from Em with his arms outstretched. He was saying something to her, and she smiled.

At least she wasn't afraid.

Johanna's heart threatened to beat out of her chest, and she moved as quick as she could toward her daughter, praying she wouldn't cause Emily to startle. *Please, God, don't let her fall!*

As she got closer, she heard Parker's voice.

Singing.

"Jesus loves me . . ."

Tears pricked her eyes. That dear man. Trying to calm her daughter and coax her to safety.

It seemed to take her forever to get close. Parker too. But he moved with slow methodical steps on the creek bank.

The crowd behind them gasped as part of the bank crumbled, and Parker slid down into the water. When he stood, the water was up to his chest, but he moved to the side of the log and reached up for Em.

She gleefully jumped into his arms, and he placed her on his shoulders, trudging his way through the water and up the muddy creek bank.

By the time Johanna reached them, they were out of the water and the crowd was cheering.

"Oh, baby, are you all right?" Johanna took her dry, grinning daughter as Parker handed her down and crushed her little girl to her chest. "Thank you, Parker. Thank you." She couldn't even look at him for the tears welling in her eyes.

Emily wrapped her arms around Johanna's neck and leaned back. "Pawker got me, Mama."

Johanna put a hand on the side of her face. "Yes, sweetie, he did." Blinking away the tears, she finally looked up at him, but he was frowning at the people gathered.

"Where'd they all come from?"

Johanna shrugged.

"I mean, how'd they know? I only found her myself a few minutes ago."

She shrugged because she had bigger questions than that. "You know small towns. News travels fast. Come on inside, I'll get you a towel to dry off with."

She headed to the house with her daughter in her arms—not wanting to let go. Where was her father? And how did Emily get out the gate?

Parker followed several yards behind Johanna and Emily because while some of the crowd moved away, several people stepped closer.

Particularly, two reporters. The same ones who had been at the lunch with Alfred. How did they get here so quick? No one from the police or fire department had arrived, and wouldn't they have been the first ones there to help rescue a child if word had gotten around?

Rather than bring Johanna's attention to them, he headed them off at the pass and put a hand up. He lowered his voice. "What are you doing here?"

"Watching you rescue a child!" One looked far too giddy and happy that a small child had almost fallen into the creek. He kept peeking over Parker's shoulder.

Parker placed a hand on the guy's upper arm and his other hand on the other man's shoulder near his neck. "This has been a traumatizing event for the family. You need to leave. Now."

"But—"

"No buts." Parker applied pressure and pushed them backward until they got the hint.

Thankfully they left without another word.

As soon as he was certain they were on their way, Parker headed up to the house.

"Where *were* you, Dad?" Johanna's sharp—almost painful—tone floated toward him.

He stopped in his tracks. Probably not a conversation he wanted to interrupt.

"I'm so sorry, Jo. We were in the garden playing. The gate was closed, I promise you. I always check it when we go outside to play so that I know even if I turn my back, she'll be safe."

"But why weren't you there?"

Silence occupied the air for several seconds. "I must have dozed off. When I saw what was happening and that Parker was out there, I came inside for towels, called the Conrads for help since they are the closest, and rushed back out as soon as I could."

Ah, so that's why he hadn't seen Daniel Easton around.

Parker took the break in the conversation as a chance to enter, praying that his presence would also help to calm down the distraught mother. "Hi. Sorry to barge in, but I could use a towel."

Johanna turned toward him and handed him the towel in her hands. "Thank you again, Parker."

"Not a problem. Emily is my favorite girl, and I was coming over here to visit when I spotted her. Kids her age are always testing boundaries. Thankfully, she wasn't scared, but I think open conversations about staying away from the water are a good idea." He smiled down at the little girl. "Especially since the treed area around the swamp north of the Conrad's house is so close."

"You're right." Johanna sat down hard. "I hadn't thought about warning her and teaching her about those things. I was only trying to protect her." Her shoulders shook and tears streamed down her cheeks. "When I saw her there . . . I—"

Daniel went to his daughter and took her in his arms. "I know. I'm so sorry. But remember that she's all right. God was watching out for her."

She nodded. "I'm sorry for lashing out at you, Dad. I know you do so much for us, and it's exhausting for you to take care of her all the time."

"No. You had every right to take me to task. It was my fault. But I don't know how I fell asleep so fast. One minute I sat watching her dig in her little garden, and the next I almost fell out of my chair and she was nowhere to be found. Until I saw the open gate and then I panicked. It *had* been closed. I'm certain of it."

"She must have learned how to open it." Johanna's sigh was long and rough. "Every day, she learns something new and gets into one scrape or another. That's why it's hard to have her in the shop with me anymore, because there are too many things that can hurt her. Can you imagine if she got a pair of scissors in her hands?" She shook her head. "We'll figure this out, Dad. We can't go on like we have been."

Parker had dried himself as best he could with the towel. It was best for him to take his leave. Their anguish was clenching his heart, and he wanted to race in like the knight in shining armor and fix everything, but he couldn't. This wasn't one of his plays. He couldn't be the hero.

"I'd better go." He handed Johanna the towel. "Thank you for that."

"Are you sure you wouldn't like a cup of coffee or something?" She leaped to her feet.

"No. But thank you. Our first performance is tonight, and I need to be back."

"Bye, Pawker." Emily rushed him and hugged his legs. "I love you."

"Love you too, kiddo." He waved at Daniel and took off like his pants were on fire rather than wet from a dunking in the creek.

His heart couldn't take it. This was where he wanted to be. But Johanna was still in love with her husband. Which was only right. So there was no room for him.

God . . . where do You want me?

10

The small clock on her dresser chimed six o'clock. Cora would be here in half an hour, and she still wasn't ready.

Under any other circumstances, Johanna would have been ecstatic to have a night off. A chance to dress up and go to a play. But after having her heart run through the wringer by Em's antics, she never wanted to leave her child again.

Johanna studied her reflection with a frown. Half her hair was up and pinned in a coiffure atop her head. The other section of her hair was hanging down her back, waiting to be twisted and pinned to finish her evening look. But every time she picked up a pin to put a lock of hair in place, her shaking fingers dropped it. So far five pins were somewhere on her bedroom floor.

She turned away from the mirror and pressed her fingers to her temples. Why on earth was she even contemplating leaving the house? The whole incident had made one thing startlingly clear. Dad wasn't able to keep up with her rambunctious daughter anymore.

The thought threatened to suffocate her. What was she supposed to do with a thriving business, a busy toddler, and a dad who was willing to help but couldn't?

Her chest felt hot and itchy. Her heart had slowed down, but there were moments she couldn't catch her breath.

It was tempting to press her face into her pillow and scream. There could have been a very different outcome this afternoon. And Parker showing up when he did? She pressed her palms against her eyes. When had her life become like one of those dramas on stage? She scoffed. Life was not easy for anyone, but these last few years had been an avalanche of difficulty and grief. Weakness weighed on her shoulders. Why would God let something like this happen? Wasn't it enough that He'd taken Gerald away when she needed him most?

All her life she sought to honor God in all she did.

Hot tears filled her eyes. Where had she gone wrong? Was God mad at her? Why did these horrible things keep happening? Why was her brother-in-law threatening her?

Johanna slipped to her knees and sobbed out her questions to God, even told Him she was mad at Him for taking Gerald away.

After a couple minutes, the tears subsided. Sitting up, she swiped at her running nose with a hankie she fished out of her dressing robe pocket.

While she didn't feel better, she did feel different. Lighter in a way she hadn't expected.

"When thou passeth through the waters, I will be with thee; and through the rivers, they shall not overflow thee."

The verse from Isaiah slipped into her soul, bringing with it a rush of peace. Fresh tears slipped down her face, but this time of gratitude. The Lord hadn't forgotten her. Hadn't abandoned her in her questions or anger. He'd simply listened. Comforted.

The clock chimed, and Johanna groaned. Only fifteen minutes remained before Cora's arrival.

Johanna sat back down and unpinned her hair. There wasn't time to finish the evening hairstyle, so she made quick work putting the thick tresses back into a serviceable braid. The verse from Isaiah continued to wash over her.

The Lord had been with Emily. And spurred Parker on to save her.

God was with her in her own distress and grief.

What a balm to her weary heart.

"Jo! Jo, are you ready? Your dad said I could come back—oh."

Cora's voice broke through her thoughts, and Johanna turned toward the doorway. Her friend looked beautiful in an emerald-green evening dress. Her brown hair was piled on her head with a single white rose nestled among the curls.

"Oh, Cora, you look stunning!"

Cora smiled, but it didn't reach her eyes. "Are you all right, Jo? You look like you've been crying."

She ducked her head and wiped at her face again. "I'm fine. But I have to apologize. I can't go to the theater with you tonight. I do hate to disappoint you, dearest, but after what happened this afternoon, I don't see how I can leave."

Her friend entered the room and shut the door behind her. In three quick steps she was beside Johanna, arm in arm, leading her to the edge of the bed. They sat, and Cora squeezed her hand. "I can't imagine what a scare that was for you and your dad. Not to mention Emily."

Flashes of the terror she felt seeing Emily on that log flooded her memory, making her head swim. "It's not a feeling I want to experience ever again. I'm grateful Parker was there."

"I am too."

The two women fell silent for a moment. What a blessing to have a friend who understood when silence was sweeter than words of comfort.

Finally Cora let go of Johanna's arm and stood, moving to stand in front of her. "I know you think that you're to blame for what happened today."

Heat spread across her cheeks, and she dropped her gaze. "Of course I am, Cora. I've put too much on my dad. With his injury and his age, he shouldn't have to contend with a toddler."

Cora grabbed her hands and squeezed them tight. "You know your dad would be so upset if he heard you say that. Emily is the light of his life, and he delights in caring for her."

"But I can't ignore what happened today! He needs help to watch her, and I can't afford that right now. And how can I go prancing off to the theater after a scare like that? It's not right."

"Well, if you were planning to prance into the theater tonight, I should very much like to see that happen." Cora chuckled. "But it is fine to take some time to yourself, Jo. Your daughter is fine. Your dad is fine. And if I know my mother, she is stuffing them both with fresh baked bread as we speak."

Her head snapped up. "Your mother?"

The look on Cora's face was a bit too innocent. "Oh. Did I not mention that? In addition to purchasing the tickets for us this evening, she's come to spend time with your dad and Emily while you're out. She didn't want you to have to worry about a thing."

Hope unfurled in her belly. "Truly? But I couldn't ask that of her. She's done so much for me already."

"Oh, tosh." Cora waved a hand. "She's offered, and I dare say you will break her heart if you deprive her of Emily's snuggles. I know it's only a one-night fix for what's troubling you, but will you let us help? So you can have a night with your best friend before she marries the most wonderful man in the world?"

She bit her lip. Would she be a terrible mother to leave her child after such a scare? Or was she simply being a ninny about the whole thing? Fear had a way of latching on . . . and fear wasn't from the Lord. Besides, Mrs. Bennett would be here with Dad. "If you are sure your mother doesn't mind, then yes!"

Cora squealed and tugged Johanna over to the vanity. "I am so glad. Now. Let's get you ready for the theatah!" she said in an affected accent.

Forty-five minutes later, Cora and Johanna were headed up the broad staircase toward the second-story McIntosh Opera House. The polished wood floors glistened in the electric lights. Guests dressed in their finest mingled and chatted. The stage awaited on the west wall, cloaked in a thick curtain, and anticipation sizzled in the air.

The row of twelve tall windows facing First Street and the four double windows facing Main Street bathed the large room with the last light of the day and the colors of the sunset.

Johanna had a hard time not stopping every few feet and soaking in the beauty of this place.

"Jo." Cora's whisper near her shoulder caused her to jump.

"Sorry, I've never been here before, and I'm enjoying every moment."

A wide grin spread across Cora's face. "I'm so glad we could come together." Linking elbows, her friend led her to their seats.

Near the front and right smack-dab in the center.

As they settled in, Johanna couldn't wait for *Romeo and Juliet* to begin. Cora had worked some sort of magic in making Johanna presentable for society in her midnight-blue evening gown. She'd pinned up Johanna's braids in a pretty coiffure.

She could hardly remember the last time she'd felt this pretty.

The lights dimmed, and the audience's conversation hushed.

The massive red curtain opened with a loud *swish*, and in a moment, she was transported to Verona. The lush costumes were breathtaking. Each actor filled their role to perfection, drawing the audience into the story of the young star-crossed lovers.

But the moment Parker stepped on the stage, fitted in his Shakespearean costume, Johanna's breath left her in a whoosh. He looked like himself, yet so completely different. He began to speak his lines, and his voice drew her in as he related his woes to his onstage cousins about unrequited love.

Her fingers clenched her playbill into a tight scroll. *My, but he's mesmerizing!* As the play went on, she found she was unable to look away every time he was on the stage.

And then Yvette came on stage. Her beauty sparkled as she traded witticisms with Parker and their characters began to fall in love.

Johanna's heart sank down to her toes.

She chewed her lip as Yvette appeared on the balcony, opining about her love—if Johanna was to let Parker back into her life, was this how it would be? Always watching him act out love and other emotions and having to trust that in real life he felt that way about only her?

Her gaze dropped to her lap, the dialogue on the stage becoming fuzzy in her ears. The girlish love she'd felt for Parker all those years ago was nothing to the depth of love she understood now. And watching him this afternoon . . . It would be so easy to love him again. But this time it would be different.

Sweat dotted her forehead. It was too warm in here. Fanning her burning face with her playbill, she looked back to the stage. Loving Parker didn't change his vocation.

He'd said that he wanted to use his gift to help draw people back to the Lord. But how was a performance of *Romeo and Juliet* accomplishing tha—?

Johanna let out a long breath. That was wrong of her. And far too judgmental. God could use any of them anywhere He chose. There was no denying Parker's gift on the stage.

Even so . . .

She'd had enough grief and heartbreak to last a lifetime. *Please, Lord, please take these feelings. Help me to protect my heart and to be wise in my interactions with him. I don't know that I can love him and lose him again.*

As the curtain closed at the end, she breathed deep. Her heart had been dragged through a gamut of emotions this evening.

The cast returned for their bows, and the audience stood and applauded.

Johanna stood, still wrestling with the discomfort that seeing Parker on stage had caused her. Perhaps her best option was to accept James. Then she wouldn't have to *feel* any of this.

A shiver ran up her arms and neck. No. That wasn't an option. How could she even *think* that?

The director came out then and announced two more showings of *Romeo and Juliet* the following day, then invited everyone to return for *Hamlet* the following week.

Johanna set her shoulders in a straight line. She enjoyed this night with Cora. She soaked up every moment of Parker's superb performance and would praise him for his incredible talent. And then?

She would make it clear to him, and her heart, that a future together simply wasn't possible.

Marvella spotted Johanna and Cora in the crowd and made a beeline in their direction, dragging her husband along with her. "Ladies, how lovely to see you here this evening. Wasn't that magnificent?"

Cora put a hand to her throat. "Breathtaking is what it was. I was so moved that I cried."

"I did as well. Why, I knew that Parker was a talented actor"— she placed a hand on Cora's arm—"but *gracious*, I didn't understand he could transport me to another time and place and make me feel exactly what he was feeling. My toes are still tingling from it all."

Oh dear. The look on Johanna St. John's face just broke Marvella's heart. "Are you all right, dear?"

Johanna blinked at her. "Oh, yes. It was a lovely performance, wasn't it." She shifted toward Marvella's husband. "Judge Ashbury, might I have a word?"

Cora stood on tiptoe. "There's Parker. If you'll excuse me?" The young woman hurried off to see her brother.

"Of course."

Marvella pulled Johanna toward them, into a little circle, while her husband leaned a bit closer.

"I'm in need of some advice about a contract I've been offered." The young widow aimed the question toward Marvella's husband.

But Marvella already knew about that. "And?"

Johanna shook her head back and forth. "Nothing else. Just the contract."

Of course she wouldn't want to bring it up here. Marvella

offered a conspiratorial nod. "Let's speak tomorrow over luncheon at our home, if that is agreeable to you?" Her husband's keen eye would pick up on what was going on.

"Thank you." Johanna glanced at Marvella, her eyes pleading for silence. "It was lovely to see you both here."

With a nod, she smiled at the young widow. Tomorrow couldn't come soon enough.

If she had to pry the truth out of Johanna in front of the Judge, she would.

James watched the crowd leave the opera house. Cora Bennett and Johanna were arm in arm as they left the theater and walked toward home.

Perfect.

Sometimes a man had to take his destiny into his own hands and direct fate.

Once the ladies were past First Avenue, he snuck back around the block and headed toward the hat shop.

Under the street lamp, he read through the typed note one more time.

It's a good thing little Emily is unharmed. Some might wonder how Parker was there at the right time. Where was your father? Isn't it interesting that a crowd formed so quick? And that the newspaper reporters were there?

Be careful around Parker Bennett, Mrs. St. John. He's using you for his own gain.

Respectfully,
A concerned neighbor

Smiling, he slid it under the door of the shop and then headed toward the train depot for his meeting. He stayed in the shadows until the woman approached and then stepped forward.

Her narrowed eyes widened when she recognized him. "What are *you* doing here?"

Allowing a sly grin, he stepped closer. "Keep your voice down, Miss Lebeau."

She placed a hand on her hip. "Is that why you told me to come in disguise?" She pointed to the wig on her head. "Because you didn't want to be seen with me?"

"No. It has to do with who you really are."

She stepped back as if slapped.

Good. She got his point. "I simply wanted to make sure that you keep yourself available to me. There may come a time when I need your assistance."

"And?"

"When that time comes, do as I say. No questions asked."

She crossed her arms over her chest. "Or?"

"I'll tell the Camorra gang that *you* were the one who stole their money. And I'll tell them where to find you."

11

Oh, Marvella was in her element! There were few things she loved more than being hostess. She poured her guest and herself cups of steaming coffee as they sat in her parlor. "I remembered that you prefer coffee to tea. I hope you enjoy this new blend. It's from a specialty store in New York City. The governor's wife sent it to us, and I've continued to order it ever since."

Johanna lifted her cup. "Thank you, it's so kind of you, Mrs. Ashbury."

"Did you sleep at all last night, my dear?"

It was nice to have this time together alone. One of the maids was playing in the room across the foyer with Emily and Sir Theophilus.

Johanna grimaced. "Not as much as I should have. I kept waking up and going to check on Emily. I'm sure that's normal after a fright like yesterday, but there's no sense in worrying. Now if I could convince my mind of that."

"Time will make it all better, I'm sure." Marvella passed

a plate of finger sandwiches to her guest. "You are doing a marvelous job raising your daughter. Be confident of that fact."

"Thank you, Mrs. Ashbury. I needed to hear that." Johanna took a sandwich and laid it on her plate.

"I'm glad you asked the Judge to review that contract for you. I'm sure he'll be back down as soon as he finishes going over every word." She held up the newspaper. "Did you see the write-up about our Parker saving Emily's life?"

She nodded, but didn't look pleased. "I did. But he didn't seem happy that so many people had gathered so quickly. How do you suppose that happened?" She frowned. "And we still haven't figured out how the gate got opened. Dad always checks it before they play in the garden area. I asked Em if she opened the gate, and she said it was already open. So how did that happen?"

No wonder the young mother wasn't getting any rest. All that worry. "Dear, you're going to run yourself in circles if you continue with this. Sometimes we have to let go."

Johanna winced. "But my daughter was in a life-and-death situation. My father is aging, and my rambunctious almost-three-year-old wears him out—"

"Again, dear. Who can add days to their life by worrying? Isn't that why you are hoping to sign those contracts? You'll be able to stay home more, and all of this will be moot."

The lines eased from Johanna's face, and she stared at Marvella. "You're right."

"Of course, my dear. I usually am." She sipped her coffee and took a bite of sandwich. "Now . . . let's talk about Parker risking his life for your little girl."

The young woman pressed her lips together, her shoulders sagging. "It moved me to tears that he was there and did what he did." She stared down at her coffee. "But I confess, I worry that I haven't told Emily enough about her father. When Parker stayed for dinner last week, Em had no problem jumping in his lap. She seemed to connect with him almost immediately. I know she needs a dad, but it crushed me to think that she might not remember Gerald."

"Are you thinking that Parker could fill that role?"

Johanna's eyes widened almost as wide as her saucer. "Oh, heavens no, ma'am! That wasn't what I was implying at all . . . I . . . um—"

So. Time to bring out her matchmaking skills again. These two floundering young people needed her help. "It's all right to have feelings for him. I know you once loved him enough to want to marry him."

Johanna blinked several times and set her cup down. "Mrs. Ashbury—"

"It's just us, dear. Call me Marvella."

"Marvella . . ." Johanna lifted her chin, tears shimmering in her blue eyes. "I did love Parker. A long time ago. Deeply. But that went away when I met Gerald. I absolutely love my husband and never ever thought of Parker while we were married."

What a silly notion. "No one is questioning your love for Gerald, Johanna. There's no reason to be embarrassed by feelings of love returning for Parker."

The younger woman shook her head. "I think it's best that those emotions remain buried."

Where on earth did Johanna get these ideas? "Nonsense. You were true to Gerald and to God, yes?"

She stiffened. "Yes. Of course."

"Then there is nothing wrong in allowing your heart to love again."

Johanna's gaze slammed into her own. Marvella stirred

her coffee, arched her brow, and waited for a response. The younger woman opened and closed her mouth a couple of times, sputtering incoherent sentences.

Finally, Johanna shook her head and put her coffee cup down. "That's a bad idea, Marvella. I can't live on the road. Besides, it would incense Gerald's brother. I can't risk him following through on his threat to take Emily away from me."

That pesky lawyer was ruining all of her matchmaking fun. Fortunately for Johanna and Parker, she never let a single meddler get in her way. She gave her young friend a smile and picked her coffee cup back up. "Let's worry about James later. The Judge will be all too glad to handle that situation, my dear. Now back to Parker . . . it appears we have a great deal to pray about."

The Judge entered the room, papers in hand. "Prayer is always the best idea. No matter the situation." He handed the contract to Johanna. "It's all in order. Nothing untoward. My suggestion is that you sign them and send them off."

Johanna beamed and put her hands over her chest. "Thank you so much! Both of you. I can't tell you what a relief this is!"

But would this actually be a relief? Marvella had her doubts. Starting with that lawyer.

SUNDAY, APRIL 23, 1905

When the director called for a rehearsal this afternoon, Parker wanted to revolt. His mind hadn't made a decision yet, but maybe his heart was making it for him.

Perhaps he was simply getting tired as he got older. The wear and tear of the job was too much.

Or maybe he was *done*. The thought ricocheted through him. That was it, wasn't it?

He stared out one of the windows of the opera house to the town that he loved. The town he'd missed more than he realized over the years.

The first few years on the road it was easy to make excuses to not come home—losing Johanna was devastating—but the disappointment from his family cut deep.

Parker rubbed his face. Maybe that was why he struggled so much now. No one had understood the depth of his passion, his certainty that a life on the stage was what he was called to do.

But that certainty had cost him. In so many ways.

And that certainty was dimming.

He watched a father and son rumble down the street in their wagon. The dad made gestures toward the horses, probably instructing the young boy on how to handle the team.

How many times had his own dad taught him the same way? Given him advice. Taught him about the Lord. He clenched his jaw, fighting the burning in the back of his throat.

Parker turned away from the window, his heart squeezing. He couldn't fix things with Dad. Couldn't change the past. Wishing it were different wouldn't make it so. He huffed at his false bravado. There was no audience around he had to play to. How many nights had he cried? Fear and regret were constant companions. Would he ever escape them?

Could his family ever forgive him for being absent? Would Johanna?

Restoration. Forgiveness. How he longed for those things. But how could he ask for them when he still felt the pull to ministry in the theatre, the very thing that kept him from his family?

And Johanna.

He still loved acting. Still knew, deep in his heart, it was a powerful way to share the gospel with people. And yet . . .

He longed for home.

Perhaps there was something he could do in Kalispell. *Maybe* . . . An idea sparked to life. Why couldn't he lead a small troupe here? Maybe even the children. He could help the next generation hone their gifts and talents on the stage. They always had Christmas programs and end-of-school-year programs.

The more he thought about it, the more he liked the idea.

Especially since, after the article in the newspaper yesterday, people wouldn't leave him alone. It was worse than ever. Ten telegrams had come in from around the state this morning. The news was traveling fast.

The rescue wasn't the only bit of news making the rounds either.

Every lie Alfred had printed about him and Yvette haunted him. News of motion pictures gaining popularity and investors hoping to help studios popped up everywhere. Along with speculation as to whether Parker Bennett would move from the stage to the screen.

Now that John P. Harris of Pittsburgh was renovating a storefront to show movies, the country was waiting with bated breath to see what happened. Would this be the start of something huge? Would Harris's nickelodeon idea take off?

If so, what would happen to the stage?

Yvette kept talking about motion pictures to everyone who would listen. And this afternoon she'd followed him around. Thankfully, they'd been surrounded by others all day, which had kept her at a distance.

What on earth was he supposed to do? One thing was becoming clearer . . . he wasn't meant to leave Kalispell again.

Not that he was ready to tell everyone. No sense putting people in the troupe into a panic. They still had a couple weeks of shows here. But the more he allowed the idea of staying here to simmer in his mind, the more he liked it.

Felt a peace about it.

The director stepped over to him. "It really is a quaint little town, isn't it?"

"Yes." Parker turned to face him. "Did you need me, George?"

The man looked around and inched closer. "Didn't I hear that you knew someone who was good with a needle? I mean, you're from here, so you know people, right?"

"I do. What do you need?" Parker crossed his arms over his chest.

George looked around again. "I don't want anyone to get all stressed over this, but the stage manager came to me. Our costume mistress left today because her mother is very ill. There are multiple things that need to be fixed before tomorrow's show and a list of things needing to be done in the next few weeks. The assistants are up to some of it, but they need someone who is an expert. Since this is your town, could you find us a replacement? Quickly?"

Parker checked his pocket watch. "Do you need me for any other scenes today?"

The director shook his head. "No, you have been flawless since we arrived. It's the others I'm concerned about, and I can run all that without you. But *please*, find a replacement— and fast."

"I'm on my way." Without glancing behind him, he headed toward the stairs.

"Parker . . . Parker!" Yvette rushed to his side. "I've been trying to be alone with you all day. Why don't we take supper together tonight? I long to talk to you privately. *C'est très important.*"

Was she kidding? "And you think we would have privacy over a public dinner?"

She wore very little but her dressing gown and all but purred as she pressed up against him. "Of course, you are right. We should meet at the hotel. Your room, or better yet, mine. No one would expect you to be there."

He stepped to the side. "Because I *won't* be there. You know how I feel about such behavior. I won't compromise either of our reputations that way."

She pursed her lips into a pout and looked up at him with tears in her eyes. Her trademark look of sorrow. So convincing on the stage.

And so repulsive right now.

"Sorry, Yvette, but I need to go."

"Where are you heading now? You are always leaving us, and the troupe suffers so. We need you here to inspire us. We need you . . . I need you."

His gaze roamed her features. How could someone be so beautiful on the outside and yet the inside . . . He shook his head. It was unkind to judge. But he needed to get out of there. "You can manage fine on your own. If you need inspiration for the show, go speak to George. I'm sure he'll be more than happy to motivate you."

George had no patience for simpering females or males. He had little trouble reducing an attention seeker to real tears if it proved necessary.

Parker hurried from the opera house.

Escaping Yvette was such a relief. What was she up to? Perhaps she was trying to gain fame by attaching herself to him. Others had tried that, and while it had helped them for a time, once Parker made it clear that they held no special place in his life, they had faded away. Or left to try their game on another.

That was the saddest thing about his life as an actor of standing—people constantly wanted something from him. It wasn't enough that he gave of himself on the stage, they always wanted more, and it was always far removed from what Parker could offer of himself . . . his hopes and dreams.

They especially wanted no part of his faith. So much so that his agent had asked him to stop talking about it unless he was privately situated, without press or other people of importance nearby.

He shook his head. How had he been so foolish as to lose sight of his faith the past couple years? His faith made him who he was. The most important thing about him was Jesus as his Savior. Not acting, nor fame, nor fortune.

At the core of the man they watched on stage was a heart that beat for God's glory.

Before *Everyman*, he'd once tried to explain it to a newspaperman, telling him about new life in Christ. The man had printed an entire article on reincarnation and how Parker Bennett was a serious believer of living more than once.

It had been eye-opening to see the world seeking ways to fill the voids in their own lives.

It didn't matter. Parker *would* see his lifelong mission to fruition, but for now he had a different mission, and it would take him straight to Johanna. Which caused all the other concerns to disappear.

A block away from the opera house, he broke into a jog. It wouldn't hurt to get there quick, and he couldn't wait to see her. Despite the years apart, she still completed him. The jog became a full-out run.

Breathless by the time he arrived at Johanna's home, he knocked on the door and then had to put his hands on his knees to catch his breath.

"Parker?" Johanna's voice brought his head up. "What are you doing here? And why are you out of breath?"

The sight of her took what little breath he'd recovered out of his lungs again. Her brows were furrowed as she studied him, and he looked away. If he wasn't careful, he'd pull her in his arms and kiss her. Tell her how she still had his heart.

Take it easy, boy.

He held up a finger. "Sorry. We have a bit of a theater emergency. Our costume mistress had to leave because her mother is sick, and it takes a lot to keep all the costumes in check. Any chance you'd be willing to help us out? I know work as a seamstress is probably a bit dull compared to creating hats, but it's good money."

She bit her lip. "I spent the majority of yesterday getting all caught up in my shop so that I could spend more time at home. Taking on something extra isn't possible right now. I need to be with Emily."

He took a step toward her, aching to hold her hand. To smooth the worry lines in her forehead away with his thumb. But he didn't have the right to do those things. So he shoved his hands in his pockets. "I can help you bring whatever you need here, and then we can transport it back to the opera house. Most of the work is repairs to the costumes. They were already fitted and tailored for each actor. You could accomplish the work at home, while the assistants can manage things during the show. Those repairs are never permanent and usually rigged to get us through the night."

Johanna's brows furrowed together. "I don't know. I mean, what if the director or actor changes their mind about a costume or someone quits and someone else has to be fitted . . . or a new costume created? That would take a lot of time."

The urge to smooth that deep *V* away with a finger was overpowering. He shoved his hands in his pockets before he did something that sent her running to the next county. "But there's no one I like to work with half as much as you." He leaned in, catching the sweet scent of honeysuckle. Her favorite. He winked, pleased when a pretty pink filled her cheeks.

Her dad appeared behind her. "Tell you what, Jo, I'll hitch up the wagon. Let's all head into town, and then we can load up the wagon with whatever you need to bring back with you. There are ladies at church you could call to help you if things get to be too much. It's for a few short weeks. That way you don't have to carry the load alone, and the community can pitch in to help the theatre troupe."

She smiled up at Parker, and it took his breath away.

"I guess there's your answer. Let me grab my things."

He scratched the side of his face as she darted into the back room, his heart in her apron pocket. He'd forgotten the power her genuine smile had over him. Oh boy, was he in deep. But he couldn't pour out his feelings to her. Not yet. Not when he didn't know what he wanted to do with his future. It wouldn't be fair to her. And with Emily in the picture . . .

He needed to handle both their hearts with care.

Johanna appeared. "I'm ready!"

He caught her gaze and gave her a smile. "After you." He gestured to the front door.

He rode in the wagon with them back to the opera house and introduced Johanna to the director. In the midst of the director outlining what he would expect, Parker felt a presence to his right. And with it came the heavy scent of lilac.

Yvette tugged on his sleeve.

"What now?" He hated to speak to her that way, but why wouldn't she leave him alone?

"I need to speak with you privately. Immediately." She tapped her fingers on his sleeve. "I told you earlier that it was important."

"Fine." He walked her over to a corner by the balcony.

She turned to face him, her brown eyes glowing in the sunlight. There was a look on her face that Parker couldn't decipher. "This is hardly the place. Why don't we go to my dressing room at least."

Not in a million years. "It's here, or nowhere."

The pout returned. "Fine. I can no longer go on lying to you, Parker. I have fallen in love with you, and the public eye on us has only proven to show me how important you are to me." She gave a hint of what he was sure was supposed to be a seductive smile. "You are all that I can think of. You entice me in the way you walk and talk. You have become everything to me. I can hardly draw breath without thinking of yo—"

This was absurd. He held up a hand. "I'm sorry, Yvette. I'm not sure where this is coming from, but it's not real. You don't love me. You don't even know me. We will be going our separate ways soon."

"But Parker"—she sidled closer and put her hands on his lapels—"I know you feel the connection between us. Kiss me now, and let your passion be mine."

He stepped back and pushed her hands away. "Yvette, listen to me. I don't feel that way about you."

She burst into tears.

Another ploy for which she was well-known. "Yvette. Stop it. Right now."

"If you refuse me, I won't be able to go on." She was almost as convincing as when she played Juliet.

Almost.

"What you really need is a relationship with God, Yvette. *He* will supply all that you need. If you want, I can go with you to talk with a pastor. Other than that, there is nothing to talk about." He turned on his heel and strode toward the director.

Maybe this was God's way of telling him he needed to be done before the troupe left Kalispell.

Johanna had barely heard what the man was telling her. She'd been fixed on Parker and Yvette walking away into the shadows. For several minutes the director rambled on and on, and finally she had to stop him. The amount of information was overwhelming.

"I'm sorry. It's been a long day for me. I can take costumes home with me and repair them in the evening, but I cannot be here at the show each night. I have a daughter who's almost three, and I cannot afford to hire someone to stay with her. My father is most helpful during the day, but I cannot expect him to give up his evenings as well."

The man looked at her for a long moment. "All I care about is making certain my actors and actresses have their costumes for our performances. I don't care how it's done, and I already told Parker that the assistants will be able to manage during the shows."

Johanna glanced around. Now where had Parker gone? "I will see to it that the repairs are made."

Relief reflected on the man's face, softening the deep lines around his eyes and mouth. "Good. You will be paid weekly on Fridays. I'll need you until our regular costume mistress returns. I have no way of knowing when that will be. Apparently informing the director wasn't uppermost on her mind."

Johanna studied the man for a moment, her heart feeling for him. His hair, what little was left, stuck out at disjointed angles, as if he'd ruffled it one hundred times that day. His tie was tugged loose and askew on his neck. Deep, dark circles lined his pale green eyes. Goodness, if this was what it was like to be a director for a big show, why continue to do it?

She shoved the question away. It wasn't any of her business.

Instead, she smiled at him and gave him a nod. "I should be available. It would work best to have Parker bring the costumes to me each evening, and then I'll make sure he can return them the following day."

"Good. Good. It will be late before you receive them, however. And we'll definitely need them by showtime."

"I understand,"

"Wonderful. Now, if you'll excuse me, I have some actors to instruct and terrify." He started yelling out names as he stormed away.

Johanna searched the stage for some sign of Parker. He came from the right, stomping toward her almost in the same fashion as the man who'd just left.

She narrowed her eyes and felt her brows knit together. "What's wrong?"

"It's nothing of importance." He put his arm around her and drew her along with him. "Come on, and I'll take you to the costume room. There may be some problems that you'll need to address before the show tonight."

Johanna allowed him to lead her to a room filled with long rows of hanging costumes. There were shelves with accessories of every kind, and two young women, who scurried around with armloads of clothes.

"Johanna, meet Neeve and Imogen." Parker nodded to the two. "They are assistants to our costume mistress, Marie."

They were hardly old enough to be out of school. Johanna smiled, nevertheless. "I'm Johanna, and I've come to help."

Parker's tone was kind as he encouraged the two young women. "Johanna is going to take over for Marie on the permanent repairs. You'll still be doing all of the last-minute and emergency repairs during the show."

One of the girls stopped directly in front of Johanna. "What a relief to know someone can help! I'm Imogen, first assistant to Marie. I can do a great many things, but I'm not as talented as Marie when it comes to making all of this work." She rolled her gaze around the room and then resettled it on Johanna. "We've done our best to keep up, but there's one of the gowns that is horribly ripped. The bodice. I think the actress is getting fat."

Johanna looked to Parker, who shrugged. "Let me see it, and we'll figure it out."

She spent the next twenty minutes reviewing the velvet and satin costume. It was in a terrible state. She looked up. "How close will anyone be to these costumes? I mean . . . can I make a repair that adds seams to the inside of the bodice without compromising the look?"

Imogen nodded. "Close up doesn't matter as much as the general appearance of the entire costume. We often put in patches and such on the underlying parts of the costume. Since the velvet overlays the satin in this bodice, you can pretty much do whatever is necessary, but I was concerned about it bulking up if I were to cut out the ripped portion and try to insert another piece."

"It can be done if you ease it in. There's a trick that I can show you. I use it all the time with my hats."

"Hats?" The girl tipped her head to the side, an eyebrow arched.

"Mrs. St. John is a millinery wizard." Parker smiled at Johanna in a way that made her cheeks grow hot. "She makes the most amazing creations."

"Oh, I wish I could afford a hat. A large blue one." This from Neeve, who had come around the corner. "I think hats are divine." She sounded like a little girl wishing on a star.

The longing in the young woman's voice tugged at Johanna. From the looks of her dress, it had been mended and patched many times over.

What if . . . ?

Johanna leaned forward, tapping Neeve on the hand with a finger. "Perhaps we can find some time, and I will give you a few pointers for making one for yourself."

Neeve's blue eyes widened, her lips in a surprised O. "Do you mean it, miss?"

"I do." The girl's delight was contagious. "But for now, I'll help you to get this costume repaired, since showtime isn't long off." Johanna made the mistake of looking into Parker's eyes as she smiled. The longing there stirred her heart into a rapid rhythm and almost took her breath away. All of a sudden, she was that young girl again.

The one who'd fallen head over heels in love with Parker Bennett.

She tore her gaze away.

No. She wasn't that girl anymore. What she'd seen had been a figment of her imagination.

12

He hadn't seen any reaction from her to the note he left. Surely that must have stirred up some feelings of distrust in her for Parker Bennett. The man was a notorious womanizer. The papers made that clear. So why couldn't Johanna see the truth of it?

Granted, she was a woman, and women were weak-willed. Even the Bible spoke of it. Men like Parker Bennett would take advantage of such women and believe it his right.

A snarl twisted his lips.

Perhaps she hadn't been to the shop yet. He'd heard through the town grapevine that she was now helping out the theatre troupe, working from home.

Well, he was running out of time. He had to do something that would bring her to her senses.

Hmm . . .

Why not take away the second thing Johanna held dear?

It wouldn't take much. Either during one of the shows. Or the wedding. Yes, that was a good plan.

He'd whittle her down until she had no other choice. No future.

Nothing.

But him.

Cora paced outside Johanna's house in the new light of the sunrise. Her skirt swished around her ankles as she walked from one end of the porch to the other, the floorboards creaking with each step. She twisted her hankie between her fingers. How could she tell her best friend the decision she'd come to?

"Cora? I think you've about worn a path clean through those boards." Johanna chuckled as she joined her on the porch.

"Oh, Jo!" Cora sniffed, fighting the tears that begged to be released. "I need to talk to you. I think . . ." She hiccuped. "I-I think I need to call off the wedding."

Her friend had an arm around her in an instant. "What? What's happened?"

Cora took a deep breath. "Can we walk? I don't want to be overheard right now."

"Of course. I'm headed to the shop anyway, and I doubt there are many people out and about this early."

The pair set off down the street, walking a familiar path to the outskirts of Kalispell.

"Now"—Johanna squeezed Cora's hand after a few minutes of silence—"tell me what's going on."

Where to begin? "You're going to think I'm being silly."

"Never."

"Well, I had a dream last night. And in it William and I were walking down Main Street, shopping for something for the wedding. The sun was shining, and we were so happy. But then we started talking about the house. How we were going to decorate. And he told me that he h-hates m-my taste in curtains. And t-tablecloths. And o-our bedr-room." She wiped at her face. "And that he wanted his *mother* to decorate our house!"

Now that she was saying it out loud, it sounded ridiculous. *She* sounded ridiculous. Her cheeks burned. "I know I'm a ninny. You don't have to tell me. But it was so real. And when I saw William today, I could barely look at him. And then when he commented that the coffee was rather weak, well . . . do you think he would ever say such a thing to his mother? Of course not! And then there was the other day when I made him cookies and he said . . . he said . . ." It was almost too terrible to repeat. "He said he preferred *shortbread* to sugar cookies. He told me I could get the recipe *from his mother.* What if he prefers everything his mother does to what I do?"

She couldn't stop the tears any longer.

All night she had been in agony. Did William really love her? Was his mother, who was a wonderful woman, disappointed in the kind of wife she would be? After all, she would *never* measure up to her future mother-in-law. That was an impossible expectation!

"Oh, my sweet friend. Aren't you at least glad he mentioned his preference? You wouldn't want him to lie to you and pretend to like sugar cookies."

Cora nodded and wiped at her eyes. How had a ridiculous dream and her fiancé's dislike for a silly cookie brought her to hysterics? Mom would never understand. She had been the perfect wife and mother from the beginning. But sometimes Cora had to work extra at enjoying all these homemaker-type things. Oh, if only her father were here. He'd take her on a hike and help her see beyond her clouded emotions.

Even worse, he wouldn't be here for the wedding.

The sobs overtook her. "But what if William . . . what if he . . . *never* likes sugar cookies?"

"Aren't our brains funny things?" Johanna's question cut through her misery. "We see our spouses, our parents, our children and siblings through such different emotions. There are times when those feelings are so beautiful and wonderful. Other times, the fear of disappointing them is intense and makes you feel things you never thought possible."

Cora regained control and gave a sniff. Then looked at Johanna.

That was it!

She was afraid.

Johanna tugged her close and squeezed her waist. "I know that your dream felt real to you. I remember all the nerves I had before I married Gerald. I worried for days if I was making the right decision."

"You did? You seemed so secure in your decision." If Cora had detected even an iota of hesitancy in Johanna, she would have given Parker's letter to her.

Johanna shook her head with a smile. "I was a mess, and my mother bore the brunt of it. But when I sat down and thought about Gerald, his character, how much he loved the Lord, and all the little ways he showed me over and over again how much he loved me . . ." She shrugged. "Peace filled me in a way I knew could come only from the Lord." She patted Cora's hand. "And I think you can have the same confidence about William."

Cora bit the corner of her lip. One of the things she loved most about William was his honesty. Even when he knew the truth would be uncomfortable. It was also how she could trust that he meant it when he told her how beautiful he found her. And how dear she was to him.

Oh dear. She *was* a ninny. "I should probably go find William and tell him the truth about my fears."

"That's a good idea." Johanna bit her lip and grimaced. "I have to be honest. I remember I had a bad dream once—one where Gerald did something to hurt me—and when I woke up, I couldn't shake it. Then I held it against him for two whole days. It was ridiculous . . . he hadn't actually done what he did in the dream, but it had been so real. When I finally told him about it, we had a good laugh. But he also took me in his arms and reassured me that it wasn't true."

The same peace that Johanna talked about now warmed her own heart.

It had only been a dream.

They rounded the corner and headed toward the shop. Cora let out a sigh. "Thank you for not dismissing my fears." She bumped her shoulder into Johanna's.

Her friend let out a giggle. "How many fears and dreams have we shared over the years? And the Lord has been faithful to us through them all." A strange look crossed her features. "That's the key, isn't it? We can't predict the future. The best thing we can do is trust the Lord in the day He gives us and go from there."

"May I ask you a question?"

"Anything."

"Knowing how much you loved Gerald and how much he loved you . . . do you think you'll be able to love again? I mean, you're still young and have a full life ahead of you."

Johanna stopped so abruptly it jerked Cora backward. Why did Parker's face come to mind as soon as her friend asked the question?

Could it be . . . ?

Did she love Parker? The warmth that rushed through her limbs made her clamp her eyes shut. Did she? After all these years?

"Whoa. Are you all right?" Cora's voice squeaked. "You're all red."

Hands gripped her shoulders.

"Don't pass out on me. What happened? Johanna?"

She opened her eyes and stared at her friend. "I loved Gerald with my whole heart, Cora. And I know God put us together. I would have been happy with him had we lived to an old age and gray hair. But we didn't have that chance. And now . . ."

Cora patted her friend's arm. "Oh, Jo. I'm sorry. I shouldn't have asked such a question. It was selfish of me . . . I was simply hoping . . ."

"That I love Parker?" Her own voice cracked.

Her friend's shoulders slumped a bit. "I'm sorry. I shouldn't have pushed."

Johanna linked arms with her friend and began to walk again. The urge to blurt it out was strong. Should she? "Will you promise to keep a secret?"

"Of course . . . you don't even have to ask."

"I think I'm falling for Parker again."

There. She'd said it.

It was Cora's turn to stop, and she placed both hands over her mouth as she gasped. Tears filled her eyes. But this time her face was full of joy.

Johanna fixed her friend with a narrowed look. "Don't you *dare* say a word to your brother. Right now, I don't see how God can do the impossible between the two of us. We are worlds apart. But at least I know now that I am capable of loving again. Losing Gerald crushed my heart, and I couldn't see past my grief most days."

"I won't say anything. I promise."

They reached the shop, and Johanna took out her key and unlocked the door. A gust of wind caused both women to reach for their hats at the same time as the door flung open and items inside the store scattered in the breeze.

Once the wind died down, Cora pulled off her bonnet, smoothing the ribbons through her fingers. "Well, this should be fun to clean up."

Johanna scanned the room. It didn't help that almost everything they used on her hats was lightweight. Ribbons, tulle, flowers, and small swatches of fabric now littered the floor of her once neat-as-a-pin shop. "Might as well get started."

Long after the work day had ended, even after a nice dinner with Dad and Emily, Johanna couldn't still the thoughts churning in her mind.

James and his threats.

Parker's return.

The contract with Sears.

Dad getting older.

Everything seemed to press down on her shoulders, and when she finally had time to pick up her Bible, it was late and the rest of the household was asleep.

Johanna sat on her bed with the Bible open to Psalm 37. She pored over the verses.

A good portion of it spoke of the wicked being defeated. She didn't know that James was necessarily wicked or evil, but his actions of late had made her apprehensive. She wanted to give him the benefit of the doubt. Perhaps he was acting out of grief. He had a good reputation in Kalispell, and people seemed to admire him. But there was always something that rose up in her spirit when he was near. Was it a warning from God?

The man had threatened to take her child. If that wasn't evil, what was? Then again, she supposed he could simply be overly concerned. Perhaps the death of his only brother had caused James to cling to what little family was left. After all, he'd been in New York when their father died. Then not long afterward he lost Gerald. Perhaps it was all too much, and James deserved her sympathy rather than her wrath.

Still, he never should have threatened her. She was a good mother to Emily, even if she did have to leave her every day to go to a job.

She read the final verses of the chapter, then spoke them aloud. "'But the salvation of the righteous is of the LORD: he is their strength in the time of trouble. And the Lord shall help them, and deliver them: he shall deliver them from the wicked, and save them, because they trust in him.'"

Peace washed over her. No matter what James had planned, no matter what happened with Parker, or what the world demanded, God was in control. And because she trusted Him, she could count on Him to deliver them.

Her eyes drifted to the little desk and the contract that sat on top. She'd meant to send it off this morning, and Cora's visit had distracted her.

She jumped up and placed it in the awaiting envelope. To-morrow morning, she would send it off first thing.

TUESDAY, APRIL 25, 1905

Parker strolled the streets of Kalispell, taking in the quiet before the shops opened. It gave him time to think and pray.

Most actors slept in until noon after late nights on stage and oftentimes parties afterward, so he wouldn't see anyone from the troupe.

A fact that brought him great satisfaction.

He couldn't deny it any longer. He loved acting. But he didn't love the life. At least, not the life he was in right now.

Making it big had only complicated things. The expectations on him were outlandish.

Honestly, he had no desire to do moving pictures.

So, it was time to make a decision. But no matter which choice Parker made, God could use him. Whether continuing on the stage, the screen, or doing something different. What mattered was his heart. His focus.

And he had no doubt about one thing. God was calling him to stay home. The whys and hows would still have to be figured out. Maybe over the next couple weeks, the good Lord would give him some insight.

"Mr. Bennett? Might I have a moment of your time?"

He turned to find James St. John standing there. The slick lawyer brother-in-law he'd heard so much about. Where had he come from?

Parker really should pay more attention to where he was going. "Mr. St. John, I believe? I don't think we've had a proper introduction." He stuck out his hand.

St. John shook it. "Thank you for rescuing my precious niece the other day."

"I was on my way to visit them—I'm thankful God had me there at the right moment."

The other man lifted his chin, his eyes mere slits. "It is *my* job to protect my brother's wife and daughter, and I intend to ensure that nothing of this sort ever happens again. While your assistance was most appreciated, I think it's best that you keep your distance from now on." He stepped forward and glared. "Good day."

As the man walked away, Parker frowned. Keep his distance? It was common for family to rally around a widow like Johanna, and for friends to do the same. But . . . was he imagining it, or had there been a hint of a threat in St. John's words?

What, exactly, was Mr. St. John afraid of?

Back at his office, James read the note for a third time.

The Camorras were on his trail.

He wadded up the paper and threw it into the fire.

What made him think he could get away with stealing from one of the most notorious gangs in New York? He'd gotten cocky, that's what.

There had to be a way to pay them off and get back into their good graces before the inheritance was settled. Because after he had that money they might come after more, and that wasn't acceptable.

His little run-in with that actor had riled him up. Now this.

No man liked another man encroaching on his territory. The inheritance was his.

And so was Johanna.

After dropping off the contract at the post office, her peace was short-lived. Had she done the right thing?

How God must weary of her. One moment she was full of praise and confidence in all He could and would do in her life, and the next she was biting her lip over the future. Was it possible that anyone else fretted as much as she did?

*God, I prayed about all of this. I know that You are in control—
that You have power over everything. So why do I go back and forth
in worry? Why can't I let go of my fears permanently?*

The Judge said the contract was sound, that it was a great
opportunity for her. Even if James was the one who set it up.

She shook her head and pushed the doubts away. Only to
have her mind turned to Parker. The local newspaper kept
touting him as a hero for rescuing Emily and praising him for
his work on the stage. Apparently, Parker could do no wrong.

Her heart wanted to agree. Wanted to latch onto this new
love for him and follow it wherever it led.

But Dad needed her here, and she needed him.

Emily needed stability.

But she also needed a father.

Johanna shook her head. If she was supposed to remarry,
God would bring the right man at the right time.

She had worked herself to the bone every waking moment
making designs to send to Sears and here at the shop making
hats for the wedding and everyone going to the theater. Then
there were the theater costumes to contend with. Along with
the mending, the director had decided he wanted a trio of new
costumes for one of the scenes in *Uncle Tom's Cabin*. There
was still plenty of time to get them made, but it was one more
thing on her ever-growing list of *things*.

Stabbing her needle through the hat she was working on,
she couldn't complain. God had provided. Dad and Mrs. Bennett had even come to the shop and helped her today. Mrs.
Bennett was talented with the sewing machine and assured
Johanna she could help with the costumes, while Dad was certain he could manage boxing the completed hats and cleaning
up the storage area of her shop. Johanna even made a small

play area for Emily, and now her sweet daughter was napping in the back.

It was all working out. They would be fine. It might take a little maneuvering, but they could make it through.

So long as Emily didn't get into any more mischief and Johanna could keep her heart from chasing after a certain brown-haired actor.

The bell over the door jangled, and she lifted her gaze.

She squashed a groan.

James.

He walked up to her and bowed—all charm and manners.

Dad stood from where he was packaging a hat for Mrs. Grisham. "Mr. St. John."

James glanced at her father, nodded, and turned back to her. "I came to see if you'd like to take a walk, Johanna."

"That is very kind of you to think of me, James, but I can't. I am swamped and want to get all caught up on these orders. As you can see, I've even asked for extra help." She motioned toward her father and Mrs. Bennett.

His smile slipped a little. "Oh, but I'm sure you could spare a few minutes. Especially since you have help. No doubt you've been at this since early this morning. Everyone needs a little break now and then." He moved toward her and offered his arm, pointing his elbow at her.

Goodness, the man did not understand the meaning of no. "James, no. I can't."

He narrowed his eyes, studying her face with an intensity that made her want to run in the opposite direction. "Come now, Johanna. There's no need for pretense here. Surely they know of our interest in one another?"

Her cheeks heated, and she coughed into her hand. "There *is* no interest, James. You are my brother-in-law and nothing more, so please do not presume upon a relationship that doesn't exist." She could feel Mrs. Bennett's gaze on her. What must the poor woman be thinking?

James didn't move.

But Dad did. He stepped closer and offered a hand toward the door. "Mr. St. John, I believe this would be a good time to leave." He said it with a smile, but Johanna saw the steel in his eyes. Surely James did too. "As Johanna pointed out, she's very busy."

Several seconds passed, and then their visitor bowed once again, said his good-byes, and left.

Thank heaven.

⁓

THURSDAY, APRIL 27, 1905

Two days later, Johanna was getting so close to completing all her hat orders that she was working in the shop in the early hours of the morning with the door locked. Whenever she came by herself, she didn't feel comfortable leaving the door open for customers anymore for fear that James would walk in again. Without her father to back her up, she could only imagine what her brother-in-law might do.

Perhaps it hadn't been smart for her to keep his threat to herself. Well, Marvella knew. Which meant the Judge probably knew. But Marvella was good at keeping a secret otherwise, and she was the only person Johanna had shared it with.

James was an unexpected problem, to be sure. He hadn't been all that active in her life right after Gerald's death, but he'd come around more and more often and now seemed so insistent. What had changed? At first she thought it might be a bit of conscience at his lack of closeness to Gerald. But in all honesty . . . she felt like James wanted to control her.

She hated it when thoughts of him surfaced. It made her uncomfortable. And there were too many happy, positive things to occupy her thoughts. She forced James from her mind.

Now what could she think about? Cora would be coming by in half an hour to talk final wedding plans. Then the wedding was tomorrow.

The wedding . . .

Parker would walk his sister down the aisle.

She let out a little sigh and stabbed her needle through a ribbon. She did love a good wedding. They always made her a bit teary. Happy couples, celebrations of love, and the way God created marriage never failed to stir her heart.

What would it be like to marry Parker Benn—?

"Stop it!" She threw down the hat she was working on, shot to her feet, and forced the question to flee. Maybe she could use another cup of coffee.

Yes, that was it.

Coffee and another treat from Marvella. The woman had been keeping them in supply. Who cared if it added an inch or two to her waist? If it helped her keep her mind off Parker, she'd eat the entire cake by herself.

13

Friday, April 28, 1905

Cora's wedding day was here!

Johanna jumped out of bed. Running to her window, she pulled back the curtain, and a huge smile lifted her lips. The sun was shining with warm rays of butter yellow stretching into the sky. *Thank You for giving my dearest friend a gorgeous day to get married.*

After a few moments, she turned from the pretty scene and took a deep breath. It was going to be a long day. There was so much to do.

She fed Dad and Em breakfast, got herself dressed, then helped Emily into her flower girl dress and fixed her hair. They were in the wagon headed across town to the orchard by 8:00 a.m.

Hopefully Dad could keep Em occupied and clean until the ceremony started at 9:30. *Clean* being the part Johanna most worried about.

When they pulled up to the orchard, a man directed them where to park their wagon. Everything seemed to be organized to a T.

William's family was well-to-do and had wanted to take

over the whole wedding and hold it at the largest church in town, but Cora pushed back a bit and offered them an interesting compromise.

Since the majority of the town would want to be at the wedding, and the only place large enough was the opera house—which was occupied—she suggested an outdoor wedding at the orchard.

The owners had been delighted and said they could easily accommodate a wedding party.

And since the cherry trees had started to blossom early this year from all the warmth and sunshine, the timing couldn't have been more perfect.

Chairs had been brought in from all over town. Tables were set up under canopies for the reception to follow.

William's father had spared no expense for the wedding as he was determined to give his only son a special day to remember, and he adored Cora. A string quartet would start playing at 9 a.m. to entertain the guests and was scheduled to play the entire day. Johanna couldn't imagine playing the piano all day for something like this. Hopefully those poor musicians would get a break at some point.

"All right, Emily. I need you to behave yourself and stay still and clean until the ceremony, all right?"

"Yes, Mama."

"Did you bring the books to read to her?" She eyed her father.

"You packed them yourself, Jo. They're in the back."

That's right. She laughed at herself. They would be fine. Today was a day to celebrate, not get all wound up in knots. "Okay. Sorry to hover. You two have fun."

"But not too much fun." Emily had a very serious face. "'Cause I gotta stay clean."

Johanna stifled a laugh. With a kiss to the toddler's cheek, she walked away thanking God for her sweet daughter and the joy she brought to her life every day.

A large tent had been set up for the bride and her wedding party. Johanna made her way there and nearly ran over Mrs. Bennett as she came out.

"Oh, good, you're here, Johanna. Cora is a nervous wreck, and I know having you close will calm her. I seem to make things worse."

"No, you don't." Johanna took hold of the woman's arm and gave her a squeeze. "I think, however, she's probably concerned about you wearing yourself out today."

Mrs. Bennet twisted the hankie in her hands again and again. "I hadn't thought of it that way. You may be right. Cora is always worrying about me overdoing it."

She gave the older woman a smile, placing her hand over Mrs. Bennett's, asking the Lord to soothe the fretting mother. "She loves you a great deal. And I'm sure she's feeling pre-wedding nerves. I remember feeling that way before I married Gerald. I was overjoyed, yet I am sure I snapped at my mother and Cora more than once, wanting everything to be perfect. I'm thankful they were so understanding." She chuckled.

"Mr. Bennett and I were so poor when we got married, it was the two of us, our families, and the pastor." Her gaze was fixed on something far away as she spoke. "I'm pleased that William was able to pay for the wedding of Cora's dreams. It makes me happy to see her happy." She sighed and patted Johanna's hand. "But I think at the moment, my girl needs her dearest friend."

Johanna slipped her arms around Mrs. Bennett, relishing in the warmth and softness of the woman's embrace. "I'll help her dress, and soon enough we'll have her married."

"Thank you, Johanna. I'll see to our guests." A smile warmed Mrs. Bennet's wrinkled face. "It's a perfect day, isn't it?"

"It is." Johanna couldn't help but smile as the woman walked toward the pastor. One problem solved, now for Cora.

Johanna found her in a dressing gown, working to pin up her hair. Without a word she put her things aside and went to take over the task. Cora gave her a grateful smile.

"I can't seem to do anything right this morning. I heard what you said to my mother, and I think you're right. I'm worried about her exhausting herself and about things running smoothly."

"As you told me the other day, rest in the Lord. Everything has come together perfectly. The ladies of the church have the wedding breakfast ready, and the pastor has the ceremony under his faithful watch. Now all we have to do is finish your hair and get you into your gown."

Cora nodded, causing Johanna to nearly drop the pin she was using to secure a final curl.

"Sit still a moment longer. We're nearly done." Johanna hurried to finish the task and then stood back. "You look beautiful, and once your veil is in place, it will be perfect."

Johanna went to where the wedding gown hung. "This is such a beautiful dress." The style would show off her friend's tiny waist with all the layers in the skirt and the puffed sleeves. The cut of the satin bodice was modest and lovely, trimmed with lace that stretched up to Cora's neck.

Cora came to stand beside Johanna. "It's everything I hoped it would be. The beadwork and lace are so delicate."

"Well, let's get it on you." Johanna carefully removed the gown from its hanger and waited for Cora to undress. The gown quickly replaced the robe, and Johanna worked to secure the covered buttons up the back. "If you're like I was on my wedding day, then you're probably in a daze. I want to say that no matter what happens today, the Lord has orchestrated your life and brought you to this point. He will faithfully walk with you every step of the way."

"Thank you, my friend." Cora toyed with the large puffed sleeves, readjusting the bands of lace that edged them above the elbow.

If Johanna could take her own advice, she might be calm enough to get through this day as well.

But in truth, the thought of seeing Parker walk Cora down the aisle was making her stomach tumble over itself. She whispered a prayer and finished up the buttons. She stood back and smiled.

"Cora, you're beautiful. Let's affix the veil, and then you'll be ready."

An hour later, she sat with Cora on a pristine bench the owners had brought out for them. Johanna's gaze darted around, her lip between her teeth. A breath eased from her when she spotted Dad and Emily walking toward them, his suit pressed and her daughter's dress looking spotless. She turned to Cora. "Are you ready, my friend?"

"Yes."

Cora took Johanna's hands. "I remember saying the same thing to you when you married Gerald. I'm so happy that God gave you the love you had with him. Even if it was for a short time. Thank you for being such a beautiful example to me all these years."

She would *not* cry. Not even happy tears. But she tucked Cora's sweet words away in her heart. "I love you, dearest, and wish you the happiest of days and a lifetime of love." Johanna squeezed her friend's hands.

The string quartet had been playing for half an hour already. It stopped.

"That's our cue." Cora stood, eyebrows raised, smile reaching her ears. "It's time."

The music started up again playing the song that Johanna was supposed to walk to. She leaned in and kissed Cora's cheek. "I guess I'll see you up there." When she turned, she bumped smack-dab into Parker's chest. "Oh."

His hand grasped her arm to keep her from falling. "Sorry about that. I wasn't trying to sneak up on you, but this grass must have muffled my steps." His words were warm and soft as he released her.

Johanna lifted her gaze to his. Big mistake. She felt her entire body begin to tremble. He was so handsome in his dark suit. For a moment she wasn't even sure she could draw breath. Why did he have to affect her this way?

"You . . . ah . . . take good care of her." Johanna turned around and took a deep breath. Gracious.

As she walked down the white silk-lined aisle between the chairs, Johanna couldn't help but think of her wedding to Gerald. It had been such a glorious day.

She reached her spot at the front and turned to watch. It was Emily's turn. Dad leaned down and whispered something in her ear and then pointed her down the aisle. Hopefully her little girl would remember the directions.

"Walk to your Mama and throw the petals on the ground as you go." Mrs. Bennett had rehearsed with Em over and over.

Now, as her big girl walked toward her, flinging petals left and right, the crowd giggled. Which only made her toss them higher, and then she started skipping. At least she stayed on the white-cloth path, but Johanna held her breath until she could safely take her child's hand.

Whew. They made it through.

The string quartet began a new song, and Parker appeared at the back with Cora on his arm.

His gaze connected with hers, and she couldn't pull her eyes away. He'd always been able to draw her like a magnet.

"Mama"—Em's whisper-shout broke the connection—"are we almost done?"

A few people in the front seats covered their mirth.

Johanna leaned down. "Look, Grandpa is right over there. In a few minutes, you can go sit with him."

"'Kay." She squirmed and shifted from foot to foot.

Parker handed Cora off to William and walked in her direction.

Without hesitation, Emily lunged at him and practically jumped into his arms.

It was a good thing Parker was quick on his feet, because he caught the frilly little girl in midair.

The pastor was saying something, and Johanna leaned closer to Parker. "Nice catch. She can go sit with her grandpa."

At that moment, the pastor announced that Cora's brother was going to sing a special song for the wedding couple.

Parker headed toward Dad with Emily on his hip. When Parker handed Em over, she started crying at the top of her lungs. "I wanna stay with Pawker!"

The crowd had a hard time covering their laughter this time. Heat filled Johanna's neck and face, but she swallowed hard and nodded at Parker.

He walked over in front of the string quartet holding Emily, who now looked like a perfect angel.

The cello and violin began to play first, and then the bass and viola joined in. Whatever it was sounded familiar, but she couldn't place it.

Then Parker began to sing. And her heart dropped to her toes.

The song he'd written for *her*.

> My heart belongs to you.
> I will always be true.
> May the Lord in heaven above
> Always bless our love.

Cora could have at least warned her about this. Goodness. Johanna fought back the tears and kept her eyes low as she tried to drown out the sound. She hadn't heard or thought of this song since the last time Parker had sung it to her.

She couldn't blame her friend for choosing it. It was lovely. But oh, if she wasn't the matron of honor, she'd run out right now.

Parker's voice washed over her. It held more depth than ever, and the youthful voice of ten years ago had matured into a heart-melting baritone.

She couldn't stop listening. Couldn't keep the words from repeating over and over in her heart.

And then the song was over, but it kept playing in her mind. As she watched Parker sit down with her daughter in his arms, more than anything she wanted to tell him that she loved him.

But she couldn't.

Because he would be leaving. And she couldn't go with him.

Holding Emily in his arms as he sang for Cora's wedding made him prouder than he'd ever felt. That little girl had held a piece of his heart since he met her. And when she unabashedly told the whole wedding party that she wanted to stay with him, he'd lost the rest of his heart completely.

Something in him had been reborn in that moment. The need to protect. The need to hold her trust and never betray it. The need to be there for her as she grew up.

How she'd wrapped him so quickly around her little finger he had no idea, but if this was what being a father felt like . . . he'd missed out.

Then there was Johanna.

His heart would always belong to her. Even after all the years away. As he sang the words he'd written for her, he meant them. Even more than he had ten years ago. The love he felt now was a new love. A deeper one.

Cora always loved the song, and it wasn't a shock that she asked him to sing it for her wedding, but singing it with Johanna right there . . . it almost choked him up. She was lovely in her green dress, her red hair piled atop her head. But it was the way she dipped her head when he started to sing that almost undid him.

It was *their* song. Most people in the crowd wouldn't know that. But she did.

As he took a seat next to Johanna's father, Emily cuddled into his lap and rested her head on his chest. The rambunctious little girl wiggled until she was comfortable, then placed her hand on top of his.

Oh, what he wouldn't give to have a family. But not just with anyone. With Johanna and Emily.

He could never replace Gerald in Jo's heart. He knew that. But he longed for her to open up her heart to him once again.

The plan he'd been mulling over now cemented into place in his heart and mind. He would let Alfred go and wouldn't replace him. There was no need for a manager any longer.

He'd fulfill his contract for the performances here and then stay here when the rest of the troupe left Kalispell.

Which meant he had a couple weeks to find a job that could support a family. He had some money saved up, and that might buy them a house of their own, but he needed to think long-term. Jo and Emily deserved the best he could give.

If he had to give up acting altogether, he'd do it. They were worth it. Leaving behind the fame, the cutthroat business, all the newspaper articles and fans . . . that would be easy. That wasn't why he did what he did anyway.

He glanced down at the sleeping girl in his arms. Maybe he hadn't been called to be a preacher like Johanna had hoped, but God was calling him to *them* now. He knew it in the very depths of his soul.

The question was . . . would she hear it as well?

14

Marvella leaned over to her husband. "Thank you, dear, for helping Johanna with those contracts." It hadn't slipped her notice that the Judge's lips had lifted in a smile underneath that bushy mustache during the song that Parker sang. The man had a soft spot for young couples in love.

And as much as he teased her about her matchmaking, he was just as involved as she was. He was merely more subtle.

He squeezed her hand and winked. "I see what you're up to, Mrs. Ashbury."

She feigned a look of innocence. "What would that be, my love?"

"You're intent on seeing Parker and Johanna together again." His whisper was close to her ear.

This man could always read her like a book. Even when she thought she was being clever. Which she was, most of the time. Even if he couldn't admit it. "Would that be so wrong?"

"No. But tread carefully, my dear. There's a lot of loss between those two." He sat up straight again as the pastor announced the newly married couple.

Everyone stood and applauded. As the clapping began

to die down, Marvella tugged on her husband's sleeve. "You keep your eye on that brother-in-law of hers. I don't trust him, and she may need you to protect her." The new couple dashed past them as cheers and hearty congratulations were thrown out.

His face hardened a bit as the onlookers began to follow the newlyweds to the reception. "He's already under my scrutiny, rest assured. Something about that man is off. At first I thought it was the grief of losing his brother, but there's something else going on with him."

"I'm glad you agree. I was worried I would have to use my superior investigative skills to show you that he shouldn't be trusted."

The Judge laughed. "No need, my dear. This has been troubling me for several months."

"Months?" She placed a hand on her hip.

"Yes, dear. Shocking, I know, that I haven't shared this with you, but I needed more information. After Johanna brought you into the conversation, I was already convinced to keep my eye on him." He held out his arm for her, and she placed her hand inside the crook of his elbow.

Excellent. She could take that item off her to-do list and focus on more important things. "Well, then. I will simply turn my attention to the couple."

"That is a splendid idea." He tipped his head toward Mrs. Bennett. "You should recruit her into your scheme."

"It's not a *scheme*." But as she glanced at Grace, she liked her husband's idea. "She does seem to be agreeable to the idea, doesn't she?"

"I would say so." He quirked an eyebrow up. "Look at how she's doting all over Emily in her son's arms."

A hundred new ideas formed in her mind. This was perfect.

Parker might be king of the stage, but he was about to fall into the matchmaking plan of the queen of hearts.

And Marvella never lost.

⁂

Landry's father had invited James to the wedding, and it was a beautiful affair.

If one liked weddings.

As he tromped through the grass, he nodded and smiled at several groups of people, all dressed in their best wedding finery. But no one stopped him to talk. Asked him if he wanted refreshment. Offered him a slice of cake.

It was a bit offensive.

Before the theatre troupe had come to town, there had been talk of James running for mayor. But now? Not a soul mentioned it. Everyone was talking about either the wedding or the shows and the opera house and the phenomenal star . . .

Parker Bennett.

Just thinking about that stupid actor and his stupid love song made James want to vomit. He'd watched Johanna. The insipid smile on her face made his stomach roll. Even her daughter clung to the man like he'd hung the moon himself. James's chest burned.

Nothing was going as planned.

Even Yvette, though biddable, thought she could manipulate James with her pouts and tears. Idiot woman. He saw right through her. If she stuck to their plan, which she'd better, he would be done with her soon.

But Johanna . . .

He needed to separate her from that Bennett fellow. She belonged to *him*. And not even Mr. Wonderful Bennett was allowed to get in the way of what belonged to James.

The seed was planted. Eventually it would come to fruition. And if Parker decided to get too close, James would simply re-iterate to Johanna his threat to take the little brat. He'd already drawn up the paperwork. Not that he could get Judge Ashbury to sign off on it. He'd have to go back to New York for that.

But Johanna didn't know that. The threat of losing her daughter should be enough incentive to push her in his di-rection.

The sharp pain in his head took that moment to rear its ugly head. He put a hand to his brow. Perhaps he needed to sit down.

But then as quickly as it had come, it dissipated.

When he looked up, Judge Ashbury was walking toward him. His stomach dropped. As if this day couldn't get any worse.

"Mr. St. John. Good to see you here at the wedding."

"Good morning, Judge."

"Are you here at the request of the bride or the groom?" The Judge sipped punch out of a crystal cup.

"The groom. William's father had me handle some things for him last year."

Emily squealed from the lawn where she was holding Park-er's hand in one, her mother's hand in the other, and pulled them into a circle.

He couldn't restrain a frown.

"They make a charming couple, don't they?" The Judge took another sip.

What? "Who?"

"Parker and Johanna. It must be good for you to see your brother's widow coming out of her grief. It's been such a dif-ficult time for her."

He ground his teeth together. No, they *didn't* make a charming couple. When he looked at the Judge, he started. Was that a warning in the older man's eyes? James lifted his chin. "I'm not sure my brother would approve of his daughter and wife being exposed to the wild and incorrigible life of an actor and theatre troupe." He raised his eyebrows.

The Judge didn't look away. He didn't soften his expression. He simply studied James. "Since your brother is in the Lord's presence, I doubt he's concerned. He knows—even better than we do—that God is in control."

James huffed a laugh. Of course. It always came back to God for these people. "Well, *I'm* not in the Lord's presence. I'm here. And I'm in control, Judge Ashbury. That is my brother's family, and I intend to do whatever is necessary to keep them from the likes of Parker Bennett."

Let the old man chew on that!

James marched over to the lawn where Johanna, Emily, and Parker still went around in a circle. Pasting on his nicey-nice face, he called out, "Johanna. Might I have a word?"

Her vibrant, joyous face fell a bit. She released Parker's hand. "Would you watch Em for a moment?" Then she turned toward James. Her face fully transformed into a frown. "What do you need, James?" Her voice was low without an ounce of friendliness.

"I've told you what I want, Johanna." He kept his face serene and smiling in case others were watching. "Gerald would not approve of you flaunting yourself here at the wedding. You need to come with me now." He held out his hand for her.

She pulled back as if his hand were a venomous snake. "*Flaunting* myself?" Shaking her head, she stepped back an inch. "I'm not going anywhere with you. And I'm appalled that you would say such a thing. Now before I call for help, I think you should leave."

He scanned the people around them. No one was watching. Except for Parker. James reached for her arm. It was time she learned her place.

But she pulled away before he could get a grip. "I will scream, James. And I don't think you want all your rich clients to see that."

Parker was at her side immediately, Emily in his arms. "Anything I can help with?"

"No." She sent him a look. "Take Em to see your mother. Please?"

The actor narrowed his gaze but walked away as asked.

She turned back to him, the look in her eyes pure rage. "Leave, James. Now."

Fine. Let her think she won. "This isn't over, Johanna."

The hint of alarm in her eyes before he turned and walked away made him smile.

Score one for me.

His gaze was fixed to Johanna as she made her way through the crowd holding hands with Emily. Parker could hardly stand still. More than anything, he wanted to be beside her again, but her conversation with her brother-in-law had made her distant. Should he should pry and ask her if she wanted to talk about it?

Did he even deserve to have a place in her life anymore?

He wanted it. And more than a place in her life—he wanted to marry her. Would she be willing?

"Son"—Daniel Easton's voice behind him made him jump— "are you going to stand there and let her get away for a second time?"

Parker shook his head. "What?"

"I think you heard me." Johanna's father laughed. "I've been watching you watch my daughter and granddaughter for the past thirty minutes. I've seen how you care for them. And not only my daughter, but Emily too."

With a swallow, Parker gave a slight nod. "I do."

"In case you're wondering? I approve. I approved back then. I approve now."

"But . . . I'm not a preacher."

Daniel stepped up from standing beside Parker to stand in front of him. "Look, you know as well as I that God is in control. I believe that He is the one who guided you and my daughter together. I also believe that He was guiding my daughter when she told you no, and when she married Gerald." He placed a firm hand on Parker's shoulder, giving it an encouraging squeeze. "Even though I don't understand how He orchestrates His master plan, I see His handiwork in everything that has happened. Look at how He's used you on the stage. Son, you have serious talent. And look at how He brought Emily into our family. Again, God is gracious and good and in control. So . . . I'm going to ask you one more time. Are you going to let her get away?"

Parker chuckled at the look on Daniel's face. "If I didn't know better, I'd say you were competing with Marvella's matchmaking. Isn't she the one who likes to put people together in this town?"

Daniel searched the crowd and pointed. "That's a great idea, I'll team up with her." He let go of Parker and made like he was going to head that direction.

Parker put a hand on Daniel's chest and laughed even harder. "All right, you made your point. I'm not going to let her get away. I do love your daughter and Em. But there are a few things that I need to figure out and fast if I'm going to make this a reality. Please don't say anything to her yet."

Daniel leaned in. "You're quitting the theatre troupe, aren't you?"

Parker nodded. "Yes. But please keep that a secret until I make it public."

"My lips are sealed."

"I do have a request for you, though."

Johanna's father stepped a bit closer. "Anything. What do you need, son?"

"Will you be praying for me—for us? One of my biggest failings was getting so busy and caught up in my life that I became lukewarm as a believer, and I never want to do that again."

Daniel reached forward and put a fatherly arm around Parker. "Why don't we pray right now?"

They bowed their heads, but a commotion interrupted Daniel's prayer.

"There's a fire downtown! We need all able-bodied men and women to help!"

15

Her beautiful green bridesmaid dress was now covered in soot and water. Johanna wanted to cry, but tears wouldn't come.

It seemed the entire town had come out to save the block from the fire. But her millinery shop was gone. All the materials, all the hats that hadn't been picked up yet. Gone.

Judge Ashbury had encouraged her to get insurance. She hoped it covered fires. If it didn't, what was she going to do?

All the designs for the hats for her contract with Sears were at home. But she hadn't sent any of them in yet. Sears would have to manufacture them, then sell them. How soon could she anticipate income from that?

Probably not for months.

Until then . . . what would happen?

Dad had taken Emily home, but Johanna refused to leave until the fire was out. And it was now. But even in the dark of night, she could see the devastation. It was all gone.

Thankfully, no one was hurt. And they'd managed to save two of the other shops on her block. But it still hurt.

Deeper than she could have imagined.

She had to shoulder all of this on her own. Providing for her child, her father, herself.

Mindless of proprieties, she plopped down on the boardwalk across the street from her dream store and stared.

Firemen picked through debris, making sure there were no more embers. Other shop owners dealt with the loss too. Spectators began to disperse.

And still she sat.

Footsteps sounded beside her, and she braced herself. If James had come to gloat or tell her that her best plan was to marry him, she might punch him in the nose.

"Hi."

She looked up at the warm voice beside her. Parker. Thank heaven. "Hi."

And then she burst into tears.

He sat down and wrapped an arm around her shoulders. "I can't believe you're still here, Jo." The use of her nickname seemed so right on his lips. It had been far too long since she'd heard it. "You should be at home, resting."

She pulled back a bit and pointed to him. "Like you're one to talk! You helped with the fire, then raced to the opera house to do your show, then came back. I can't believe you're not dead on your feet!"

"In a good community like Kalispell, everyone pitches in, right?"

With a nod, she looked back to her shop. The tears still slipping down her cheeks. "I can't believe it's gone."

He didn't say anything. Didn't try to give her false words of hope. He let her grieve as he held her. When the worst of her tears had passed, he gave her a tight hug.

She sniffed. "I only had the shop because Gerald insisted on having life insurance. I thought it was silly and expensive, but then he died, and I thanked God for Gerald's forethought. It's the only reason I was able to buy the shop."

"Seems like a good investment."

She shook her head.

"It did seem so at the time, but maybe I should have put the money in the bank or invested it. I did seek counsel before I bought it. Judge Ashbury was so good to guide me and help me find the right place. He insisted I purchase insurance on the business, so I'm hopeful that I will be able to get some money back." Tears blurred her vision once again. "But it's never been about the money. It was more . . . it's as if Gerald provided for Emily and me, and now that's gone. I don't know what I'll do to provide for Em and Dad in the future. James arranged a contract for me to design hats for Sears, so I suppose I have that."

Her voice broke a bit, and she sniffed back tears. "I don't even know what happened. How did the fire start? Was it bad wiring? I don't remember there being anything left on to cause this. I always shut the iron and lights off."

"Jo, this isn't doing you any good. You can make guesses all day long, but in the long run you'll have to wait until the fire chief investigates. They're good at figuring things out." He paused for a long moment, then added, "Besides, even when you know what happened, it won't take away the fact that it's all gone. I'm so very sorry."

She regained control of her emotions. There was no sense sitting on the street crying. That part of her life was done. "I'm sorry that I'm such a mess. I know that God is still in control. Whatever His reason for allowing this to happen, I trust Him."

"Trusting in Him won't ever let you down." He smiled as she looked his way. "God will never leave us or forsake us. We can count on that. I don't know why this happened, but I do know that He has already made provision for your future."

Oh, to be able to believe that right now. "I know in my head you're right, but my heart is still heavy and worried."

"It's been a long day. Why don't I walk you home?" He stood and then pulled her to her feet.

She didn't argue and held onto his arm for the long walk home.

Parker talked about the show that night and his excitement to get to share *Everyman* with people next week. Then he talked about Emily and her cute stories she'd shared with him at the wedding.

"Emily charmed everyone around her, including Mrs. Ashbury. The sweet woman asked Emily if she thought she'd like to get married one day, and she replied that she'd rather have a dog."

Johanna couldn't help but laugh. "I'm sure there are probably women who would agree with her."

Parker chuckled. "I'm sure there are men who feel the same. Without the right person, a dog would be better company."

"And the cleanup might actually be less." Johanna looked at Parker in the streetlight and laughed. "For all his good and positive aspects, Gerald was a messy person. If he saw a cleared space, it was as if he thought it his duty to put something there. I'm not sure what he had against clean spaces, but apparently they begged for a book or newspaper or whatever else was at hand."

"Cora told me he was a good man to you."

"He was." Even as she spoke the words, she caught her breath. It didn't hurt to share this with Parker. "He was quiet and a deep thinker. There were times we spent entire evenings in silence."

"I can't imagine that. I always feel like I have so much to say to you."

She looked away. Strangely enough, she felt the same. There were at least a dozen things she wanted to say to Parker.

"I'm glad he was good to you. When Cora told me you were getting married . . . well . . . I thought maybe you were settling. That it wasn't really love."

"There was plenty of love." Her voice was a whisper. "It was different with Gerald than it had been . . . with you. But then . . . I was older and had a different view on life."

"And now?"

What was he asking her? Given all that had happened, Johanna wasn't sure she even wanted to know.

She stumbled, and Parker tightened his hold. "Easy there."

Her strength was giving way. At least she wouldn't have to go into the shop tomorrow. Maybe the day had worn Emily out as much as it had her. Maybe she'd sleep late. Maybe they could both sleep late.

By the time they reached her home, she realized she hadn't said anything in response to Parker's question. It was just as well. She wasn't sure she had an answer. Instead, she focused on putting one foot in front of the other. Exhaustion overtook her as they headed up the walk to the front steps, and she couldn't go on any longer, but words wouldn't come.

She felt her body collapsing, and there wasn't a thing she could do about it.

Strong arms swept her up. "I've got you." Parker whispered the warm, comforting words in her ear, and she closed her eyes and let the darkness descend.

SUNDAY, APRIL 30, 1905

James hadn't even heard the sermon that morning. He had gone to church certain that Johanna would seek him out. Perhaps burst into tears as she told him about the loss of her shop and how much she needed him.

Instead, upon his arrival he found her actually smiling and in the company of that wretched actor.

Why wasn't she devastated? Why was she walking with Parker? Her hand was even in the crook of his arm. Again. Not only that, but the actor was carrying Emily.

This was *not* how things were supposed to go. Not after the accident with the gate. Not after the fire.

James had slipped away during the benediction, desperate to rethink what was to be done. What more could he do? What would be the most effective?

He only began to think clearly again when he was safely home. He took to his office, and a plan came to mind. He rang for the housekeeper, then scrawled a note.

Mrs. Simpson looked less than happy to have to find a boy to deliver it, but James didn't care. The old biddy could take it herself if she wanted to be difficult about it.

He leaned back in his chair and closed his eyes.

The throbbing pain behind his left eye started up again, and he clutched his head. Fool headaches. If he and Johanna were married, she could massage his head for him. Of course, that brat of hers made enough noise to bring down the house. He would situate the nursery on the top floor in the New York house. The rowdy creature could remain in the nursery with her nanny. Johanna might not approve at first, but in time he would bend her will to his.

A tap on his door forced him to open his eyes. He drew a deep breath and struggled to his feet. Had they found him? He licked his lips. Good grief, the door handle was turning. "What do you want?"

Yvette sauntered in and shut the door behind her. No wig this time and very little makeup. "You sent for me?" Hands on her hips, she studied him.

"Don't be impudent."

"You don't look so good."

"You look less than perfect yourself."

She scowled in a most unbecoming fashion. "I just awoke. I had no time to groom myself, and my maid was busy elsewhere." Her eyes narrowed. "But you . . . you've obviously been up and dressed for some time, yet your face is ashen, and your eyes look as though they might pop from your head."

"I'm *fine*." He walked around his desk. "Now, let's get down to business. I heard about your little stunt with Parker. Well played."

"I told him I could not live without him." She smiled. She really was one of the most beautiful women he'd ever seen. If not for the money, James might as easily have imposed his will upon her rather than chase after that bore of a sister-in-law.

"That's perfect. But now I need you to follow through."

She seemed taken aback. "What do you mean?"

"I mean, if you can't live without him . . . prove it. Right now those are grandiose words. Prove the point to him."

"*Kill* myself?" She backed up a pace as James moved closer.

"Yes, my dear. At least give it a good pretense. I suggest you take poison or pills. Have your maid tend to something for

220

you . . . something that will bring her right back to find you on the floor having succumbed to your heartbreak."

"But I could die."

Her face told him she wasn't willing. Well, she would be.

"Not if you work it out right. Good grief, must I plan everything? If your maid comes right back from whatever task you send her on, she'll realize what you've done and send for the doctor. The doctor will come and pump your stomach, and you'll live to act another day. Hopefully, Bennett will see the seriousness of the matter, and since he doesn't seem inclined to be seduced by you . . . well, he can be persuaded by concern."

"It seems a bit extreme. Maybe I can pretend to have taken something."

James laughed. "You aren't that good of an actress." He went to his desk and pulled out a bottle of the pills he used for his headaches. "Here, use these. Take the entire bottle. No, take all but a few, and strategically position the empty bottle and several pills in your open hand. Be sure to lie upon the floor rather than the bed. No sense in the maid mistaking you taking a nap."

Yvette drew back, her hand pressed to her throat. "You cannot be serious."

James grinned and paced. He could see the scene in his mind. People screaming and gathering. The doctor arriving in the nick of time. Or perhaps not.

He smiled.

Either way would serve his purpose.

He pinned her with a glare. "Do whatever you have to do to get Bennett at your side. I'll take care of the rest."

"And then you'll finally leave me alone?"

Beautiful or not, she was growing tiresome.

He tilted his head to look at her. "Why*ever* would I do that?"

MONDAY, MAY 1, 1905

It was early, but Parker had no doubt that his mother had been up for an hour or two, having her quiet time with the Lord and making breakfast. He took the porch steps two at a time, then stopped short at the door. His stomach twisted, feeling like it was up in his chest rather than in his abdomen. Sweat slicked his palms, and he wiped them on his pants to dry them.

It was silly to be this nervous about talking to Mom.

But nervous he was.

He'd put off asking her about Dad's passing for too long. And now the guilt and the shame were eating at him with an intensity that made it difficult to think at times. He needed to know what his father really thought of him. Once he knew, good or bad, at least he could move forward.

Taking a deep breath, he twisted the knob and stepped into his childhood home. "Mom?"

"In the kitchen, dear!"

Parker followed the familiar path to the kitchen, where the delicious smells of bacon and toast wafted in the air.

Mom sat at the table, a steaming cup of coffee and a full breakfast plate before her. A smile lit up her face as she stood and held her arms out. "Well, good morning, son."

He stepped into her embrace, relishing the comfort only a hug from his mom could give. "It smells wonderful in here."

She let him go and turned to the stove. "Take my plate. There's plenty here. I had a feeling I'd be seeing you this morning."

Parker took a seat and tugged Mom's plate toward him. "You did? Why is that?"

She took a moment, filling a second plate with breakfast, and sat down next to him. "Say grace, Parker. And then I'll tell you."

He prayed over the meal, then dug into it.

"I knew you'd come here because big events always stirred you up in a big way." Mom smiled at him. "You have such deep feelings, and those emotions usually get all tangled after events—happy or sad."

He took a long sip of his coffee, contemplating her words. It was both comforting and disconcerting to be so understood. "I appreciate that you've never been afraid of my big emotions."

Mom chuckled. "Never. Although . . ."

He felt her gaze burn the side of his face.

"I think today *you* are afraid of them."

Leave it to her to cut to the heart of the matter. The bite of eggs and bacon he'd taken tasted like dirt. He swallowed and pushed his plate away. Where did he begin? Words and feelings tossed about like waves inside him, but it was as if his throat had a big fat cork in it. What would his fellow actors say if they could see him now? Parker Bennett unable to utter a single word before an audience of one.

A warm hand covered his, and he glanced up. Mom's face was serious but soft, her brows drawn together over her dark brown eyes. "It's all right, son. Tell me."

Her tenderness was his undoing. "I need to know if Dad was disappointed in me." His eyes dampened with tears.

She looked at him for a moment and then smiled. "Oh, Parker, of course he wasn't." She scooted her chair closer to him. She rubbed his back and let out a long sigh.

"It was a stupid thing to ask." He wiped at his face with his napkin. "I know he was . . . disappointed that I didn't follow in his footsteps and become a preacher. But what about the path I did choose? Did he go to his grave hating what his son did, what he became?" The more he spoke, the easier it was to confess the burden he'd been carrying for years.

Mom made a humming sound. It was the same sound she made when Dad would ask her about one of his sermons or her thoughts on a book they were reading together. Nine times out of ten, wisdom was soon to follow.

"Your father was as proud of you as any man can be of his son. There was never any doubt in his mind that you were following God's plan for your life. Did he struggle with what that looked like for a time?" She let out a light laugh. "Of course. We all do when the Lord steps in and shows that our plans and His don't match. But that didn't mean for one second he wasn't proud of you."

Parker let the words sink in, clinging to the truth in them, asking the Lord to help him hear what she was saying. That the truth would cut through the lies he'd let himself believe.

"I know it was difficult for you to be in Europe when he passed. It happened so fast I could hardly take it all in. But I think it was actually an act of grace on the Lord's part to keep you away when He took your father home."

Parker's head shot up. "An act of *grace*?" How could she say that? It had been the single most devastating moment of his life. The pain of not being with her and Cora, of not being able to say good-bye, haunted him.

"Yes. Because I think if you had come home when Dad died, you would have left what you were doing." She pulled her hand away from his back and picked up her coffee cup, took a sip, then continued. "It would have been premature. Jesus had things He wanted to teach you, and as hard as it was to be apart, I was always at peace that He kept you from coming home."

"Well, *I* haven't had that peace." He rubbed his face with his hands.

"I know."

The words hung between them, and Parker let out a long breath. "Did Dad say anything about me before he . . . he passed away?"

Mom put her coffee cup down. "Wait right here."

She left the kitchen and was back a moment later, a thin, white envelope in her hands. She put it in front of him and patted his cheek. "He wanted you to have this as soon as you got home. But I knew it needed to wait until you were ready. We didn't exactly start off on the right foot because of all those lies in the newspaper. That riled me up, and I'm sorry about that, son. Now you read this, and I'll be in the living room when you're ready to talk a bit more." She pressed a kiss to his head, much like she had when he was little, then left.

Parker nodded and picked up the envelope. Studied his name written in Dad's thick scrawl. He tapped it against his palm once, twice, then without overthinking it a second longer, tore it open, took out the letter, and began to read.

Dear son,

I miss you. I don't say that to make you feel bad for walking down the path the Lord put before you. I say it because it's true. Your presence around town, in our house and church and lives, is sorely missed.

But I can't tell you how proud I am knowing you are out using the boldness and love God has put in your heart to share His story with a hurting world. Though it is not the path I thought you would take, I have assurance from the Lord it is the path He has put you on. And I know you are bringing Him glory.

I also know that the life you're living has many temptations and will bring many doubts your way. Never forget the day you gave your life to Jesus, when you made a promise to follow Him and His word, no matter what. He will help you and guide you, and I have no doubt you will listen to Him. Seek Him with all your heart, and He will direct your paths. Rest in His love. Be confident in His mercy. Rejoice in His forgiveness. Be thankful for His grace.

There isn't a day that goes by that I don't pray for you and love you, my dear son.

Always,
Dad

Parker's shoulders shook with deep, heavy sobs. His dad's words, the truth that rang in them, covered him. Seeped into him.

His father had never stopped loving him. All the fear and insecurity that had filled Parker's mind for so long slipped away.

Thank You, Jesus.

After a few minutes, he wiped his face, folded the letter back up, and put it in the envelope. Tucking it in his back pocket, he went in search of Mom.

She was in her favorite chair, a small sock hanging from a crochet hook.

"Thank you." He sank into the comfortable couch. "That letter . . . Dad always had a way with words. It's what made his sermons so powerful."

Mom nodded as she finished a stitch. She put her work to the side and smiled at him. "Feel better?"

"I do. Dad answered so many questions for me. It's a comfort to know he was proud of me."

"He was. We all were. Gracious, Cora and I still *are*. Parker, wrestling with the Lord and His word doesn't mean that you've failed. It means you want to know His will. That you are choosing Him over yourself. That is never easy."

He leaned his head back against the cushion and let out a chuckle. "I feel like I've been wrestling with the Lord for a lifetime."

"Don't we all?"

"After Dad died, my fear that I had disappointed him . . . It clouded any confidence I had in what the Lord called me to do." He lifted his head and looked at Mom. "But coming home, I've gained so much clarity about what I need to do next. And Dad's letter was the cherry on top."

Mom studied his face for a long moment. "You are a good man, my son. And I'm not surprised to hear that the Lord has given you some wisdom about what He has next for you."

Parker nodded. He had wanted God's leading before, but on his terms. Now he knew better. "Thank you for always being here for me, Mom. I hope you know how much I love you."

"And I love you, my dear son. But now, I think you have things to do."

"You always know . . . sometimes even before I do."

"It's a mother's job to stay two steps ahead of her children." She laughed. "Although now that you're grown, I believe I've earned the right to resign."

He got up and kissed the top of her head. "Maybe rest from that now. Then one day you can take it up again with your grandchildren."

That afternoon, Parker went to see his manager. Alfred had returned to Kalispell with the movie man, Louis Delecort, in tow. Parker didn't care, but some of the others were bubbling over with excitement, including Yvette.

"Oh, Parker, isn't it *merveilleux*? We will soon be able to perform for Mr. Delecort. They say he is a positive genius."

"I hope it works well for you, Yvette." He moved past her on his way to the small room Alfred had taken for his office. Over half of the troupe called the man their agent, so it behooved Alfred to keep in close contact.

"Parker, don't go." Yvette put her hand on his arm and pulled him away from the others. "I haven't seen very much of you and long for your affection."

He frowned. "I have no affection to offer you, Yvette."

She gave a pout and widened her eyes. She would be so good on the screen, where facial expressions were more important than fluid body movements. "Parker, you know that I love you. We are, I am sure, destined to be together. Everyone thinks so. We work so well and look so beautiful together."

He blew out a long breath. Her obsession with aesthetics was exhausting. *Give me patience, Lord.* "We may look great playing roles together, but that's all it is. An act. I have no feelings for you."

She pressed herself against him and encircled him with her arms. "That cannot be true. I know you care for me. I've seen it in your eyes. You want me as much as I want you."

He jerked back, prying her off him and taking a step back. Jaw clenched, he tried his hardest to sound firm, not disgusted. "No, Yvette. I do *not* want you. You may have conquests all over the world, but I am not one of them." He winced. Her lilac fragrance assailed his senses. As soon as he said his piece, he was going to the hotel to change. But first, he was going to ensure Yvette had no doubts about his feelings for her.

"The woman I desire is one of substance . . . one who loves

God first and foremost. She is honorable in every way and determined to serve others first. You, on the other hand, are clearly your own biggest fan. You manipulate and scheme to get all those around you to do your bidding. I wish you only the best, but there is no future for you that includes me."

"You cannot mean such words." Tears streamed down her face.

Goodness, but the woman could cry on a moment's notice. He would feel bad had he not watched her pull the same trick hundreds of times. On stage and off.

"I am heartbroken if you say you have no love for me. You made me believe that you cared. I cannot possibly go on without you."

Parker couldn't help himself. He clapped and gave her a bow. "You play your roles so well, Yvette. It's impossible to tell where the actress ends and the real woman begins."

"I am always real with you, Parker." She tried again to take hold of him. "Without you, *je mourrais.*"

He took hold of her hands and held her back. "You will not die, Yvette. Not for me or any man. Now, if you'll excuse me, I have to see Alfred."

She jerked away, and her lips twisted into a sneer. She stomped the floor, fisting her hands on her hips. "You'll be sorry, Parker Bennett. You'll be sorry."

Enough, already.

He left her standing there and went to Alfred's office. The man was bent over a stack of papers and looked up frowning when Parker knocked on the door.

"I haven't got time for you."

Parker went to sit in a chair. "Well, I'm sorry to hear that, but you'd best *make* time, because what I have to say is going to change a great deal for you."

He had Alfred's attention now. The man leaned back in his chair. "So have you decided to leave the stage and seek moving pictures as your medium?"

Parker leaned back. "Well, I have decided to leave the stage, but I'm not yet certain what I will do instead. I will finish out my contract for Kalispell and then remain here when the troupe moves on."

Alfred's face contorted as he jumped to his feet. He hurried to close the office door and returned to his chair, shaking his head. "No doubt something happened in my absence, but, my boy, you *cannot* leave acting. The world hails you as the greatest actor alive. You must continue to serve your public."

Parker smiled. "I'm afraid not. You only say that because you make a lot of money off of me. But I've felt for some time that God was leading me elsewhere. When I came home, I finally realized what He's been telling me. I'm to remain here."

The man began to sputter. "But . . . but—you . . . See here, Parker—"

He held up his hand. "I know this comes as a surprise, but this is how it will be. I will finish the work here and be done."

"But we have a contract!"

"That I am terminating today. You are no longer my manager." Parker got to his feet. "Now, if you'll excuse me, I need to speak to George. Oh, and you might want to talk to my understudy. This will be a great opportunity for him. I believe he's more than ready to take over a leading role."

For the first time since he'd met Alfred, the man had no words. His jaw hung open, reminding Parker of a large whitefish he'd caught with his dad years ago. A smile tugged at the corners of Parker's mouth.

There was no stab of regret any longer when he remembered Dad. Only joy. And gratitude.

The Lord was so good to him.

He clapped Alfred on the shoulder and walked away whistling *It Is Well with My Soul.*

And indeed, it was.

16

Sitting at the table with her business ledgers in front of her, Johanna surveyed the loss. The fire insurance would help, but it wouldn't replace all the hours and hours of hard work. Her fingers trembled as she flipped another page.

She would not break down. Nor would she faint again like some weak-kneed female. No matter how lovely it had been to be in Parker's arms.

Oh, for heaven's sake! She pushed the thought away. Now was not the time for flights of fancy.

Dad sat across from her, drinking another cup of coffee. "Well?"

"It's not as bad as I thought." She pasted on what she hoped was an semi-encouraging grin.

"That's good. God always provides. *That* we can bank on. No matter what."

"I'm so glad we decided to keep the theatre costumes here at home. I can't imagine how we could have ever replaced them had they been consumed by the fire." She grew quiet again and stared at a landscape picture her mother had hung on the wall. A peaceful meadow with a stream meandering through the center. Cattle grazing. How she longed for the comfort that scene suggested.

Dad set his cup down with a rather loud clunk. "Jo, why don't you tell me what's really on your mind, hmm?"

Shuffling the papers in front of her, she took a moment to think through her response. Dad had been with her through thick and thin. She closed the ledger and tucked everything else inside. She met his gaze. "Losing the shop has made me think about what God is trying to tell me. I mean, I felt like I was on the right track—especially when the offer from Sears came—but what if I've been wrong? What if God called me to be a preacher's wife, and that was Gerald?" She paused.

"And?"

She scrunched up her nose. This next part was difficult. "What if . . . God is now calling me to something different? To be someone else's wife. Someone who isn't a preacher. So He allowed the things that tied me here to be taken away, because I was being stubborn and not paying attention."

"Have you been particularly stubborn and not paying attention?"

"Playing innocent doesn't become you, Dad." She groaned. "You know very well how stubborn I can be."

"That is true, but putting that aside, let's talk about what you feel like He might be calling you to."

Biting her lip, she squinted at him. "Marrying Parker."

"All right . . . and?"

He was going to make her say it, wasn't he? Lacing her fingers together over her books, she tapped her thumbs together. The Lord had done so much in her heart toward Parker's chosen vocation. She was willing to meet him halfway. Still, doubts lingered.

"My struggle is not that he's an actor—especially after

watching him on stage the other night. He's fabulous at it. But the thought of living in New York City or traveling with a troupe, like he is now . . ."

She glanced away from Dad's thoughtful gaze. He always saw too much. Seemed to know how she felt about things before she said a word, then made her put her raw emotions out there. "And then there's all the newspaper reporters following him around all the time and the crazy stories they write. I mean, seriously, the hero story they wrote about him rescuing Emily was positive and complimentary, but it was also so blown out of proportion, it was ridiculous. The negative stories are even worse. I don't think I can live like that."

Dad was quiet for a minute, an inscrutable grin on his face. "Well . . . have you talked to Parker about it?"

"Gracious, no!" She straightened. "We haven't even talked about our feelings for one another or courting or anything. Certainly not marriage. But God brought him back here, and I can't deny how I feel."

"Believe me, he can't deny how he feels either." Dad winked at her. "I'm sure the entire town sees it, no matter what those newspapermen want to write in their little columns."

Her cheeks warmed. She'd suspected that Parker was feeling like she was, but the confirmation of it, even if it was second-hand, made a world of difference. "All right. What should I do?" Getting all of this out had really helped, but she needed answers. And soon. Because Parker wasn't going to be here for long.

"Grab your Bible, Jo. Let's read together and pray and then wait for the Lord to show you His will."

Of course. Why hadn't she thought of that? She got up and went over to the fireplace to grab her Bible.

"By the way, speaking of Parker"—Dad scooted something

across the table next to her cup—"I have a little surprise for you to help take your mind off all the stressors of the past week."

"Oh?" She sat back in her chair and set her Bible on the table. She reached for the papers. Tickets? She turned them over in her hands. "What is this?" But she couldn't help a smile.

"I'm going to take my daughter out for an evening on the town, so to speak." He held up a hand. "Now don't worry about a thing. Grace—uh, Mrs. Bennett—is coming over to spend the evening with Em, and these didn't cost near as much as they say. I had a little bit set aside to do something special for you."

Jumping up from her seat, she clutched the tickets to her chest and ran over to hug her father. "Thank you."

"They're for tonight, so let's get to praying and studying. They're doing that play that made Parker famous." He reached across the table and grabbed her hand. "Father, we come to You now with a heavy weight on our hearts as we seek to follow Your will—"

A loud knocking at the door made Johanna jump.

Who on earth . . . ?

She went to the door and found the fire chief. "Yes, sir. Is everything all right?"

"Mrs. St. John, I'm sorry to have to tell you this, but we've learned the fire was set on purpose."

The words reverberated through her, like an echo in a canyon. "O-on purpose?"

"Yes, ma'am. Since this is now an arson case, we have to ask if you have any enemies."

"What? Why would you ask me that?"

"The fire was started in your millinery shop."

"My shop?"

His expression softened. "I'm afraid so. Can we step inside, Mrs. St. John?"

Johanna nodded and stepped back to allow the fire chief in the house. She led him to the living room. "Won't you sit?"

He shook his head, working his hat brim with his hands. "I'll just be a moment, ma'am." His gaze searched her face with such intensity, she almost felt compelled to admit to crimes she hadn't committed. "As I said, the fire started in your shop. It was clear to see that was the origin, and the way in which things were burned in your shop suggested an accelerant."

"Accelerant?" The word felt like marbles in her mouth. Wait. Was she hearing him right? Someone hated her enough to destroy her livelihood? She sagged down into Dad's favorite chair.

"Probably kerosene. So I have to ask again, do you have anyone who might have wanted to threaten you or . . . hurt you?"

"I can't think of anyone who would wish me harm." Wait. What about James? No. He couldn't have done this. Not to his family. But he *was* threatening her. Threatening to take Emily. Should she mention that?

What if she was wrong and she besmirched a man who was well-known and powerful? She bit her lip. "I'm sorry. I hate to mention it. But there is someone . . ."

Hours later Johanna's thoughts were still consumed with the fire chief's questions. Was it possible James had set the fire? And if not he, then who? Who would want to risk burning down all of Kalispell to hurt her? Fires were every town's nightmare. Who would do something so heinous?

The more she thought about it, the more it tormented her.

Had someone wanted to hurt her? Whoever it was had purposefully waited until the wedding, knowing she would be gone from the shop and busy all day.

Still, it *was* done during working hours. How was it that no one had seen anything?

"You need to forget about what the fire chief said and enjoy the evening." Her father took her hand. "There's nothing you can do about what happened, but you can let tonight be a rest from the routine and the problems."

She smiled and nodded.

Hard to believe this was the second time within two weeks that she'd had the incredible opportunity to be seated in the McIntosh Opera House. Dad was right. She could gain nothing by fretting over what had happened. She drew a deep breath. Tonight was special, and her father had been so gracious to arrange this for her.

She read the playbill and acquainted herself with the story. She'd never seen a morality play before. She smoothed the paper on her lap, then tucked a stray hair behind her ear. What time was it? How much longer until the curtain rose? Johanna licked her dry lips. This wasn't the first time she'd seen Parker on stage. So why was she so antsy tonight?

Her excitement wasn't just her own, though. The entire room seemed to buzz with it. Especially since everyone knew that this was the play that had catapulted Parker to stardom.

The lights dimmed, and the crowd hushed. The director stepped to the middle of the stage and explained a bit about the play and how it was written and portrayed.

Johanna straightened in her seat.

The director left to a round of applause, and the curtain opened to one man:

The Messenger.

I pray you all give your audience,
And here this matter with reverence,
By figure a moral play;
The Summoning of Everyman called it is,
That of our lives and ending shows
How transitory we be all day:
This matter is wondrous precious,
But the intent of it is more gracious
And sweet to bear away.
The story saith: Man, in the beginning
Look well, and take good heed of the ending . . .

Another man appeared. Fearsome, in grand robes of white with gold embroidery.

God spoke.

I perceive here in my majesty,
How that all creatures be to me unkind,
Living without dread in worldly prosperity;
Of ghostly sight the people be so blind,
Drowned in sin, they know me not for their God;
In worldly riches is all their mind,
They fear not my rightwiseness, that sharp rod;
My law that I shewed, when I for them died,
They forget clean, and shedding of my blood red;
I hanged between two, it cannot be denied;
To get them life I suffered to be dead . . .

Hot tears trailed down Johanna's cheeks as the actor playing God continued to speak. Then another entered.

Death.

Almighty God, I am here at your will,
Your commandment to fulfil.

The crowd gasped at the eerie form of the character and his words.

God spoke again.

Go thou to Everyman,
And show him in my name
A pilgrimage he must on him take,
Which he in no wise may escape;
And that he bring with him a sure reckoning
Without delay or any tarrying.

Death spoke again, and when he noticed Everyman walking, he called out to him to stand still and asked:

. . . Hast thou thy Maker forgot?

Parker stopped and faced Death.

Why asketh thou?
Wouldest thou wete?

Johanna sat forward in her seat. As Everyman sought for someone or something to help on his journey, her heart wanted to weep for all of those who didn't know the truth. For everyone who didn't understand God's grace and mercy—who couldn't grasp the sacrifice that Jesus made for their salvation. Who thought their good deeds were enough.

The world needed Jesus. They needed the truth. The gospel. They needed to know that salvation was completely free—that they couldn't find it in and of themselves.

Yet as the play progressed, the sting of conviction rose in her conscience. All her fretting and worrying about the future. How prideful she'd been! Tears gathered in her eyes as Everyman crumpled to the ground, crying out to the Lord. But she didn't see Parker, or Everyman, or anyone else.

She saw herself.

Lord, forgive my pride and my stubborn heart. I've depended on my own ideas about how my life should go and not fully surrendered to Your will.

She stopped trying to wipe the tears away. Letting them fall, Johanna fixed her gaze on Parker, who was pouring his heart and soul into the character on the stage.

Everyman spoke one last time.

> Into thy hands, Lord, my soul I commend;
> Receive it, Lord, that it be not lost;
> As thou me boughtest, so me defend,
> And save me from the fiend's boast,
> That I may appear with that blessed host
> That shall be saved at the day of doom.
> *In manus tuas* of might's most,
> Forever *commendo spiritum meum.*

As Everyman commended his soul into God's care, he went into the grave.

"Amen." The word broke out of her on a whisper. Her heart felt like it would split open, it was so full of wonder, joy, and gratitude.

A stunned silence permeated the opera house. Johanna couldn't help herself. She burst to her feet in applause. "Bravo!" All at once, the audience followed suit, coming to their feet and giving such a thunderous standing ovation the floor vibrated.

The cast returned and took their bows. While the audience continued to applaud, Johanna wiped her eyes.

She'd never been more proud.

Parker's smile was wide as he took his bows, waving to the cheering crowd. But it was as if she was seeing him for the first time.

Was this how Paul had felt after the scales fell from his eyes? As if the world around him was suddenly sharper and more vast and beautiful than he'd ever imagined?

Johanna pressed a hand to her mouth. How blind she'd been! And now . . . ?

Now she could see.

She plopped down in her chair, the revelation rolling over her, seeping into every part of her being. There were hurting, broken people who might never step foot in a church. Who might not even know that there was a God who loved them and died for them.

Even in her humble town.

If the Lord could touch her heart and convict her through this beautiful play . . . why couldn't He do the same for others?

Parker and his troupe had displayed the gospel as powerfully as Gerald had from his pulpit. She had been so wrapped up in the idea of being a pastor's wife, she'd forgotten that they were actually called to minister to others wherever the Lord planted her.

Parker had heard the call of the Lord and obeyed. In spite of her rejection. He'd lived out the truth that each and every man was given talents to use for the people around them to see the light of Christ.

Johanna bit her lip. Yes, she'd been called to marry Gerald, to serve the Lord alongside him. But now . . .

God was calling her to something different. Something beautiful and wonderful.

A smile burst across her face.

However life looked for her and Parker and Emily and Dad in the future . . . she didn't need to worry. She would do what she should have done from the beginning.

Get down on her knees and pray for strength, because she didn't want to miss what Jesus had in store for her sweet family.

Marvella tugged her hankie out of her sleeve and dabbed at her eyes. If one person in this town wanted to disparage Parker Bennett for becoming an actor to preach the gospel, she would challenge them to a duel of some sort in the town square.

Everyman was simply one of the most moving experiences she could remember. And she'd seen plays in Paris, London, and New York City. She stuffed the bit of cloth back up her sleeve and glanced at her husband. "Simply marvelous, wouldn't you say, my dear?"

The Judge's mustache twitched as he took a deep breath. He wasn't prone to public displays of emotion, but it was clear he had been deeply moved. "That Parker Bennett is gifted. What an incredible thing to see in our town."

"I agree, I agree." Her gaze slid across the audience to a lone figure two rows ahead of them.

Johanna St. John was still in her seat, her eyes transfixed on the stage, though all the players were gone and the crowd had mostly dispersed.

Marvella had enjoyed Parker's performance to be sure. But watching Johanna watch Parker through the whole of the play had been something else entirely. If that young woman didn't come to her senses, Marvella would be forced to take drastic measures.

Fortunately for these two lovebirds, drastic measures were her favorite thing to take.

"I see Johanna St. John over there. I'm going to speak to her for a moment."

The Judge grunted. "You leave that young woman alone, Marvella. She's had enough happen to her lately. She doesn't need your meddling."

"I think that is *exactly* what she needs. Why, how is she to face the monumental loss of her livelihood without Parker's strong support?" She cocked her head in her husband's direction. "That woman needs more than her aged father—who needs rest himself, mind you—and a young toddler for encouragement and support. Honestly, I don't know why you doubt my superior instincts. Look at Mark and Rebecca. Ellie and Carter. And countless other matches. Indeed, my love, *you* were hardly immune to my charms as a young woman."

The Judge's booming laugh rippled through the theater as he stood. He clasped her hands and pulled her up, tugging her close in the circle of his arms. Pressing a kiss to her cheek, he whispered, "Indeed you are right, dear wife. And never forget, I am not immune to them now." Pulling back, he settled his hat upon his head. "Go, talk with Johanna. I'll come find you in a few minutes."

Marvella watched her husband walk away and snapped open her fan. How grateful she was to the Lord to have only grown deeper in love with that man. Despite his occasional proclivity for trying to ruffle her in public. Still, she couldn't keep the smile from her face as she went to see her young friend, who was still seated, chatting with her father.

"Good evening, friends." She smiled at the duo, noting the

sweet rose color in the widow's face. "Well, Johanna, aren't you a vision of loveliness. Navy blue never looked so elegant. Although I think it's high time we saw you in some lighter colors. You're well past mourning."

Daniel stood and gave Marvella a nod in greeting. "While I agree with you about my beautiful daughter, Mrs. Ashbury, if you're about to talk fashion, that's my cue to step away. I see a few old friends to say hi to."

The two women laughed as he left.

The younger woman stood and offered Marvella a sweet smile. "Mrs. Ashbury, what a pleasure to see you tonight. I'm afraid with all of the work and careful budgeting I've had to do, upkeep with my wardrobe has suffered. You, on the other hand, look like a fashion plate. That plum color looks rich on you. Perfect for tonight's performance. It's Parker's favorite play, and I know he'll be very touched that you came."

She patted Johanna's hand and motioned back to the chairs. "We wouldn't have missed Parker's performance for the world. Of course, I've always been a great supporter of the arts. As you well know. But tell me, what did you think about the performance?"

A dreamy smile stretched across her features, and her eyes strayed back to the stage. "I've never seen anything like that. Parker was brilliant, as you said. But the whole play, the presentation of the gospel . . . of Jesus' love and of the consequences of sin and forgetting the Lord . . ." She fell silent, then turned back to Marvella. "I never realized the gospel could be so powerfully presented in that way."

"I agree. It is incredible to see a representation of your own state before the Lord. It makes you examine your heart and motives before God. But also provokes a deeper sense of gratitude for what Jesus has done for us."

"Exactly!" The young woman toyed with a loose curl on her shoulder. And then her whole expression brightened and a lovely pink tinted her cheeks. "Hello, Parker."

Marvella turned and gave the young actor a grin. Oh, he couldn't have played into her plans any better. "Well, here is the man of the hour himself." She stood and took his offered hand. "What a stunning job you did tonight."

He bowed slightly over her hand and gave it a squeeze. "Thank you, Mrs. Ashbury. I'm pleased you were able to make it tonight. Is the Judge with you?"

"Yes, he should be along shortly. I know he is eager to pass along his own congratulations."

Parker nodded, and his gaze moved to her companion.

The glow of love was quite unmistakable to Marvella's trained eye.

"Hello, Johanna. It's wonderful to see you."

Johanna stood and took a step toward him, the pink in her cheeks deepening. "Oh, Parker, it was simply wonderful. Even better than *Romeo and Juliet*. You were marvelous."

Marvella watched as a similar blush now lit up the young man's face. Honestly, why didn't they get married tonight? What on *earth* were they waiting for?

Well, Lord, it's clear I'm going to need to step in and, with Your help, get these two lovebirds together.

She smiled at them both. "It is so fortunate, you coming out here like this, Parker. For I have had the most wonderful idea. I think I shall put together a tea for you at my house. A small group of intimate friends. After all, your success deserves to be celebrated. What do you say?"

His gaze tore from Johanna to Marvella, a distracted grin on the young man's face. "What? Oh, you don't have to do that, Mrs. Ashbury. Besides, I'll be spending time at Johanna's shop, helping her clean through some of the rubble."

"Ah, yes. I am so sorry about the loss of your shop, dear."

Some of the light left Johanna's eyes. "Thank you. Actually, I am glad to know the Judge is here with you tonight. I need his advice."

As if on cue, the Judge appeared at Marvella's elbow, giving the small group a wide grin. Johanna's father was on his heels and took the open spot by his daughter.

The Judge took his wife's arm. "My ears were burning. What's this about needing advice?"

Johanna twisted the strap of her small evening bag between her fingers, and Marvella frowned. What was on the girl's mind? She'd become so pale.

Johanna's voice was low. "The fire chief stopped by my house earlier today and gave me some devastating news. He said the fire at the shop was arson."

It was as if someone had doused all the candles in the building, so swiftly was all the joy sucked out of the room.

"*Arson?*" The Judge's expression darkened. "Please give me all the details."

Johanna related the specifics, and as she spoke, Marvella glanced at Parker. His face was about as angry as the Judge's, and that was saying something. The care and concern for Johanna were evident in the way Parker watched her every move, absorbed every detail of what she shared.

When Johanna finished, the Judge motioned to Daniel and Parker. "Gentlemen, would you follow me for a moment? I believe I'll need your help with the information Mrs. St. John has shared."

The men left, and Marvella slipped an arm around Johanna's waist. "My dear, I am absolutely shocked to hear this. And

I am so very thankful that the Judge is springing right into action. The truth is, we must also do the same."

"Do the same?" Her eyebrows bunched together. "What do you mean?"

"Why, you can't weather this horrible storm alone! So instead of throwing a celebratory tea for Parker, I insist you come to my house for a luncheon. Bring Emily—she can play the day away at my home. And Parker must come as well. It's about time we had some resolution between you two."

"Resolution?"

Marvella almost rolled her eyes. "Johanna, have you become a parrot? Of course resolution. It's time you two star-crossed lovebirds get back together. You *need* each other."

The look on Johanna's face almost made Marvella laugh.

"Mrs. Ashbury, I don't think that I can do—"

Marvella patted her hand. "Hush, dear. Whatever you are about to say, I will assure you, you *can* do it. Trust me. I will set everything up to perfection. Let's plan on Wednesday. Then . . ." She gave Johanna her brightest smile. "How would you feel about a late summer wedding?"

17

Tuesday, May 2, 1905

The morning had not gone well.

Emily had unwound five spools of costly ribbon. Johanna had burned not only the biscuits but the bacon and coffee too. And now she was trying to comfort her child, who had a long gash on the palm of her hand thanks to a pair of sharp scissors.

Emily was crying. Johanna was crying. And there was blood all over the floor, Em's dress, Johanna's apron, and Dad's favorite pair of denims.

Lord, I don't know what You're trying to teach me, but I might need a second attempt at conquering today. Please?

She held a thick rag tight against Emily's palm. "Shhh, sweetie. It'll be all right. I promise. Let's remember next time that you are never ever *ever* supposed to touch Mama's scissors or needles, right?"

"Yes, Mama. I won't never do it again. It ouchies!" The sobs started in again, and Johanna pulled her close.

She sent a pleading look to her father as he walked back into the room.

He nodded to her. "Remind me to thank Mrs. Conrad for insisting we have a telephone. That's the second emergency we've had in a few short weeks." He pointed his thumb over his shoulder to where the telephone was on the wall. "Lettie said she'd send Doc over right away."

"Thank you." She released a breath. The last thing she needed right now was to go into town and have James find out that Emily was injured. He would surely use that against her.

"Knock, knock." Doc opened the screen door and poked his head in. "I hear I have a patient with a cut."

Emily sucked in a great big breath, and her bottom lip quivered as she stuck out her hand. Doc loved children, and they loved him because he always had treats.

Half an hour later—after a bucketful of tears, four stitches, and a penny stick of candy that Doc crushed into little pieces—Johanna was able to sit down in the parlor with Dad and release a sigh. "My arms are killing me from having to hold her so tight for so long. I was worried Doc wouldn't be able to get it stitched."

Dad leaned his head back and closed his eyes. "I don't think I've ever seen a small child be so strong and put up that much of a fight. I'm glad he gave her something to calm her down."

"Me too." Johanna looked toward the upstairs where her darling little girl was sleeping in her bed. "Hopefully the throbbing and aching will have died down by the time she wakes."

"We can only hope." Dad stood. "I better go take a nap myself so I can be prepared to help you. I don't think the next day or two are going to be easy with her recovery and keeping it clean."

She glanced at the list from Doc. "I have a feeling we have

our work cut out for us." She waved him off. "Go rest. I'm going to put my feet up for a few minutes before I try to chase down all the ribbon that is strewn all over the house."

Dad chuckled as he limped his way up the stairs.

How she wished she could take the result of his injury away. But like he said over and over, it was a miracle he still had both legs, and he would be grateful every day.

As she put her feet up and closed her eyes, another knock sounded on the door.

She got up quick so it wouldn't wake the sleeping duo and rounded the corner for the door.

One of the firemen stood there outside the screen door.

"May I help you?"

"Mrs. St. John?"

He must be new because she didn't recognize him. "Yes?"

"Chief sent me over here. I found this at your shop the other night when we were trying to put out the fire. It was smashed in the door's hinge, and I shoved it in my pocket. I was sent down to Missoula and forgot it was there. When I pulled it out, I thought it was trash, but then I read it and took it to the chief. I'm sorry. But you need to see it." He held out a wrinkled and soot-smudged paper.

The screen door creaked as she opened it and took it. "Thank you."

"I've got to get back. But the chief will want to talk to you about it." He hopped off the porch and jogged down the street.

Johanna unfolded the paper and read.

It's a good thing little Emily is unharmed. Some might wonder how Parker was there at the right time. Where was your father? Isn't it interesting that a crowd formed so quick? And that the newspaper reporters were there?

Be careful around Parker Bennett, Mrs. St. John. He's using you for his own gain.

Respectfully,
A concerned neighbor

It took her a minute to realize the note was about the creek incident. But that was over a week ago. Someone had left this at her shop? Why?

She read it again and then one more time. The accusation behind it sinking in.

Could it be true?

Had Parker—or his manager—arranged Emily's accident so he could get publicity?

No. He wouldn't do that. Not Parker.

She wouldn't believe it, but still . . . She had to find out for certain. Too much had happened lately, and her little family had been through far too much to allow manipulation and lies.

She raced up the stairs, took off her apron, and woke up her dad so he would know that she was going out.

"Where are you going?" His groggy voice told her he was still half-asleep.

"Don't worry. Rest. I'll lock the doors, and you listen for Em, okay?"

"Mm-hmm." He set his head back down on the pillow.

Emily should sleep for several hours, Doc said, so that gave her some relief that her daughter wouldn't need her or her poor father while she was gone.

She shoved the note in her pocket and headed toward the opera house. If she didn't find him there, she would scour the town until she did.

Fifteen minutes later, she huffed her way up the steps to the

251

opera house and marched across the wood floor to the stage where they were rehearsing—most likely for *Uncle Tom's Cabin*, which was supposed to show this weekend.

"Parker Bennett." She didn't say excuse me. Didn't even care that they were in the middle of a scene.

Everything on the stage halted while Parker stepped forward.

Johanna didn't flinch. "I need to speak with you right now."

The director moved toward her. "Mrs. St. John, while we appreciate all your help with the costumes, this isn't a good time."

She flashed him a glare.

Parker hopped off the stage. "Give me a few minutes, George."

The director's hands flew up.

Johanna marched back across the stage and down the stairs as fast as she could.

Parker followed. "What's going on? Why do you look madder than a hornet whose nest has been knocked down?"

She pulled the note out of her pocket and shoved it at him.

Reading it, his face blanched, and then reddened. Then that muscle in the side of his jaw started twitching. "Where did this come from?"

"A fireman brought it to me. Said they found it caught in the hinge of the door to my shop the night of the fire." She paced at the bottom of the stairs. "I cannot believe that you would do such a thing, but I still need to hear it from you, Parker." Hearing her voice echo in the wide stairwell, she glanced up and saw several cast members attempt to disappear. "Let's go outside."

Parker followed and took her elbow once they were alone. As he spun her around to face him, the urgency in his eyes was real. "I had *nothing* to do with this, Jo. I promise. You know I was headed to visit your Dad. I had no idea what I would stumble upon, and I certainly wouldn't have invited the press along. Do you really think me capable of such a horrible thing?"

Gazing into his eyes, she shook her head. "No. I needed you to . . . needed . . . " She fell silent and her shoulders sagged. "Why would somebody write this?" The weight of everything from that morning compounded on her, and she lifted a trembling hand to her brow.

He put his arm around her shoulders. "I don't know, but maybe we should talk to Judge Ashbury about it. He'll be able to discern if it's something to be concerned about."

She nodded. "Can we go now?"

"Give me one minute." He ran back inside, then was back quicker than she expected, shrugging into his suit coat. "All right, start at the beginning. Have any other odd things happened?"

It was a fair question, but the pit of her stomach began to churn. "Before we go to the courthouse, I think there's a lot I need to tell you."

"Go ahead. I've got time."

"Are you sure?"

"The director knows that I have my part down pat. It's the rest of them that he has to worry about. Besides, I told him this was more important."

Wonderful words for her hurting heart. She didn't want to do this alone anymore. "We better find a place to sit. This is going to take a while."

There were several empty lots by the train station, so they headed that direction and found a bench under a tree that afforded them a bit of privacy.

Johanna launched into everything that had happened with James. How the oddities had increased and the way he treated her had escalated.

The scowl on Parker's face deepened the more she conveyed. "So the little conversation at the wedding wasn't the first time."

She shook her head. "But he had threatened to take Emily, and I wasn't sure if that was the grief talking, or if I should do something about it." Placing a hand on his arm, she gave it a squeeze. Had she waited too long to tell him? "The Judge knows a good bit of this already."

The lines in his face eased a bit. "Good. Because James St. John sounds dangerous. What if he's the one who left the note?" He paused. "Or opened the gate so he could accuse you of not taking care of Emily?"

"What does he have to gain?" She looked off down the train tracks. "That's what I can't figure out. He doesn't actually seem to care for me or love me, so why would he want to marry me?"

"Other than you being a beautiful and caring woman?"

She toed the dirt with her boot. "It doesn't make sense, Parker. He must be hurting or feeling a loss of family closeness. Yet he and Gerald weren't close . . . not like brothers should be."

Two fingers slipped under her chin and tilted it up. The warmth in Parker's gaze was almost at odds with the fierce scowl on his face. "Don't feel sorry for him, Jo. Don't do it. He might try to take advantage of you when you're vulnerable. We can figure out the why later. Right now, we need to decide how to proceed." He dropped his hand and took a step back.

But his touch had warmed her face. She knew her cheeks were pink, but she wasn't embarrassed. Instead, she took a step, recovering the distance he'd put between them. "We're supposed to have lunch with Marvella and the Judge tomorrow. Maybe we can fill the Judge in then?" She fought the smile tugging at her lips. "Sorry, but Marvella is up to her matchmaking again, and I couldn't tell her no." Her heart began to pound as a soft smile tipped Parker's mouth. She hadn't been imagining things. He *did* still care for her.

"Speaking of matchmaking"—he took both of her hands in his—"I can't keep this to myself any longer. Johanna Easton St. John . . . I love you."

Though he'd said the words to her before, all those years ago, this moment was much sweeter. She returned his smile. "You love me?"

He reached up to caress her cheek. "I've loved you since I met you, but I didn't understand back then what love was. Didn't understand *how* to love you well. I've learned a lot about life in the last ten years, and coming home proved to me that I love you more today than ever before. This is a new and deeper love. I know we haven't had a normal relationship. We haven't courted or anything—at least not recently."

His fingers trailed to her neck and cradled the back of her head. His touch was familiar and new all at once. "But I had to share my heart. I don't know what God has in store for us, but I want to serve Him with my whole heart and spend the rest of my life learning to love you more and more. Emily too. That little girl of yours—"

Johanna laughed. "Wait until you hear what she got into this morning."

"Oh boy. Well, that little rascal already has my heart as well. I love her so much, I feel like my heart could burst."

Her heart was in a similar state, overflowing with thanksgiving at the kindness of the Lord. Of Parker's love. Tears streamed down her cheeks. Goodness, she was a mess. But a joyful one.

Parker thumbed the wetness off her cheeks, his smile disappearing. "Have I scared you off for good? I don't want to push you. But—"

She gasped out a laugh and covered his heart with her hand. "These are the happiest tears I've cried in a good long while." Johanna locked her eyes on his. It was time. "I love you, Parker."

"You do?" His arms encircled her waist, drawing her close.

"I do." She cupped his cheek. No more holding back her heart from him. "Seeing you again brought all my old feelings to life. When you first left, I buried it all . . . my love, my feelings, my hopes and dreams. Time passed, and Gerald came into my life, and he was so different from you that I dared to allow his love to stir my heart. I let myself hope again. He was such a good man. You need to know that. Our love was real, and I believe it was God's purpose for my life at that time."

Parker nodded. "And now?"

"Now everything has changed." She patted his cheek and stepped back. He snatched her hand in his, and tingles zipped up her arm. "I know Gerald would be the first one to encourage me to love again . . . and allow myself to be loved. He'd want Emily to have the love that only a father can give." Her words came out in a rush, a tiny sliver of insecurity worming its way into her happiness. "I know you love Emily, but she is a handful. Energy for days. Always talking. Cranky and—"

His finger covered her lips for a moment, stemming her worries. "I want to be there for all of that . . . and more. But only if we do it together."

Her insecurities melted. "Oh, Parker. I have a lot to work through. *We* have much to talk about. I can't begin to tell you how amazed I am by your talent on stage. You are clearly called to it. That gift is from God, I know that. But I am so unsure about everything that comes with it. Give me some time, and we w—"

"Parker!" The shout of one of the stagehands startled them both as he ran toward them. Johanna stepped to Parker's side and tucked her hands behind her back, her cheeks heating.

"Tom, what is it?"

The young man's chest heaved as he delivered his news. "I'm so glad I found you. Come quick! It's Yvette! Her maid thinks she's dead."

18

Parker ran all the way back to the opera house, with Johanna close behind him. Yvette was dead? No. Who would do such a thing?

But then their last conversation hit him. Had she really been that distraught? She said she would die without him. Surely the woman wasn't in love with him. She loved *herself* too much.

There was the crux of the matter. She loved herself too much to do herself any harm.

Something else—or some*one* else—was behind all this.

As they raced up the stairs together, the crowd of cast and crew was seated on the stage as they waited for word.

The doc came out looking grave, Yvette's maid trailing him.

George surged forward. "Well?"

The doctor scanned all the faces.

George pushed. "We're all family here. Please. Is she still alive?"

"Yes, but I'm afraid she attempted to take her own life. Took too many pills. I've pumped her stomach, and she will be all right, in time, but she will not be returning to the stage any time soon." He turned to the director. "I need some assistance getting her back to my office."

"Of course."

Johanna placed a hand on his arm. "Thank God she's alive."

Everyone began whispering among themselves, while several men followed Doc back to the dressing rooms behind the stage.

Parker lifted his gaze to the domed ceiling. *Thank You, Lord, that she's still alive, but why do I feel like something worse is coming? Please show me what to do.*

Yvette's maid was in front of him when his gaze came back down.

"You. You did this." She thrust a piece of paper at him and then stormed off.

Several of the cast stared at him and whispered behind their hands.

Parker opened the note and read:

Dearest Parker,

I can't go on without you. I wish you would have listened to me.

We could have changed the world from the stage. You and me.

I hope you'll remember me when I'm gone. Je t'adore, chèri.

Yvette

"What does it say?" Johanna studied his face. "And why did that woman say you did it? Did what?"

"Come with me." He took hold of her arm and led her out of the opera house. They headed down the street in silence.

What on earth was really going on?

"What was on that note?"

He sighed. No more secrets. "Supposedly it was from

Yvette saying that she couldn't go on without me. Earlier she had thrown herself at me, but Johanna, it was all an act." He stopped and took hold of her. "Yvette has never cared one whit about me, much less loved me. She's new to the troupe. Relatively new to the stage groups in New York. She wouldn't commit suicide over me, that's for certain. She cares far too much about her own well-being."

"But she took those pills."

"Yes, and I know I sound callous, but I believe it was all an act. Actresses do it all the time to get attention."

Johanna's eyes widened. "How awful!"

Parker blew out a breath. She didn't know the half of it. "I know. Before we came here, the newspapers reported at least three suicide attempts from actresses in New York. The stories could have all been lies as so many of the stories are. It gets attention, and then people want to show up at the plays and see the actress who tried to kill herself. It's a sort of morbid sense of interest."

"I can't even imagine." She wrapped her arms around her middle, her gaze fixed on something in the distance. "What a terrible thing to do to people . . . to yourself."

"I agree. If Yvette's maid hadn't returned at the right time . . ." Johanna looked too pale. Parker led her to a bench and tugged her to sit next to him. "If the doctor hadn't been available . . . hadn't pumped her stomach . . . Yvette would be dead."

The tension in the air grew thick as Johanna processed what he was saying. "And she was willing to risk that for attention?"

Parker paused. He'd rattled off his comments as if *he* were a newspaper journalist. Cold. Just the facts.

When had he become so callous? Had he become so immune to Yvette's acts that he'd lost all sense of care for her as a person? As a soul the Lord desired to save?

Forgive me, Lord.

He gentled his tone. "I know it sounds far-fetched, but it is the darker side of the theatre. So many broken, hurting people desperate to be noticed. To be loved."

When Johanna didn't respond, he continued. She needed to know his suspicions. "What I don't understand is, why here? Why now? Kalispell is a small town, and getting word out to the rest of the world isn't easily done. Then there is the moving pictures director, who, I suppose, could be impressed with her doing such a thing. But this could also make him not want to be involved with a temperamental actress who might die during one of his projects. So again, I see no profit in her doing this here and now."

Her soft hand covered his, lacing their fingers together. "Is it possible that she has really fallen in love with you?"

He looked at her and saw the love in her eyes. "No. Not even the remotest possibility. She's made all sorts of flirtations, but that's the way Yvette operates. She's used to being the object of desire, and when a man shows her no interest . . . well, sometimes it makes her try all the harder. But not with me. She knew my feelings. Because I made them clear to her. I almost wonder if someone wasn't putting her up to this."

A frown creased her forehead. "Like your agent or the director?"

Could they have done this? "Alfred might, but to what purpose? I fired him, and he wasn't happy, but there's no way Yvette attempting suicide could cause me to hire him back."

"I'm so sorry, Parker." She tightened her fingers around his. "I wish I could help you."

Her offer warmed his heart. And yet, if Yvette was willing to go this far to get him to be with her, what would she do if she knew he was in love with Johanna? "It's okay. I'd just as soon keep you as far removed from all of this as possible. In fact, I want to get you home, where you'll be out of the way of reporters and such. I'm sure this will be all over the newspaper by tomorrow."

Johanna nodded, and they stood. She looked so beautiful in the afternoon light. All the worry and shadows he'd seen on her face the last few weeks were gone. The past was where it belonged, behind them. Once this mess with Yvette was settled, they could seek the Lord for the future of their family. Together.

Johanna laughed. "That's a pretty pleased smile on your face."

"Only because you've put it there." He tugged her close and pressed his lips to her temple. "Get home to our girl. I'll visit later."

Johanna stood on her tiptoes and kissed his cheek. "I can't wait."

He watched her make quick work of the path home until she disappeared from his sight. Parker turned, his spirit lighter than it had been in years, and moved back toward the opera house. He shoved a hand in his pocket and sobered. Yvette's note was still in there.

And that's where it would stay. He had no desire to read it again.

Or to have anyone else read it.

Walking through the lobby, Parker searched for the director and spotted him coming from the theater. He headed for him. "Has anyone else been around Yvette's dressing room?"

George studied him for several seconds, then narrowed his gaze. "I wouldn't know for sure. There's a lot of people backstage during the shows." He tipped his head closer and glanced around. "What are you thinking? Is someone targeting the troupe?" His lowered voice held a hint of fear.

He didn't really think so, but that didn't mean he couldn't use the possibility to his advantage. "I don't know. But we've got to keep this under wraps. No talking to the press. Not until we can get the facts, agreed?"

George crossed his arms over his chest and looked around the large room.

Parker could guess what was going through his mind. Outlandish stories and newsworthy items like this were what helped sell tickets.

He fixed George with a hard look. "People could be in danger. And no amount of ticket sales is worth that."

✺

WEDNESDAY, MAY 3, 1905

James watched his former sister-in-law stroll down the street toward the ash heap that was her precious little shop.

But she didn't look one bit downcast or desperate. She appeared almost . . . happy.

How. Dare. She?

She should be pounding on his door, begging for his assistance. Clearly, she grossly underestimated his power and seriousness in following through on every threat he'd made.

Pushing off the lamppost he'd been leaning against, he made quick work of the distance between him and the object of his desire. As soon as he drew close enough, his hand shot out and wrapped around her upper arm, whirling her around to face him.

She let out a squeal and went stiff beneath his touch. "James! What are you doing? Let me go this instant! How *dare* you grab me like that." She swatted at his hand, but he tightened his grip, watching her wince.

"Don't you take that tone with me, *Mrs.* St. John. Have you forgotten that I hold your whole world in the palm of my hand? I gave you a deadline a couple weeks ago. What will it take for you to understand I am not a man to ignore?"

Though her face was pale, there was still a spark of anger in her blue eyes. "You don't own me, James. And I have been as clear as can be. I will not marry you."

He tightened his grip once more.

"And I have been clear as I can be with you, but still you refuse to believe me. So hear me well, Johanna. If you spend any more time with that actor, I *will* take Emily. I will not allow you to corrupt her through the questionable morals of a man like Parker Bennett."

Johanna stilled and shook her head. "You don't have the power to take Emily, and you know it. In fact, why don't we go speak with Judge Ashbury right now?" The fire in her gaze grew.

He curled his lip. "You shouldn't question my power, Johanna. Ask Yvette Lebeau. She trifled with me, and look where she ended up."

Her face went ashen, and all of her bravado seemed to vanish. "*You* were responsible for Yvette attempting to take her life?"

"You would be astounded at the things I'm responsible for, my dear. I'm powerful. Why, in New York they fear me as much as they do . . ."

Stop. Don't say their name.

He shrugged. The less she knew the better.

But then the fire was back in her gaze, and she struggled

against his hold. "You are despicable! I'm going to report you to the authorities."

Who did she think she was? "Oh, sweet, delusional Johanna. Don't you understand? Those men are in my pocket. Besides, who do you think they would believe? A single mother who can't keep her daughter safe—yes, I know about the latest injury, even though you tried to keep it from me—or a prestigious lawyer who has the respect of everyone in this town? Why, I heard this afternoon that they will be seeking to question Parker because he abrogated his vow to marry that actress. Which is ungallant, considering how he compromised her."

She twisted and jerked her arm from his grasp, falling back several steps. "No. You're wrong."

Oh, what joy watching her world crumble around her, knowing he held the key to rebuilding everything. "I guess we will have to see, won't we."

Johanna studied his face for a moment. Indecision and insecurity flashed across her features. He could practically taste the victory.

Then her spine straightened. She took one step back toward him. "You. Are. A. Liar."

She emphasized each word with a firm poke to his chest. "Parker would never do that. He is a man of honor. Unlike *you*." She let her hand drop to her side and straightened her shoulders. "I am telling you for the last time, James. Stay away from me, my dad, Emily, *and* Parker."

"Or what?" He should kidnap her right now, in broad daylight, and teach her a lesson.

Her eyes seemed to darken, and her expression was like cold, hard marble. He'd never seen such a look on her face before and—

It sent a shiver up his spine. This was a Johanna he didn't know.

"I wouldn't suggest you find out." She turned on her heel and strode away from him, her chin held high.

There was something almost mesmerizing about the slow, steady pace she set. Why this sudden confidence?

Who *was* this fierce woman?

James took a step to follow her, but halted.

Johanna thought she was so clever and powerful, but he'd prove her wrong. She was about to learn what happened to those who made James an enemy. He straightened his jacket.

Time to start the next phase of his plan.

Parker's heart pounded as he walked into Doctor Foster's practice. "Hello?"

"In the back! Unless you're with the newspaper, in which case . . . get out!"

"It's Parker Bennett, Dr. Foster."

"Come on back, son."

He turned his steps down the hallway toward an open door. Dr. Foster appeared, wiping his hands on a towel.

"She's back here."

Parker entered the room to find a small ward with three beds. It was like a small hospital, but Yvette was the only patient in residence.

"You can see for yourself that she's doing much better today, but she's still weak."

Parker drew closer. Yvette was lying on the small bed in the corner, her fine features pinched and pale. Her eyes were closed, but Parker could see the steady rise and fall of her breathing. She was merely asleep. Not dead.

His shoulders relaxed a bit, and he glanced at the doctor. "Is she going to be all right?" He kept his voice low.

The doctor looked up from his notes, pushing his wire-rimmed glasses back up his nose. "What? Oh. Yes, yes. She will be fine. We've emptied her stomach of all its contents. I'm sure you were there when I mentioned it."

"Yes, I was, but I wasn't sure that some amount of the medication got into her system."

"No, I don't think so. At least not enough to cause harm. To be sure, she will be exhausted for the next day or two and need some rest. But after that, right as rain."

Yvette stirred and turned her head, her eyes blinking against the bright light. "Parker?" Her voice sounded scratchy and low. Nothing like the cultured tone she usually took with him.

He stuffed his hands in his pockets, staying right where he was. While he was glad she was going to be all right, he wasn't about to let himself get drawn into more drama.

The doctor finished his notes and stood. "I've got to file these away and let the police know she will be fine. I shall return shortly."

Parker watched him leave, praying the doctor's definition of *shortly* matched his own.

With stilted movements, Yvette pushed herself up into a sitting position and rubbed her face. Her hair was disheveled, and some of her eye makeup had smeared across her cheek. "I'm sure I look a fright." She pushed her hair off her shoulder. "But I am so happy you came."

"I'm glad to hear you will make a full recovery." His words sounded cold, even to his own ears.

Tears filled her eyes. She held her hands out to him. "*Chèri,* don't you know it was all for you? I can't live without you. Why can't you see that?"

Lord, please give me wisdom. "Yvette . . . I don't love you. I have never given you any reason to think that I do. Or that us being together was even a possibility. Where is this coming from?"

She simpered, fluttering her lashes at him. Perhaps other men thought that was attractive, but to him it looked like she had something in her eye. "Come now, Parker. You know I have always found you attractive. And think of our chemistry on the stage! Why, we could be one of the most powerful couples on Broadway. Or in the movies! We could be an overnight sensation in moving pictures. Imagine what we could accomplish!"

He rubbed his face. It was almost like they were speaking two different languages. *Lord, how do I make this any clearer than I already have?* Taking a settling breath, he tried again. "I have no desire to go into moving pictures, Yvette. In fact, the future I have in mind wouldn't bring you any happiness at all."

"Why can't you see that marrying me is the best step you will ever take in your career?" She reached out to try to grab his hand.

"*No!* I have tried to be kind, but now you've left me with no choice." *Guide me, Father.* "I don't love you, Yvette. And I never will. I love someone else. When I get married, it will be because God has put me and the woman I love together for His purpose. Not to further my career or to be famous. If you think that's my motivation, then you don't know me at all."

In an instant, her pleading gaze turned hard. Her lips curled into a snarl, and she catapulted out of the bed. "*Cochon!* Pig! You worthless excuse for a man!"

Parker took a step back. What on earth was she doing?

She plunged her fingers into her hair, pulling on it. Parker blinked. Was she having some sort of episode? He took another step backward toward the door as she advanced toward him, rage darkening her brown eyes to black. "I've wasted *months* on you. Simpering and preening. Look at me! I am everything you could *ever* want in a wife! How dare you reject *me*!"

"Yvette, I'm not trying to hurt you. But this is exactly why we could never—"

She grabbed the pitcher off the table beside her bed and took another step toward him. "I will tell everyone you compromised me, Parker. I will absolutely destroy your precious reputation in your stupid hometown. And then—" She let out a low chuckle. "Oh, yes, and then I will go after that silly little widow. You can be sure of that!" She heaved the pitcher at him.

He ducked and heard it shatter on the wall behind him. She was trying to kill him! Where had that confounded doctor gone? Yvette needed help. Now. "That's it. I'm leaving." He'd tell the doctor about her erratic behavior on his way out.

Without a word, she grabbed the basin on the table, and Parker turned to run out the door.

But he wasn't fast enough.

The porcelain basin caught him on the back of the head, sending him tumbling to the ground. Light sparkles danced before his eyes as he slumped down.

"What is this madness?"

The doctor's voice sounded far away and fuzzy.

And all Parker heard was the echo of Yvette's wails as the doctor threatened to take her to the asylum.

Then the world went black.

19

Johanna marched up to the Ashburys' stately home and stood outside staring at the exterior. She'd been halfway here to unleash her tirade about James when she realized the luncheon was today. She didn't feel much up to a luncheon, but they were expecting her. And she would get to see Parker.

Ever since he'd returned to town, her life had been in upheaval. Still, it was hard to imagine life without him now. An involuntary grin lifted her lips. All the upheaval was worth it to have him back.

The thought sent her stomach into flips. She and Parker hadn't settled anything—simply shared their feelings. But with the threats that James had made, she was more than ready to move forward. When she and Parker were married, her brother-in-law would leave her alone.

Not that her longing to marry Parker was to get James off her back. She put a hand to her forehead. Goodness, no.

Lack of sleep and anxiety had obviously messed with her good sense.

Running footsteps from her right caused her to turn.

One of the young boys in town that the mercantile hired out as messengers ran up to her. "Mrs. St. John?"

"Yes, I'm Mrs. St. John."

"Got a letter for ya." He handed it over and took off back the way he came before she could even pull a coin out of her purse.

She ripped into the envelope and pulled out a small slip of paper.

Don't say a word to the Judge about the fire or about me. This is your last warning.

Even though it wasn't signed, she knew exactly who it was from.

Well. She wasn't about to be held hostage by her husband's brother. She would speak to whomever she pleased about what she pleased. What made him think he could control her?

Marching up the steps to the beautiful home, she ran all the events with James through her mind.

Yes, this luncheon was a perfect idea. She would tell the Judge and his wife and Parker absolutely everything. No longer would she be riddled with fear over what a powerful man like James could do. She had God behind her. And the Judge.

She rang the bell.

"Hey. Fancy meeting you here." Parker's warm voice greeted her from behind.

She turned, then gasped at the sight of the bruise discoloring his forehead. "What happened?"

Parker's smile faded. "What do you . . . Oh." His fingers brushed the mark, and he waved off her concern. "I'll explain later. I want to know what's happened. I know that face. What's wrong?"

Shoving the note at him, she ground out the words. *"This is what's wrong. And I'm tired of it."*

The door opened, and the Ashburys' butler greeted them. "Please come in."

"Thank you." Putting at least a bit of effort into not looking like she was ready to explode, she smiled.

"My dears, I'm so glad you made it." Marvella glided into the foyer.

"Mrs. Ashbury, I need to see your husband. Right away." This couldn't wait until all the niceties were over.

The older woman's face turned serious. "Of course. Let's go see him now. He took a few moments in his study before lunch."

Marvella led them into the bookcase-filled room. Beautiful cherry wood gleamed from a fresh polishing. The fireplace was empty since the spring was warm this year, and the lush leather chairs invited them to sit.

But Johanna chose to stand. "Sir, I need your help."

He stood and waved all of them in. "Is this about your brother-in-law?"

"How did you know?" She handed him the note that had been delivered.

He took it and put on a pair of glasses, then scanned the note.

Marvella spoke to one of the servants and asked them to bring luncheon to them in the study.

"Sit down, Johanna. Parker, you too." The Judge removed his spectacles and rubbed the bridge of his nose. "Let's go over every detail."

Johanna rolled up her sleeve. There was a bruise turning a variety of ugly colors.

Marvella gasped.

Parker's nostrils flared as he tenderly brushed his fingers over the dark marks marring her skin. He caught her gaze, his jaw tight. "He did this to you?" Johanna could hear the anger in his tone, yet the tenderness of his touch brought tears to her eyes. How blessed she was to be loved by this man. She nodded. "He told me not to go to the police because they were in his pocket, and they wouldn't believe me. But these bruises show what he did—in broad daylight, mind you—and I can't allow him to do anything else. Especially not to Emily."

She turned to Marvella. "I'm sorry for ruining the lunch you had planned, but with everything that has happened this week, James grabbing me this morning, then this note, I can't take anymore. I can't. I am certain he's responsible for the fire. He hasn't admitted it, but in this note he mentions it. Why else would he do that?" She fought against the tears burning the corners of her eyes.

Parker slid his hand around hers, his thumb rubbing the side of hers. He didn't say a word. Just waited for the Judge.

Who looked like he might be ready to go out and wring James's neck all on his own. "Yes, why indeed."

Johanna leaned forward. Her body felt very heavy all of a sudden. "I'm sorry. I wasn't sure what to do. He's threatened to take Emily away and even told me to look at what he did to Yvette. How it all fits, I have no idea."

Parker jerked back like she hit him. "He did something to Yvette?"

"I think he somehow forced her into staging her suicide attempt." Johanna bit her lip.

Inhaling a deep breath, he squeezed her hand and looked at the Judge. "What do you think about all of this?"

"First, you did the correct thing by bringing it to me, Johanna." The Judge stood and paced around the room. "We need to catch James in the act of evildoing. He might think that he has the police in his pocket, but I have my own relationships with them. Upstanding and honest relationships. If there are those willing to work for bribes, that's criminal activity, and I'm sure the police chief will be all too glad to know that and weed them out."

Another horrid thought hit her. "Should I be worried about Emily and my dad? What if he goes after them when I'm not there? Especially after all James's threats to take Emily from me. I'm supposed to attend the first showing of *Uncle Tom's Cabin* tomorrow evening"—she gazed at Parker and then back at the Judge—"and James knows it."

The Judge nodded and continued pacing. For several moments, he didn't speak, and the only sound in the silent room was his soft footfalls on the carpet.

He stepped behind his desk and steepled his fingers on top of it. "This is what we're going to do."

Sweat beaded his forehead. Pulling a large handkerchief out of a desk drawer, James rubbed his forehead then threw the offending fabric to the floor. The last thing he needed was to start this brief again. He couldn't afford another setback with this client.

Especially when he had so many other things to do.

Picking up his pen, he began writing.

"You have some explaining to do, Mr. St. James."

Judge Milton Ashbury's voice boomed through his office like a cannon.

Relax. Stay calm.

James capped his pen, set it down, then leaned back, staring at Kalispell's most prominent law official. "Why, Judge Ashbury, is this any way to greet an old friend?"

Reginald appeared behind the Judge, his eyes wide. "I apologize, Mr. St. James. I told him your explicit instructions were to be left undisturbed for the day."

James waved a hand. "I always have time for Judge Ashbury, Reginald. Don't be silly." He glanced at the large man who was still glowering at him. "Would you like Reginald to fetch us some tea? Coffee? Water?"

Judge Ashbury narrowed his eyes. "No. Thank you."

The thin clerk nodded and rushed out of the room, slamming the door behind him.

James fought a frown. He really had to get a more intimidating clerk. In fact . . . he picked up his pen and jotted a note down. Hiring a bodyguard was his next priority. The last two days he'd noticed a couple of strange men following him.

He couldn't afford a dustup with the Camorras, not while he had unfinished business with Johanna. Besides, he'd paid them off.

He put his pen aside and shuffled his papers. Then he glanced up at the Judge, who was still standing there, glaring at him. "You have interrupted me on a particularly busy day. Please say your piece, then leave."

"I couldn't give two figs about your busy day, James. I'm here to ask you why Johanna St. John, your *sister-in-law*, has come to me with complaints of your heinous threats. And don't you lie to me. You forget I've seen your court antics."

James leaned back in his chair, fighting the smile that wanted to bloom. So Johanna had gone and found herself a big protector, hmm? "Judge Ashbury, I am a well-respected man of the community, with deep ties here. Why, at one point my name was being bandied about as a candidate for mayor of our fair town. How is it possible you are taking the word of a grief-stricken, addled young woman over my sterling reputation?"

"Johanna has been a member of this community longer than you have." The Judge snapped. "And when a woman comes to me, complaining of not one, but multiple instances of harassment, the latest of which caused bruises on her arm, I am going to deal with the man face-to-face. I will ask one more time, why are you causing her so much grief?"

Blast those bruises. He knew he'd held her too hard. Still, if she hadn't fought him, she wouldn't have hurt herself. "There is no grief in family, Judge. I am concerned about Johanna and Emily. And that is all I have to say about the matter. It's private, between Johanna and myself."

The Judge closed the gap between him and James's desk. He pressed his large hands flat against the desk and leaned over. "I would suggest"—his voice was low and calm—"you talk about it now. Before I haul your sorry carcass into court for harassment and abuse."

James studied the older man's face. Judge Ashbury's reputation around Kalispell was unimpeachable. There was no way he could go against him and win. Not if he wanted to keep his own reputation intact. There had to be another way. What had his old friend always told him? Ah, to use that swell mouth of his to get out of any scrape.

"I appreciate your clear care for Johanna, Judge. It pleases me that she has people who are willing to help her in such dark times. That is what I am trying to do as well. It's ludicrous to think that I would threaten her or try to harm her in any way. I've simply offered to marry her and care for her and Emily. I have a large house and would hire additional staff to help. All I've ever wanted is to honor Gerald's memory. It's what he wanted. He told me so himself many times."

"I suspect that's a pretty tale you've told yourself to assuage your guilty conscience of any wrongdoing." The Judge stepped back and tucked his hands in his pockets. He looked so smug. So self-righteous.

James's fist itched to knock that sanctimonious clown right to the ground.

His eyes sized James up and were unimpressed. "I propose this. You leave your *former* sister-in-law alone. You cease your unwanted proposals of marriage. And if I hear that you've gone near Johanna or her child or her father, I will take you to court myself."

Heat burned in his chest and up his face, so intense he thought he would burst. He would not tolerate being talked to like this! "You've meddled with the wrong man! Do you know who I have at my fingertips? Who I could call in New York City and have out here in a snap to ruin you and your empty-headed wife and your stupid town?" James stood and rounded his desk, getting nose to nose with the Judge. "I can ruin you in a minute! Do you hear me?" Spittle flew from his mouth and flecked the Judge's face.

The Judge took a step back and plucked James's pocket square from his jacket pocket. He wiped his face and tucked it right back where he found it. "You wouldn't happen to be speaking about the Camorra gang, now, would you?"

How did this infuriating man stay so calm? James pulled back. And how did he know about the Camorras?

"I think *you* are the one who has meddled with the wrong man. You don't frighten me, James. I've dealt with your type before and won't tolerate you causing harm to someone I've come to care about a great deal." He met and held James's gaze. "I *will* be watching you."

20

Friday, May 5, 1905

Tonight was the night. Parker peeked through the slit in the side curtain at the packed house. They had sold 1,132 tickets for tonight's show. People were jam-packed into every square inch. He even noticed a couple of people seated on each of the windowsills. Well, if there was a way to go out, this was it.

No one knew his plans to retire from the stage, or that he would announce it tonight. He'd let Alfred go, and Yvette was gone. Doc had sent her for a mental evaluation, but she'd disappeared.

Thankfully, the press hadn't printed any outlandish stories about her suicide attempt, thanks to Judge Ashbury. He had a close friendship with the paper's owner and had explained how best the paper could help.

Now Parker prayed he could finish well.

The past two days had been difficult for Johanna with the last-minute costume fixes, but they'd snuck away to pray together twice for a couple minutes, and that had been all he

needed. Tonight he would surprise her with his announcement, and then after the show, he would propose.

Once the troupe left town, he'd have plenty of time to spend
with her, talk about their future, and plan a wedding. He shrugged.
Maybe it was doing things a bit backward, but it felt right.

He let the curtain slip shut. Right now, he needed to protect
Johanna and her family from James until the Judge finished
his investigation and handled things. All the Judge would tell
them was that there were shady characters in town, and he
was going to get to the bottom of it.

It had been hard to just stand by, but Parker trusted the
older man's wisdom.

A tap on his shoulder made him turn around. "Hey, George,
what's up?"

The director nodded at him. "Wanted to make sure you
were ready to go." The smile on his face was wider than Parker
had ever seen it. "The place is packed."

"Ready whenever you are."

"Good. Get ready for cues." He walked away and out in
front of the curtain.

The crowd responded with thunderous applause as George
introduced the show.

Johanna managed to slip back to the costume room at in-
termission. She hadn't paid attention to the play at all.

Something wasn't right.

Had she forgotten something important? Was Dad all right
at home?

It didn't make sense. This was supposed to be the best of the
best for the troupe, and Parker was on stage, but she couldn't
focus.

At all.

Well, at least she could make herself helpful to Imogen and Neeve. The girls had a ton of work to oversee each night.

"Weren't you enjoying the play? It's been so popular." Imogen went back to ironing recently washed shirts.

She shrugged. "My mind isn't on it. Parker gave us vouchers and my dad was supposed to come with me, but at the last minute, he changed his mind. I think his leg was bothering him. Besides, there are so many people in there that I almost couldn't breathe." Johanna picked up a discarded costume. "I see Henry has made a mess of this again." The rather portly man had a terrible time not ripping out the seat of his pants. "I'll get right to work on this. Shouldn't take but a couple of minutes to fix."

"I hate sewing up Henry's clothes. The man smells like liniment and beer." Imogen put her fingers to her nose, causing Neeve to laugh.

"You would be surprised by all the smells." Imogen went back to her ironing. "Miss Lebeau's clothes always smell like a mix of lilac, lavender, and a hint of sage. There are three girls in the chorus who insist on wearing L'Origan. They bought one bottle and share it between them."

"Bathe in it, don't you mean?" Neeve giggled and continued affixing ribbon trim to a bodice.

Johanna smiled, but her heart wasn't in the chatter. She wanted to see Parker take his bow amid what was sure to be thunderous applause . . . But even more than that, she needed his steadying presence.

Maybe that would help her shake this feeling that something was wrong.

"Isn't it strange the way Miss Lebeau disappeared?" Imogen glanced up from her ironing. "She became very popular in the theatre, and it seems strange she would go into hiding like that."

"Perhaps she's afraid of something." Johanna could only imagine what hold James might have on the poor actress. If he made her life as miserable as he'd made Johanna's, the farther she ran, the better off she'd be.

"I think she's very beautiful." Neeve sounded like a little girl fawning over her favorite star. "I'd love to wear the clothes she wears. They're all so . . . so . . . *French*. Ooh la la."

Imogen rolled her eyes and shook her head. "That one is dreaming all the time. She wants to be an actress."

Neeve scowled. "And what's wrong with that?"

Johanna finished Henry's seam and put the needle and thread away. "I suppose I should reclaim my seat and watch the troupe take their bows." She rose and dusted thread off her skirt. As soon as the play was over and Parker walked her home, everything would be all right. It had to be.

Parker relaxed his shoulders and released a long sigh when the curtain fell for the final time. The show was over. He was done. Now he could focus on a new future.

His heart picked up its pace. After curtain call, it would be time for him to make his announcement. The director, cast, and crew would probably be in shock and furious with him for not telling them in private first, but it couldn't be helped. This was the best way.

"Hey, Parker. This came for you." Jerry, one of the stage-hands, handed him an envelope.

Parker tore it open.

I have Emily.

*Johanna's father is dead, and if you—Parker Bennett—
don't leave town immediately, Emily will be next. Then Johanna. Don't say a word to anyone. Leave now!*

No! Please, God, no! He rushed out the side door while
everyone else gathered on the stage for curtain call. Could
it be true? Or was it just an empty threat? He couldn't risk
alerting anyone else until he knew for sure.

Several hackney cabs were outside the theater, and he
jumped into one and gave them the address. "Hurry. As fast
as you can."

The driver urged the horse into a gallop.

When they reached Daniel and Johanna's home, Parker
jumped down before they were even stopped and ran into
the house. The door was standing wide open.

In the middle of the floor, Daniel Easton lay unmoving and
covered in blood. Parker kneeled and put his head on the man's
chest. *Please, God, let him be alive!*

After several moments, he heard a faint thump of the man's
heart and a very shallow breath.

"Hold on, Daniel. I'll get help."

Parker ran back out of the house and went straight to the
Conrads'. Surely there would be someone there who could
help. He banged on the door, and one of the servants opened
it. "Please, someone has attacked Mr. Easton. I need the doc.
And the sheriff. *Anyone* that can help."

When the girl nodded, he ran back to Johanna's home,
charging through the house, searching every nook and cranny
for Emily. She wasn't there. He went through the house again.
Then out to the garden. By the creek.

But no Emily.

When he went back inside, the sheriff was standing in the doorway, and the doctor was kneeling at Daniel's side.

The sheriff frowned at him. "What happened here?"

Parker showed him the note. "This was given to me at the end of the show tonight. I raced over here and found Daniel on the floor, injured but still alive. I ran for help, then came back to search for Emily, but I can't find her anywhere." His voice choked on the last word.

Doctor Foster looked up from treating Daniel. "This poor family has had more than their share of troubles. What happened?"

Parker shook his head. "I'm not sure. According to the note, someone tried to kill him, and now that person has Emily."

Doc shook his head. "I'm going to need to get Daniel to the hospital. The injuries are too extensive for me to treat here."

"I'll get their wagon. It's out back." Parker headed for the door.

"Hold on just a minute." The sheriff narrowed his gaze at Daniel's still form, then turned to Parker. "How do I know *you* didn't do all this?" He waved the note in Parker's face.

Parker wanted to slug the man. Didn't he realize Johanna's little girl was out there? "I was on stage at the McIntosh Opera House until a few minutes ago. Ask anyone. You need to get word to Johanna. She's at the opera house."

"If you were on stage, then how come I had a phone call right before the Conrad house called? It was a man who said you were the one who hurt Mr. Easton."

Parker shook his head. "Who is this eyewitness?"

"A well-respected lawyer in this town, Mr. James St. John. Said he saw the whole thing and that you weren't at the curtain call at the end of the show. He said there's over a thousand eyewitnesses."

Wiping a hand down his face, Parker took a long, slow breath to calm his temper. "How exactly did Mr. St. John see the whole thing? And if he did, how did he know I wasn't at the curtain call? You need to talk to Judge Ashbury. He'll agree with me that Mr. St. John is the one responsible for Daniel's wounds."

The sheriff put his hand on his gun. "You're under arrest, Mr. Bennett."

"Now that seems a mite bit hasty, sheriff." Doc stood up. "If Mr. Bennett had beat this man, he would be covered in blood. But *look* at him. The only bloodstains are on his hands, probably from when he came in and checked on Mr. Easton."

"He could have changed his clothes." The sheriff lifted his chin.

"And *when* exactly would I have had the time to do that?" Parker surged toward the man. "It's *you*, isn't it? You're the one St. John has in his pocket! How much did he pay you?" He grabbed the man's collar.

The police chief rushed through the door with several deputies. "What's going on here?"

Parker refused to release the weasel in his grip. "This man has been bribed by Mr. St. John." He jerked the so-called sheriff closer to his face. "Now tell us where he has Emily!"

The man didn't say a word.

Parker shoved him toward the deputies. "We're wasting valuable time. Someone *please* get word to Johanna that we're taking her dad to the hospital. And we've got to find Emily. Who knows what St. John could do to the child if he would do *this* to an old man?"

Where had Parker gone? It was so out of character to not see him come out at curtain call. And he told her that he had a surprise at the end, but that hadn't happened either.

Johanna helped put costumes away and listened to the buzz in the opera house. Everyone was talking about what a magnificent play it was and how talented the troupe was. Especially their very own Parker.

Speculation about where he went ran rampant.

Marvella rushed to her backstage. Her cheeks were flushed, eyes wide.

Johanna's heart plummeted. "What is it? Is it Parker? Is he all right?"

The Judge walked in after his wife. "I'm so sorry, Johanna, but someone beat your father, and he's at the hospital."

Her hand flew up to cover her mouth. "No. Not Dad!" Then the world stopped. She couldn't breathe. "Where's Emily?" Had James finally gone through with his threat?

"I had two men keeping watch outside your home this evening, and the police found them bound and gagged in the wagon shed." The Judge was calm, but the storm of fury in him could not be missed. "I'm so sorry, I thought we could stop him."

Tears clogged her throat. "Where's Parker?"

"He's with the police chief looking for Emily. But there's more . . . The reason Parker wasn't here was because someone sent him a note saying your father was dead and that Emily and you would be next if he didn't leave town. So he went straight to your house to check on them. The sheriff tried to arrest him, saying he got a phone call from James, who said he witnessed Parker beat your father. But Parker confronted the sheriff and figured out he was James's paid man. Thankfully, the police chief and his deputies showed up."

The Judge's face swirled before her. She couldn't breathe. Her legs buckled, and she fell to the floor, her face in her hands. "This can't be happening." Looking up, she pleaded with the Judge. "Please tell me they know where to find my little girl." Johanna's stomach lurched. Her daughter was missing, and Dad was badly hurt. Would he survive the night? *Oh, God, help! Please! We need to find Emily . . . and please help the doctor to be able to save Dad.*

She closed her eyes. How could she have been so stupid as to leave them alone?

"Let's go see your father, and then we're taking you back to our home until they find Emily." Marvella pulled Johanna to her feet. "I'm sure she'll be fine. The whole town will help find her. I'll sit up with you all night if necessary. Now . . . let's go, dear. There's nothing more we can do here. It's time to rally everyone to pray."

21

The banging at the door jolted him from the chair. Killing Daniel Easton had invigorated him, but by the time he got home and placed the call to the sheriff, he was beyond spent.

The pounding came again. Where was Mrs. Simpson, and why didn't she answer the door? Wait. She had the night off. She'd gone to that ridiculous play.

James straightened and forced his body to comply. He slipped through the dark to the study where he could see who was on his porch.

The police chief? Odd . . . where was the sheriff?

He opened the door, and the chief spoke first.

"James St. John?"

"Yes. How can I help you?" He turned on the outside light without thinking.

"Where's Emily?" Parker surged forward out of the shadows.

James motioned to the lawman. "That man has made multiple threats against me, and tonight I saw him kill Daniel Easton. He had a big club and hit him over and over. Why have you brought him here?"

"He's brought me here so we can find Emily. Where is she, James?" Parker pushed toward the door.

James shook his head. "I don't have Emily. *He* does. He probably killed her the same as the old man."

Parker leaned closer, his nose only an inch from James's. "*The old man,* as you call him, is alive. Mr. Easton has been delivered safely to the hospital."

James swallowed what felt like a lump of coal in his throat. "Alive, you say? Well . . . that's good news."

The officers moved forward. "We need to ask you some questions."

"And we need to find Emily." Parker looked over James's shoulder.

"I don't know where the child is. When I saw you kill . . . ah, *wound* Mr. Easton, I made a run for it, fearing you'd kill me. I called the sheriff and did my duty. Now if you'll leave me, please, I have nothing of value that I can add to what I told the sheriff earlier. I saw Mr. Parker bludgeon Daniel Easton. I have no idea what happened to the child."

He turned to close the door, but Parker was faster and grabbed the front of his coat. "We know you've paid off the sheriff."

"Help! He's going to kill me!"

Parker gave a hard yank on his coat, popping the buttons that held it closed, then frowned. "Look! Look at all the blood."

Before James could think, Parker pulled the handkerchief out of James's vest pocket to reveal even more blood.

Two deputies took hold of James. And the chief got in his face. "How do you explain this?"

What was happening? Did they actually believe this actor over him? "I fell. As I ran back from Easton's place I . . . uh

... well, I fell. I hit my nose and it bled. Bled quite a bit, as you can see."

The chief shook his head. "For a man of the law, you'd think he'd know better than to give us such a tale."

Parker pushed into the house, several officers close behind, turning on lights as they went.

"Emily! Emily, it's Parker! I've come to get you, sweetheart. Emily!"

James looked at the deputy holding his arms and found the man watching him with a scowl.

James sniffed. "She's not here. I assure you. Parker is the one to blame. Not I. He must have taken her."

The deputy shoved him into the front sitting room and all but tossed him onto the sofa. "I think you'd better start telling me what happened tonight. Why were you at Daniel Easton's house?"

Drat the man! Where was the sheriff? "I . . . uh . . . I go there all the time. Johanna is my sister-in-law."

"Emily!"

Footsteps raced up the stairs to the second floor. That horrible actor! All his yelling and stomping could raise the dead.

"So you went to the Easton house to see your sister-in-law?" The deputy stood over him, hands on hips.

"Yes . . . uh . . . yes. I went to see her and . . . uh . . ."

"Emily! It's Parker, Emily!"

"Tell him to shut up!" James could hardly take it anymore.

"He's trying to find a missing child, and you'd better pray she's all right when he does."

James looked at the officer's face. Hard and unforgiving.

Enough! How dare this fool treat him like a criminal. He started to get up, but the deputy knocked him back.

"You're stayin' right there."

Parker returned from upstairs. "I tore through the rooms, and she's not up there. I'll keep looking down here."

A noise sounded somewhere in the house, and both men looked to James.

He shook his head and laughed. "It's the cat, gentlemen. Just the cat."

"Didn't sound like a cat." Parker took a step forward. "Why don't you let me beat it out of him. I'm sure he'd confess after one blow."

James pushed back into the sofa. "*He's* the killer. I'm telling you, I saw him beat the old man with his fists."

The chief tilted a look at him. "So now he beat him with his fists? I thought you said he hit him with a club of some type."

The infuriating man! "Both! He did both. He's—"

The noise came again, followed by what sounded like a crate opening and something falling to the floor.

James held his breath. No! That little monster! Why couldn't she stay where he put—

The chief turned toward the hallway arch, while Parker moved to the hall. The sound of little feet running pounded inside James's aching head.

Emily appeared and stumbled into Parker's arms, wrapping herself around him. "Daddy, you found me."

Parker nestled her close and kissed her over and over. "I'm here, sweetheart. I found you. Daddy found you."

Of all the unmitigated—"*You* aren't her father! You aren't her *anything*!" James jumped to his feet. If he could make a dash to the open window, he could jump out and get away.

The deputy had hold of him in a heartbeat. The man's fingers dug in tight as James fought against him.

There *had* to be a way of escape. He was too close to having it all. Too close to lose now—

His hands were jerked behind him. Handcuffs were snapped onto his wrists. "James St. John, you're under arrest for the attack on Daniel Easton and the kidnapping of Emily St. John."

Johanna was at her father's side when Parker appeared in the doorway of the hospital room. For a moment she feared the worst, but then he gave her a simple nod.

Oh, praise God! Emily was all right!

She jumped to her feet and flew into his arms. Clutching him close, she thanked God over and over for saving them.

"Emily is with the doctor right now. James gave her laudanum, but otherwise she is unharmed."

"Oh, thank God. Thank You, God!" Johanna's tears flowed down her cheeks. "I've got to see her." She pulled away and glanced back at her father's bandaged form. "Doctor Foster says he's badly wounded and only time will tell. But he's a fighter."

"Come on, I'll take you to Emily."

She let Parker lead her, his protective hold on her giving her courage. She wasn't alone, and neither was Emily. They entered the small examination room to find Emily sitting on the table while Doctor Foster checked her over. Her little girl looked fine, but until she held her—touched her—it wouldn't be enough.

She rushed to her baby's side and, mindless of the doctor, scooped her into her arms and kissed her face. Stroking her daughter's baby-soft hair, Johanna gave her a quick once-over. "Are you all right, sweetheart? Did you get hurt?"

"I fine, Mama. Daddy found me."

Daddy? Johanna raised an eyebrow at Parker.

He smiled and shrugged. "She said it. But I am happy to take on the title and role, if you approve."

She covered her mouth. Warmth reddened her cheeks. This day continued to be full of surprises. But if he was asking what she thought he was asking, she knew what her answer would be. "Are you proposing to me, Parker Bennett? Here in the hospital in front of the doctor and his staff?"

An older woman who served as the doctor's nurse actually snorted, while Dr. Foster did nothing to hide his grin.

She looked back to Parker, who seemed ready to burst into laughter.

Emily patted her arm and gave a yawn. "Can we go home? I wanna sleep."

Cheeks burning, Johanna glanced away from Parker to her daughter. Had she misread Parker? His intentions? Why didn't he say something?

She ran a hand over Emily's hair. Perhaps once Emily was asleep, she could have a good cry before bed. The day had been overwhelming enough without her trying to add an engagement to it all.

"I think that would be wise for all of you." Dr. Foster came back to the table. "Emily seems fine, but she'll need to sleep off the effects of the laudanum."

"And Dad?" Johanna bit her lip.

"As I told you, only time will tell. But we will have people here around the clock to watch him. He's older and less able to withstand trauma to his body. And anytime the brain is involved . . . well . . . we don't know enough. Until the swelling goes down, he'll probably remain in a coma. There's no telling when he'll awaken."

While she'd hoped for miraculous news, this was better than her father no longer being with them on this earth. "We'll go home and return in the morning." Johanna looked to Parker. At his nod, she reached to pick up Emily.

"I want Daddy to carry me." Emily reached up to Parker.

Johanna stepped back and watched as Parker took Emily in his arms. Her sweet little girl placed her head on Parker's shoulder and closed her eyes. The child had utter peace and confidence in the man she now called her daddy.

God, let me have that kind of confidence in You . . . my Father.

Johanna drove the wagon back, Parker cradling Emily as she slept. They didn't speak. There was really no need.

When they reached the house, Parker carried Emily to her bed. While Johanna undressed her and readied her for bed, Parker cared for the horse and wagon. By the time Johanna came downstairs again, he was standing by a window in the darkened front room.

How she loved him.

"Come here."

He knew she was there? Of course he did. They could sense the other's presence. And his tender whisper sent chills dancing through her. She went into his arms.

Parker kissed the top of her head and held her close for a long while. Johanna rested her head against his shoulder, much as her daughter had. There was something so perfect in the action, in his strength and tenderness surrounding her.

Everything would be all right.

"I love you, Parker, and I want you to know I'm done being scared. I'm saying yes to us. I don't know how to fit in your world, and the idea of it scares me. But not more than the thought of living my life without you. So I will do my best to support you in what God's gifted you to do."

His arms tightened around her, and she felt his lips against her hair again. "My world is right here, Johanna. I'm leaving the stage—at least any stage that requires I leave Kalispell. My home is here with you and Emily, and I don't need anything else."

Johanna's head jerked up, and she looked into his face. Had she heard him correctly? Light from the entryway gave very little illumination, but she saw he spoke the truth. His smile was gentle, and there was a peace in his eyes she hadn't seen in a long time.

Swallowing back the lump that threatened to clog her throat, she hugged him tight. "I never even dared to hope that you would say such a thing. I was preparing to follow you wherever you went."

His chuckle rumbled in his chest beneath her cheek. "I love hearing that. But I've prayed a lot these past few weeks. Leaving the troupe, staying here with you and Emily and your dad . . . it's the right thing to do."

"What will you do for a job?"

"It won't be preaching. I hope that won't alter your decision."

Johanna reached up to touch his cheek. "It doesn't alter anything. I married Gerald and fulfilled my calling to be a preacher's wife. God has given me a new calling now."

"And what is that?"

She smiled. "To love you."

Parker had never felt such completion as he did in that moment. For all of his life he had worked to serve God and share His love, and there had been much satisfaction in that. But holding the woman who would be his wife, thinking of the child upstairs who would be his daughter . . . it was as if all of the roles he'd ever played had come together in one grand finale. *This* was the part that he'd always been meant to play. This was a real and holy calling that God had given him.

When he looked down, all he could see was love in Johanna's eyes. Love for him. He lowered his lips to hers and savored the moment. How amazing God's blessings were!

"I wish you could stay here tonight." Johanna whispered the words as he stepped back.

"Me too."

"We could call and wake up the Judge." She smiled.

At the thought, he roared with laughter. "For all Marvella's matchmaking and tender interference, I'd say they *deserve* to be awakened. We could always have a formal wedding in the days to come."

"I agree. Do you want to call them, or should I?"

He waggled his brows. "How about I head over to their house right now?"

Johanna would never understand how Marvella managed it, but her music room was decorated with rose-trimmed garlands, long white candles, and a small side table complete with refreshments. Her staff was dressed and standing to one side, ready to act upon a moment's notice. Parker's mother stayed with Emily while Johanna and Parker went to the Ashburys'.

They hadn't even bothered to change their clothes, although Marvella had offered them a change if they so desired. Was there *anything* that woman didn't have at her disposal?

Sir Theophilus danced around them as the Judge set the ceremony in motion. The Ashburys' butler, Tobias, acted as Parker's witness, while Johanna could think of no better person to stand with her than Marvella herself while Cora was on her honeymoon. The older woman was actually stunned silent at the request, which the Judge said was a first.

When it came time for the exchange of a ring, Johanna gasped when Parker produced a small gold band.

His smile was tender and sweet. "It belonged to my mother. She and Dad had the best marriage that I could ever imagine. She gave it to me tonight and prayed a blessing over it and us."

Johanna's eyes dampened as she accepted the gift. If only Dad could be with them as the Judge pronounced them husband and wife, but then again, he was. It was his wish that they marry, so when he regained consciousness he'd be delighted to hear that they had gone ahead and done it. Maybe it would even give him incentive to recover quickly.

"You may kiss your bride, son." Judge Ashbury nodded to Parker.

Her beloved moved so quickly to take Johanna in his arms that she couldn't contain a gasp.

Mrs. Ashbury chuckled and stepped closer to her husband. "You don't have to tell that boy twice."

If the Judge replied, Johanna didn't hear it.

22

Monday, May 8, 1905

He did *not* belong in shackles. How humiliating for a man of his status in the community to be treated in this fashion. On top of that, Judge Ashbury suggested he might want a lawyer to represent him at this hearing. A lawyer!

Who did he think he was dealing with? James *was* a lawyer. The best Kalispell has ever known. Everyone knew that.

He wanted to shout to the rafters that they had no right to treat him in such a fashion. Not only that, but his head was killing him. The pain was severe, as it had been since the night he'd dealt with Daniel Easton.

The police chief sat to his right, and the court reporter, Rebecca Andrews, sat to the Judge's right. It was all so uncalled for. Why should he be forced to endure this charade?

The last people to enter the room were—well, well. Geoffry Brandenberg, one of Kalispell's finest lawyers. James had once had respect for the man, but that would certainly change if Brandenberg was tied up in this mess.

After Brandenberg came Parker, carrying Emily, and last

. . . Johanna. They took their seats without even looking in his direction.

How rude.

That Parker again had Emily in his arms was atrocious! The fiend! What was he trying to prove by stealing James's niece away?

No one would get away with this travesty of justice.

"It looks like most of us are here." Judge Ashbury inclined his head. "So let us get started. First, for the record, we are reviewing the events of Friday, May 5th, the year of our Lord, 1905. Events that took place at the home of Daniel Easton, his daughter, Johanna Easton St. John, and her daughter, Emily St. John. On the night of May 5th, Daniel Easton was attacked in his home and bludgeoned to an unconscious state. His grand-daughter, Emily, was then removed from the home without permission and later found at the residence of her uncle, James St. John. This hearing is to ascertain the facts of the evening and hear the explanations of those involved. Daniel Easton has regained consciousness and has issued a sworn statement to be read." The Judge produced the paper and held it aloft. "I'll read it now and then will allow Mr. St. John to respond."

He'd *better* let James speak. He had the right to let them know exactly what he thought of this farce. He . . . *he* had spent *three nights* in the jail and had been treated poorly.

"Unca James is a bad man."

The child's voice caused every head in the room to turn. James looked at his niece. Oh, how he hated that creature. "Shut her up."

"No." Judge Ashbury motioned Emily to continue. "Tell us why your uncle is a bad man, Emily."

"There was blood." Emily shifted in Parker's arms. She

pointed her finger and shook it at James. "He . . . he . . . he's bad. And he has . . . bad candy."

"Bad candy?" The Judge's eyes narrowed. "What bad candy did he have, Emily?"

She screwed up her face and shook her head. "He said it was good, and I ate it, but it was bad."

Johanna spoke up. "The doctor said she was given laudanum."

"She was upset." James didn't even try to hide his disgust. "Her grandfather was hurt, and she was upset. I simply tried to help the child calm down."

"Emily, I have a question for you." Judge Ashbury smiled. "Tell me why you think your Uncle James is bad."

"He hit Pawpaw. He made Pawpaw have blood."

"You saw him hit your grandfather?"

"*Outrageous!*" James surged to his feet. "She's a stupid child. She's only saying what Parker and Johanna have told her to say. This is ridiculous. I refuse to be accused by a *child*."

"Sit *down*." The police chief glared at him. "Judge, Mr. St. John bribed the sheriff and lied about witnessing Mr. Bennett hit Mr. Easton. However, it was St. John who had blood on his coat and shirt."

"I tried to help get Easton to the hospital." James rubbed his head. "I'm sure I got blood on my clothes when I attempted to help him."

"You didn't do anything to help."

How could that horrible Parker tell lies with such calm? Ah yes, he was an actor.

Parker went on. "When I arrived at the Easton house, you were nowhere to be found, and neither was Emily. I'm the one who attempted to help Daniel."

299

James let out a harsh laugh. "That's the word of an *actor*. A man who tells lies on the stage for a living."

"Even the best of men can go bad, Mr. St. John." The Judge shook his head. "I think the wise thing is to let Daniel Easton speak for himself. I'll read his deposition, which was obtained this morning at the hospital. Present were myself, Mr. Brandenberg, attorney-at-law, and court reporter Rebecca Andrews."

The Judge put on his glasses. "'I, Daniel Easton, do solemnly swear that the information I am about to give is true.'

"Question by Mr. Geoffry Brandenberg: 'Mr. Easton would you tell us where you were and what you were doing the night of Friday, May 5th?'

"Answer by Daniel Easton: 'I was in my home taking care of my granddaughter, Emily, while her mother attended a play at the opera house.'

"Question by Mr. Branderberg: 'Please tell me in your own words what happened that evening.'

"Answer by Mr. Easton: 'After we had supper, I read Emily several Bible stories—'"

"Pawpaw read about the lions and Daniel. Pawpaw's name is Daniel. Just like in da Bible."

Would *no one* silence that brat?

Johanna took her daughter from the doting Parker. "Shh, Emily. You need to be quiet unless they ask you a question."

The Judge smiled at the little monster. Actually smiled! What was *wrong* with these people?

"I like that story very much, Emily. I'll continue reading now.

"Answer by Mr. Easton: 'After we had supper, I read Emily several Bible stories and then had her go get her nightgown so we could get her ready for bed. There was a knock on the door. I answered it, and James St. John was there. He asked if he could speak to me. I invited him in, then when I turned my back, I was struck with a hard object. I turned back around, and James hit me again and again. I fell to the ground and almost immediately lost consciousness.'"

"It's a *lie!*" His outburst wouldn't endear him to the Judge, but so what? This was all a sham anyway. "I refuse to sit here and be treated this way. You have no proof. How dare you believe the rantings of an old man, who suffered a head injury and can't be trusted to remember, and a child, who has been prompted by her mother. A mother, I might add, who has continually endangered said child's life. Why, even now the poor thing has her hand stitched from injury. Who can say how it even happened? The child lives in danger with her mother, and I am petitioning the court to release Emily St. John, *my* niece, to *my* custody. *That's* why we're here."

Why was everyone staring at him? They were frowning and whispering. Well, let them be confused.

He rubbed his temple.

"Mr. St. John, you are not here to petition for anything." Judge Ashbury gave him a most severe, even reprimanding look.

He was always doing that in court. Someone should call attention to the old man's wandering mind. He couldn't keep track of anything.

The Judge set the paper in his hand aside and leaned forward, folding his hands together. "Are you well, Mr. St. John?"

At the back of the room, the door opened. James turned to see who it might be. Hopefully someone had come to his rescue and would put an end to this lunacy.

Yvette Lebeau strolled into the room as though she were on a stage. She was dressed in her finery—feathers and lace and a hat big enough to shade three people. James scowled. A lot of good she could do him now.

Judge Ashbury nodded to her. "Miss Lebeau, thank you for coming today. I wonder if you might take the seat to my left?" He waited until she was seated and then smiled. "I expect the truth and nothing but the truth, young lady. We're trying to sort through what happened on Friday night. I wonder if you might tell us your part in all of this?"

"*Bien sûr.*" She leaned forward, pretending to be on the edge of her chair.

The Judge was buying her act. Stupid man.

"First, let's establish for the sake of record who you are."

"My name is Yvette Lebeau. I am an actress. An internationally known star of stage."

The Judge nodded. "And how is it that you have come to be a part of this matter?"

That Rebecca woman's constant scribbling was beginning to get on his last nerve. Why must her pencil make such horrid scratching on the paper? *Make. It. Stop.*

"I came to Kalispell with our theatre troupe. We have been performing at the opera house for several weeks now. Mr. St. John was known to me in New York City, where our social circles often . . . entwined. Mr. St. John asked for my help and, since we both owed the same men a lot of money and he offered me a substantial amount to do what he asked, I agreed. It was a job, *c'est tout.*"

"And what was it that Mr. St. John asked you to do?"

James shook his head. She wouldn't dare.

But she did. "He wanted me to entice Parker Bennett and make him believe I was in love with him, so that the papers would say we were a couple and that Johanna woman wouldn't want anything to do with him."

Judge Ashbury raised an eyebrow. "And did you attempt to do that?"

"I did. I quickly came to see he loved another, however. I continued to try to convince Parker that we should be together, but he was not interested. James then told me I had to do something rash. He gave me a bottle of pills and told me to pretend I wanted to kill myself. He suggested how to do this so that I would not really die."

"And you took the pills?"

"I did. I didn't want to, but I needed the money." She looked at Parker. "I was the one who sent the note on Friday night. James told me I had to get someone at the theatre to give it to you before the final curtain call so that you would be gone from the stage. This way he could place you at the house where he told me he planned to kill Mr. Easton."

"That's a lie!" James tried to jump to his feet only to have the deputy push him back into his chair.

The Judge turned on him, pointing a beefy finger in his direction. "Remain seated, Mr. St. John, and refrain from further outbursts. I will have you removed if you fail to comply."

Fine. James sat still. There was no sense in arguing. They had already rigged everything against him. He would have to do something drastic. But what?

The Judge nodded to Yvette. "Miss Lebeau, you may continue."

"I delivered the message to one of the stagehands and told them Parker must receive it before the final curtain call." Again she turned toward Bennett. "I'm so sorry, Parker. I never meant for this to happen. If I hadn't needed the money, I would never have listened to Mr. St. John. He assured me that he only wanted to set matters in motion to have you arrested and out of his hair so that he might marry Mrs. St. John."

"Miss Lebeau, did Mr. St. John tell you why it was so important to him to marry Mrs. St. John?"

"He told me that they would come into money once they were married. That's how he intended to pay me."

James could barely control himself. He should kill her for revealing the situation with the will! He *would* kill her when this was over, and he was acquitted!

"All right, thank you, Miss Lebeau. You may go." The Judge looked to James. "Very well, Mr. St. John, since you are so determined to speak, now is your chance."

James squeezed his eyes shut as white searing pain ripped through his head. Not now! He had to think clearly. He had to present his case. Yvette stood and started past him.

Better yet, why not kill her *now*?

He lunged at her, gripping her slender throat in shackled hands, ready to squeeze the life out of he—

White-hot pain washed through him. With a groan, his hands dropped to his sides. The room disappeared from view.

And he fell into the dark.

FRIDAY, JUNE 2, 1905

Finally, life was getting back to at least a semblance of order.

Johanna sat down to dinner at the Ashbury's table. The Judge had said he had news to share with them this evening, and Marvella insisted they all come to supper. Dad was even recovered enough to attend. In fact, he was more like his old self every day, thanks to spending a great deal of time with Parker's mother.

Johanna almost giggled. Another wedding might be taking place soon.

The Judge offered grace, then smiled at those gathered. "I am glad you could all come this evening. I know that Sir Theophilus will enjoy his time with Emily and Mimi in the garden. Cook set them up with a darling little picnic of their own."

"She was over the moon." Johanna thought of her daughter's exuberance as they walked to the Ashbury mansion. "I told her what you had planned and, well, you saw her delight when we first came through the door."

"Indeed. What a precious child." Marvella motioned to the servers to begin. "She seems no worse for all that happened."

"No." Johanna knew a miracle when she saw one. "I believe God is moving us all past what happened. Even Dad said he feels like a youngster again."

"It's true." Her father gave a chuckle. "Of course, I can honestly say that Parker's mother has something to do with it. She keeps bringing me various dishes she's made. Claims they have healing properties."

"Perhaps *she's* the healing property." Marvella gave her husband a knowing smile. "I think I should have her to tea."

Johanna suppressed a snort. If she knew Marvella, she'd find a way to invite Dad too. She sipped her water. Perhaps a Marvella Ashbury push was what the two needed to see their feelings for one another. She caught Marvella's gaze, and her friend gave her a wink. Johanna let out a chuckle.

The woman was the definition of incorrigible.

Once the food was served, the Judge cleared his throat. "I suppose the dinner table seems a strange place to strike up a serious conversation, but I thought to get this out of the way so that we could enjoy the rest of the evening together."

Parker reached for the salt. "Of course, Judge. We're eager to know what you've learned."

Eager might not be the word for it. Johanna was grateful that Judge Ashbury was spending his time and efforts learning what James had been talking about in his crazed diatribe. But she was also a bit anxious. What could it all mean?

"James died of a cerebral hemorrhage, like his brother. But he also had a tumor behind his left eye, which is what caused his delirium there at the end. In rare cases, it can be genetic. Of course, his lifestyle didn't help, what with all the drinking and gambling and angering the wrong people."

Johanna faced that news with mixed emotions. She never wanted James to die, but his behavior had been terrifying.

"The important thing"—Marvella patted Johanna's hand—"is that Emily is safe, and James can do no further harm."

The Judge cleared his throat. "As for the money he spoke of . . . his father's inheritance . . . it seems his father disinherited him some time ago and named Gerald St. John as his sole heir. The will was never changed, even after Gerald's death, but James declared it had been. He waited a good bit of time to settle his father's estate, because he hoped certain people known to the family would forget about his father's decision to omit him from any inheritance.

"One judge, a good friend of James's father, did remember and questioned James on the matter. Soon after, though, there was an accident, and the judge died. Apparently the authorities now believe the judge's death was murder. And they are investigating whether James's and Gerald's father's death was murder as well."

Johanna let go a gasp. Parker reached over and took hold of her hand. James had murdered his own father? It was horrific to imagine.

Parker continued to hold on to Johanna, gently stroking the back of her hand. "What happens now?"

The Judge nodded. "Back to the will. The one presented by James, which named him as a beneficiary, was determined to be a fraud. A handwriting expert was brought in when word got out after the judge's death. The handwriting was James's rather than his father's. So the original will stands, and Johanna, you are now to inherit the entirety of the St. John fortune. It's substantial."

The words crashed into her like a wave. There was a St. John *fortune*? "How? Why? I mean, Gerald was always so frugal. Talked about how poor his childhood was. I . . . I don't understand."

"It seems that Gerald's father was a part of a group of inventors, and something of theirs took off." The Judge scratched the side of his face. "The details are a little unclear. How he earned his money is now irrelevant. The point is it now belongs to you."

She looked to her husband, whose eyes were as wide as hers. "I can hardly believe this. How quickly life can change. One moment I was worried about how to provide for my family, and now you're telling me I have an inheritance." A thought burst the stunned bubble around her mind. "But what about the people he owed money to? I don't want anything to do with it if people are going to come after my family."

The Judge shook his head. "The judge in New York sent a representative to the Camorras. James had paid his debt, and the head of the Camorra gang insisted that they were turning over a new leaf and working with the Catholic Church to reform the streets of Brooklyn. They had no idea about James's father or his fortune."

Johanna's father leaned back in his chair. "I, for one, am happy to see this thing resolved. I think we all need to put these last, awful months behind us and look to the future. Parker, didn't you have some good news to share?"

Everyone looked at Parker and Johanna. Parker had started to eat and paused once more. "I do. Johanna and I discussed it and decided that I will open a drama school and theatre troupe here in Kalispell. I saved a bit of money over the years and will use this to invest in a building, costumes, stage equipment, and so forth."

Johanna's heart swelled. The joy in Parker's voice was contagious. "Parker is also going to work with the children at church, and once a month they will put on a play that ties in with the pastor's sermon." She suppressed a giggle. Who would have ever thought she would be excited about a drama school? About acting?

Marvella applauded. "Wonderful! Perhaps we can come to visit your church when the first performance takes place. I would love to see what Parker can accomplish."

Parker dabbed his mouth with his linen and gave Marvella a nod. "I appreciate your support. My prayer is that it will make the Bible even more real to the children . . . perhaps the adults as well. I've always loved working with younger people. They are so enthusiastic."

Johanna had never been prouder of her husband. She couldn't resist giving him a smile. "There's additional news"— she glanced at Marvella—"and for this I will need to enlist the help of Mrs. Ashbury."

The older woman put down her fork and leaned forward. "Oh, do tell, my dear. What is it? I'm all ears."

Johanna laughed. "Well, as you know, Parker and I married without a formal ceremony. We would like to have a party to celebrate our marriage. I was hoping perhaps you could advise me on how to go about it. I've never hosted such a thing."

Marvella pressed her hands to her ample bosom, her smile wide. "It would be my delight. We'll hold it here, of course. We shall need two weeks to set things properly in motion. I will talk to Cook immediately, and tomorrow you will come over and we'll plan the menu."

"Oh, but I never wanted to burden you with *all* the plans." Johanna looked to Parker and then to the Judge. "That wasn't my intention."

The Judge let out a hearty laugh. "My dear, Marvella lives for these moments. You might as well ask the sun not to shine. There are two things my wife is good at. Throwing parties and matchmaking. Since she has no new couples to see married at the moment, a party is exactly what she needs to keep herself busy."

"Who says there are no new couples to see married?" Marvella gave them a conspiratorial look and settled her gaze on Johanna's father. "God continues to send lonely souls my way. It's all a matter of doing His work."

Epilogue

Marvella strolled around the garden making certain that everyone seemed to be enjoying themselves. "My dear. Splendid job as always." The Judge was at her elbow, and he steered her over to the gazebo.

"Thank you, Milton, but if you haven't noticed, we have many guests to attend to." She put on her best smile and attempted to tug him in the other direction.

But he held fast.

She sputtered and twirled around to see a broad grin on his face. Narrowing her eyes, she crossed her arms over her chest. "What are you up to, Judge Ashbury?"

He led her into the gazebo, where a vase was filled with roses and flower petals covered the floor.

As she took in the romantic little space, her hands fluttered to her chest. "You did this?"

He nodded.

"For me?"

Another nod. This time he stepped closer and pulled her into his arms. As if on cue, the string quartet in the garden began to play. Milton kissed her on the lips and then waltzed her around the gazebo.

It had been ages since she'd been in his arms dancing, and she didn't mind the way he swept her across the floor. Not one bit. When he ended the dance by twirling her around, a giggle escaped her lips. He pulled her close again and kissed her.

"What has gotten into you?" She breathed against his lips.

His mustache twitched. "Oh, probably just watching you have fun with your matchmaking. Love is in the air."

She swatted at his chest.

"In all seriousness, my dear, the young people have a surprise out there for you, but first . . . I wanted to give you a gift."

"Whatever for?"

"Because I love you, that's what for." He released her and handed her an envelope.

She slid the flap open and pulled out the tickets. Her eyes widened. Lots of tickets.

"We're going to see the country, my dear. I know you're not fond of ships anymore, so I decided Europe was out of the question, but we can take trains all over the grand US of A and explore whatever your heart desires."

Flinging her arms around his neck, she pulled him close. "I love you, Milton Ashbury. I can't wait to have Johanna make me a new hat . . . oh, and I'll need to have someone tend to my roses while I'm gone." The list in her mind grew by the second.

"Don't get too carried away with your planning. We still have Johanna and Parker's reception today."

Her eyes widened. "Our guests! Oh my, I had forgotten about them."

"Well, I know you planned this day for them, but there is that little surprise I was telling you about." He took her hand

and led her back out of the gazebo and to the party in the garden.

Everything stopped, and people around them stood and applauded as the Judge led her to the front where Johanna and Parker, Rebecca and Mark, and Carter and Ellie all stood hand in hand.

Rebecca stepped forward, and the crowd quieted. "Marvella, would you join us up here?"

She glanced at her husband. No one had ever pulled off a surprise for her before. No one. What a smart man she'd married.

He helped her up the two small steps and then hurried away.

"While we are here to celebrate another beautiful couple in our town, Johanna came to me with an idea to honor the woman who brought us all together." Rebecca motioned to someone in the crowd.

Mary and George walked up. Then Phyllis and Dwain. Garry and Judy. Charles and Elizabeth. And four other couples.

"We've all been 'victims' of Marvella's matchmaking, and we couldn't be happier!" Ellie grinned.

The crowd roared with laughter and then applause. Each couple came forward to share little stories of Marvella's antics to bring them together, and then told the crowd how long they'd been married and how many children they had.

The couples all surrounded Marvella and showered her in hugs and kisses on the cheek.

People cried out, "Speech! Speech!"

For the first time in all her years, Marvella didn't know what to say. She looked out upon the crowd of friends and townspeople, and her heart swelled.

A yip sounded from the back of the crowd. Marvella's eyes widened as Sir Theophilus barreled toward her, his leash streaming behind him. Tobias ran after him, his face flushed.

"Let him go, Tobias." The Judge waved the butler away. "It's too late now that he's spotted her."

Chuckles rippled through the crowd as Marvella bent down, arms wide, and her dog leaped into them. He yipped and wriggled, giving her face wet kisses. Oh, how this little rascal filled her heart with joy.

After a few moments, her sweet pet settled in her arms. She caught Milton's eye as he winked at her.

And suddenly she knew exactly what to say.

"I've had the privilege to be married to my true love all these years. I simply wanted *everyone* to experience the unexpected grace and incredible love that God has given us."

Her gaze drifted from Rebecca and Mark, to Carter and Ellie, and Parker and Johanna. Though the Lord had not seen fit to give her children, He had blessed her beyond measure with these souls and so many others. *Father God, what a blessing you've given me in the people of our dear town.*

Tears welled in her eyes as she looked at her wonderful husband again. "I suppose it would behoove me to keep it brief for the first time in my life. So I will leave you with a verse that has carried me most of my years here on this earth. Psalm 63, verse 3. 'Because Thy lovingkindness is better than life, my lips shall praise Thee.'"

The crowd roared in hearty agreement: "Amen!"

One

"I cannot tell what the years may bring, life is a scene of change."

~Earl Douglass

SUNDAY, JUNE 2, 1878 · SETTLEMENT OF WALKER CREEK, WYOMING TERRITORY

Home.

A seemingly innocuous word. A place she loved. And yet, every time Anna Lakeman returned there, her insides begged to differ.

She could see it in the distance, just a few minutes away . . . the house where she grew up, where she learned to sketch and paint.

The wheels of the wagon bumped and rolled their way along the grass- and weed-covered lane. A testament to her absence.

What was it about coming home that made her want to run away?

With each return from a dig with her father, she pondered

the same questions. Never getting any answers. Or perhaps she'd been avoiding the answer for too long.

Memories of her mother were beautiful and made her feel warm and loved, so it wasn't the loss of the woman who gave her life that brought these feelings.

Then there was the loss of her best friend, Mary. It had been a decade since her friend went missing, but Anna felt the absence in her heart and soul every day. Some people said that grief lessened over time. And if she was honest, she could say that yes, the grief was less. But the loss . . . she knew that as keenly today as she had the day Mary didn't return.

Home was where she had the best memories of Mary and of Mama.

So why was it an uncomfortable place? This time she didn't silence the answer.

She knew why. Because *he* wasn't there.

It was best to face facts. Her struggle came down to the loss of her first and only love, Joshua Ziegler.

She drove her wagon up to the door and set the brake, her shoulders sagging with a long exhale. It exhausted her to deny that struggle over and over. The effort it took to shove it down so she wouldn't voice the words weighed heavier each day.

But that was the path of great loss.

And even though the loss wasn't in death, she felt it as such.

Three years had passed since he'd gone back east for medical school. Three years since their spat. Three years since they'd talked. Shared their hearts. Talked of dreams of the future. Until he left, she would've never dreamed of life without him. The community expected them to marry. Their families expected them to marry.

She'd expected them to marry.

The rumble of her father's wagon brought her thoughts

around. This was no time for her pondering. She had work to do.

Every inch of Anna's body ached as she stepped from the hub of the wheel into the tall, dry grass in front of her home. She stretched but it didn't help the soreness that seemed to scream from every muscle. With a glance around, she took mental notes of the scene. One she'd sketched a thousand times and would probably do a thousand times more. Other than the growth being too tall around the house, not much had changed in the months she'd been gone with her father.

"I don't know if it's me and my old age, but the road seems to get rougher every time we travel it." Dad's soft chuckle brought her gaze around.

"It's not you, I can promise you that." Turning on her heel, she stretched one more time and then stepped toward the supplies that needed to be unloaded.

A bone-jarring wagon ride over the rough Wyoming terrain for the past five hours had given her insides the impression she was eighty years old rather than a young twenty-one. But such was the life of a traveling paleontologist and his daughter. He went wherever the bones called. She tagged along to sketch and paint everything.

As they unloaded crates, bags, and fresh supplies they'd purchased from the large mercantile up in Green River, she longed to get back to all her sketches from the trip. The bones of the horse-like creature they'd found fossilized in the rock layer weren't the greatest find her father had ever had, but they *were* interesting. Quite exciting to draw too, since she'd never seen a bone structure quite like it.

As a child, she'd wanted to be a paleontologist just like her father. She'd hung on his every word, watched his every move, and read every tome written on the subject.

But over the years, she'd learned the harsh truth.

Women didn't pursue science like that. And they most certainly didn't dig in the dirt. That was unacceptable. And vulgar—according to the women of society who knew about such things.

Although, she had to admit that she'd always admired the work of Mary Anning from Lyme Regis, England. The woman had been a fossil collector pretty much her whole life, and even though she wasn't given the credit she deserved, her name was still well-known in paleontological discussions. Why couldn't Anna do the same?

If only she could have known the woman. But Mary Anning had been gone for thirty years and had lived half a world away. Besides, her fossil collecting had been her means of support after her father's death when she was eleven. Probably why it had been somewhat acceptable. The pity of the public gave allowances now and then.

Anna released her breath as she set down another satchel. Even though she longed to be the one to find the next great discovery in paleontology, her gifting truly was in the sketching. Oh, how she loved every little detail.

Now that they were home, Dad would sequester himself with all his notes and specimens, and she would need to put the house to order once again. After that, she could spend all the time she wanted going through the sketches and reliving their last dig.

They worked together hauling and sorting, enjoying the quiet camaraderie that had become habitual. It didn't take long to set things in their proper place since they'd left everything clean and in order. The one addition was the layer of dust, which Anna eliminated with the removal of the sheets covering the furniture and quick use of the broom.

"I'll be in my study, Anna." Dad's nose was in a book as he walked down the hall.

She'd figured as much, but unlike her usual desire to get back to her sketches, her insides swirled. The unsettled feeling called for something different from her usual routine. "I think I'll go see the Zieglers then, if that's all right with you?" she called after him. "Louise will return tomorrow to help around the house."

"That's fine." His voice vanished as the door clicked behind him. Whether or not he'd heard what she said was the question of the hour, but he'd likely stay buried in his study for the rest of the afternoon anyway.

Anna hauled the tub into her bedroom and filled it with warm water. Washing away all the dirt from the travels made her feel a bit more like herself. She dunked her head to rinse the soap from her hair. She couldn't wait to see Mary's family. When her best friend disappeared ten years ago, Anna had spent days and weeks helping the community search for her.

When no trace of her friend had been found, she'd mourned with the family, begging her father to allow her to stay at their home for a few days. Each night, she'd cried herself to sleep in Mary's bed while Mrs. Ziegler sat in her rocking chair staring out the window at the dark.

It had taken the community months to recover from the loss. Mary's parents did their best to find joy in their faith and family, but the sorrow never left.

Over the years, Anna spent a lot of time at the Ziegler home. Martha and Joshua were older but had never seemed to mind when their little sister and her best friend tagged along. After Mary disappeared, Anna continued to spend a lot of time with the family. If she wasn't at school or out on a dig with her father, she could be found at the Ziegler home.

Then Martha got married, which left Joshua and Anna. They'd been comfortable with one another the entirety of their childhoods, but things changed. In the evenings they would read with his parents, she would show them her sketches, and he soon insisted on seeing her home each night.

It didn't take much for her to develop a deep crush on Joshua. For a long time, she thought it was mutual.

Anna shook those thoughts away along with the droplets of water from her bath. There was no sense in pining for the man who hadn't even bothered to write.

After dressing and pinning up her hair, she grabbed her bonnet, went out to her horse, and saddled Misty for the short ride out to the Ziegler ranch. With the wind at her back, she hunched over the mare and gave her free rein to race along the trail they both knew so well.

The pounding of her horse's hooves shook the rest of her ill thoughts away. A chat with Mrs. Ziegler—who'd been like a mother to her—would certainly settle her down again and help Anna to get over this melancholy.

But the ranch yard was empty. No smoke rose from the chimney. The barn doors were shut. Animals corralled close to the house.

It was clear no one was home.

"Bother." Anna allowed her shoulders to slump. They must be in town.

The choice before her stretched. Go to town in search of her friends? Of course, she'd have to see other people as well. That made the option a bit less desirable. Or . . . head home?

Her shadow disappeared on the ground as she contemplated. A cloud must have covered the sun for the moment. As her gaze shifted upward, the sky darkened, and gray clouds staged themselves in the distance to roll in and cover the sun for the rest of the afternoon.

It might blow over and it might not. What to do?

A crack of thunder made the decision for her.

She'd have to head home. What had been a beautiful day now seemed downright gloomy. Sad how it matched her mood.

Turning her mount back to the trail they'd just ridden, she pulled her hat down and tightened the string. Fat drops of rain dotted the dusty road. "Time to go, Misty. Let's hope those clouds don't have much to spill."

She shouldn't have voiced the words. Because within minutes, the sky opened up, and a storm like she'd never seen before gushed from the heavens. The trail almost disappeared before her eyes and Misty's unease vibrated through Anna's knees and thighs as she held on. Slowing her horse to a trot so she could gain her bearings, she couldn't see anything but the downpour of water. Misty's head bobbed up and down with her discomfort with the thunder and lightning.

There was no shelter and no other choice than pray that her faithful mare could find her way home. Anna's dress, her underclothes, and every inch of her were now soaked.

Lightning struck a nearby tree and Misty reared. Anna held on with all her might and clung to her horse's neck. "Whoa. Easy, girl. We need to get home in one piece, all right?" She soothed the mare and rubbed her neck, keeping her words calm. Which grew increasingly difficult as the storm built.

Tension grew in her neck and shoulders as she gripped the reins. If she couldn't see where they were going, how would Misty? Her beautiful mare was getting up in years.

God, please help us to make it home. The prayer left her mind as the sky seemed to open its floodgates and dump oceans of water on top of them.

Misty's head was visible but not by much. Anna's bonnet was completely flattened from the deluge, and rivers of water raced down her face and body. Bending over her horse, she held the reins and hugged Misty's neck. "Get us home, girl. You can do it."

Misty whinnied and shook her head as thunder rumbled overhead in a constant rhythm. Then the mare trotted forward.

Anna counted each second in the minutes as they passed, hoping and praying they would reach shelter soon.

She had tallied eleven minutes when the roar sounded behind her. What was that? She sat up and looked around, but she couldn't see anything through the sheets and sheets of rain that continued to pour down from above.

The roaring grew. Accompanied by massive explosions— snapping and cracking. What was happening?

A wall of water barreled toward her.

"Giddyap, girl!" she yelled in Misty's ear.

Her mare didn't hesitate and raced into a furious pace.

But they were no match for the water.

Just as they crested a hill, Anna felt the horse underneath her lift with the wave.

God . . . help!

Tracie Peterson (TraciePeterson.com) is the bestselling author of more than one hundred novels, both historical and contemporary, with nearly six million copies sold. She has won the ACFW Lifetime Achievement Award and the Romantic Times Career Achievement Award. Her avid research resonates in her many bestselling series. Tracie and her family make their home in Montana.

Kimberley Woodhouse (KimberleyWoodhouse.com) is an award-winning, bestselling author of more than forty fiction and nonfiction books. Kim and her incredible husband of thirty-plus years live in Colorado, where they play golf together, spend time with their kids and grandkids, and research all the history around them.

Sign Up for Tracie's Newsletter

Keep up to date with Tracie's latest news on book releases and events by signing up for her email list at the link below.

TraciePeterson.com

FOLLOW TRACIE ON SOCIAL MEDIA

Tracie Peterson

@AuthorTraciePeterson

Sign Up for Kimberley's Newsletter

Keep up to date with Kimberley's latest news on book releases and events by signing up for her email list at the link below.

KimberleyWoodhouse.com